Midnight in Rome

Midnight in Rome
A Wandering Mind in a City Eternal

{a novel}

Michael J. Gyulai

iUniverse, Inc.
New York Lincoln Shanghai

Midnight in Rome
A Wandering Mind in a City Eternal

Copyright © 2008 by Michael J. Gyulai

All rights reserved. No part of this book may be used or reproduced by any means, graphic, electronic, or mechanical, including photocopying, recording, taping or by any information storage retrieval system without the written permission of the publisher except in the case of brief quotations embodied in critical articles and reviews.

iUniverse books may be ordered through booksellers or by contacting:

iUniverse
2021 Pine Lake Road, Suite 100
Lincoln, NE 68512
www.iuniverse.com
1-800-Authors (1-800-288-4677)

Because of the dynamic nature of the Internet, any Web addresses or links contained in this book may have changed since publication and may no longer be valid.

This is a work of fiction. All of the characters, names, incidents, organizations, and dialogue in this novel are either the products of the author's imagination or are used fictitiously.

ISBN: 978-0-595-47375-5 (pbk)
ISBN: 978-0-595-71114-7 (cloth)
ISBN: 978-0-595-91653-5 (ebk)

Printed in the United States of America

Based on the actual adventure ...

Welcome to **Wells Fargo** Online Banking …

Your statement as of **November 01, 2004** is

Cash Accounts

Account	Account Number	Available Balance
CHECKING	XXX-XXX0385	$4,659.24
SAVINGS	XXX-XXX6608	$100.02
		Total $4,759.26

UNO

The automatic doors at the head of a bustling Termini station parted, and I strode into a mass of thick Mediterranean air. It crawled across the exposed skin of my face and forearms as I moved. It was robust, aromatic, unmistakable.

"I can make it through March!"

"Explain to me how you've possibly projected yourself spending less than one thousand dollars a month?"

I pressed my phone firmly to one ear, fighting to keep Dad on the line, as I marched determinedly past a series of taxi drivers lingering at the trunks of their vehicles, snapping at me clichéd Italian and broken English. The sprawling lot beyond them was a frenzy of careening tour vans, airport shuttles, and an abundance of rumbling local buses. Between the mechanical giants zipped petite motorinos, spitting swirling streams of gray in their wakes. The noise was constant—the roaring of the buses, the buzzing of the motorinos, anonymous horns and whistling, and endless human chatter.

"I'm going to eat more pasta and less meat."

"Stop being ridiculous."

"I'm not!" I was, though, sort of.

I caught myself at the edge of a crosswalk. The roadway was wide, four lanes, cobblestone edge to edge. The cross traffic saw its light change and together orchestrated a crescendo of engine noise—a textured symphony of revving mechanisms. It departed from the edge of the intersection and began a thunderous forward procession. I followed the assembly with my eyes as it continued down the street to my right, led by a tight cluster of motorinos. The group moved like a school of fish—individually sporadic, yet collectively uniform.

"I think you need to reconsider your budget before making a commitment like this."

It had sounded like so much money—one thousand U.S. dollars a month—but the exchange rate was skewing everything for the worse, and the transformation of the numbers was astounding.

Rent: €550 became rent: $715.

Food: €187 became food: $243.10.

Add those two together and the cost to exist in Rome for one month—to simply feed and shelter myself—totaled over nine hundred U.S. dollars. How was that possible?

Then there was the mobile phone, a virtual necessity by now. Or a drink or cheap pizzeria dinner with Ayden and Aleksia and Nina, refusal of which would have been social suicide for an unemployed American transplant. Somehow, one thousand dollars a month had been rendered an overly optimistic, practically unworkable budget. How could that be? It could not be. There was no way.

"In all seriousness," I projected into my mobile phone, "my first week here I had to eat out every night because I was staying at the hotel, then I had to front my first month's rent and a month's deposit …"

The traffic signals changed, and I moved through the intersection alongside a dozen other pedestrians. To my left, a new buildup of snarling fenders growled at my shins.

"And I had to pay a ridiculous one-time registration fee with the phone company. And there was even—"

"I get it, Mike," Dad interrupted with a laugh.

I cut onto the narrow sidewalk of the quieter Via Principe Amedeo. Broad, salmon-colored buildings fitted with stone trim and bearing beige terraces rose from either side of the short street. Double-parked cars encircled the outdoor seating of a humble pizzeria in front of me.

I passed under the first of three large umbrellas and pushed through a shifting gauntlet of casually dressed waiters. An older man, holding paper menus in hand as he lingered at the restaurant's door, glanced up at me. He had slim reading glasses placed low on his rounded nose and asked if I was hungry. I shook my head.

"This whole budget scenario is assuming I can't find anything—absolutely *nothing*—to make some Euro over the next few months. If I can make a few hundred over the next, say, three months, then I can make it through March for sure—no problem. If I can find something that makes me a little more

Euro, maybe I can move my flight even further—until summer, or possibly after summer."

There was a pause, then a deep exhalation.

"How is the apartment you found?"

"It's very ..." I hesitated, "practical."

"And the people you live with?"

"They're ..." *not Italian* immediately came to mind, "nice people."

I neglected to elaborate, hoping instead to create a lingering appeal for return to the previous subject.

"All right," I could hear a reluctant compliance in Dad's voice, and it made me grin. "What is it exactly you want me to tell the travel agency?"

"I'll e-mail you their phone number and my ticket number. Just tell them I want to move my return flight from next week, where it is right now, to the first or second week of April."

April. Spring. Flowers covering the Spanish Steps. It was going to be spectacular.

"And why can't you do this yourself?"

"Because it would cost a fortune with all the hold time."

"Why can't you have them call you, like we did, so you don't have to pay?"

"If you want to give them my number and try to convince them to work out the time change and ring me—"

"All right, all right," he laughed again. "I'll call them later this week."

"Thanks. And thanks for hearing me out."

"A pleasure, as usual. I'll look for your e-mail this week?"

"Okay, great."

"We love you, Mike."

How are things with Mom?

"Love you guys too."

Working themselves out, I'm sure.

Click.

DUE

June. Saturday. My feet are tapping the floor of Royce Hall along with the other two hundred twenty-five University of California, Los Angeles, communication studies graduates. Our program director, flanked by the entirety of the Communication Studies Department, looks out across the audience from his position onstage behind the podium. He leans to the microphone.

"Ladies and gentleman, faculty, family, and friends,"

The rumbling swells. Parents begin to whistle.

"By the power invested in me by the trustees of the University of California, it is my honor to present …"

Leighton, sitting next to me, slouches low in her seat. She cups her hands around her mouth and begins a sustained howl.

"The graduating class of 2004 in the Department of Communication Studies!"

The hall erupts. The organ blares. We hug, clap, and spin circles in the narrow spaces between our seats.

Our row moves right, toward the main aisle, the whoosh of our black gowns drowned by the applause. I follow Leighton straight along the red velvet seats, then down the alley of unnamed cheering relatives, each new locking of the eyes instilling an ounce more satisfaction.

"Mike!" It's coming from the left. I look.

Flash.

Mom has the camera out.

Our train of black-gowned bodies spills across the rustic brick and immaculately groomed lawn of the outdoor quad, followed shortly thereafter by a river of anonymous family members. Soon the entire plaza is overrun with racing children, wandering students, euphoric grandparents, and orchestrating mothers and fathers. They are everywhere—along the brick, down the stairs, across the grass. I hug moms I know, meet dads for the first time, update mental catalogues of siblings, and piece together family trees.

As I bounce between parents and grandparents, aunts and uncles, it seems every remark from an elder follows the same theme—that of welcoming me into adulthood and postacademia. Even if they are not saying it directly, the undertone is there.

"You made it!"

Welcome.

"It's so exciting to see all of you joining us out in the *real world*."

Welcome.

"Before you know it, you'll be looking like me, sending your own kids off to college."

Welcome.

I am expelled into a dispersing crowd of mostly strangers and spot my parents on the western edge of the lawn. My younger brother, Philip, is disinterestedly texting away on his phone while Dad, next to him, stares up at the asymmetrical towers of Royce Hall.

"Mike!" I hear Leighton call out from behind me.

I turn and see her approaching across the battered grass.

The afternoon sun casts sharply angled shadows extending from the feet of the families dotting the square behind Leighton. The sky above burns a pale and milky blue. It is that typical Los Angeles blue, the kind emitted from a television screen which has the brightness level turned up too high, washing out any vivid color with a casting of bright white.

"How's it going?" I ask.

"If one more person asks me what my *plan* is, I'm gonna lose it. I feel like printing *moving to New York to work for a PR firm* on an index card and stapling it to my chest."

I crack a smile.

"How are *you* handling the *plan for the future* interrogations?" she asks.

"Doing my best to tactfully deflect the question."

Leighton glances over my shoulder.

"Uh oh," she murmurs.

I turn to see her parents appear in front of mine, and the four begin conversing.

"Worlds colliding," I say.

"Let's let them gossip. You wanna stick our feet in the fountain?" She motions to the west end of the square.

"Hell, yeah."

We move in synchronization, gowns still swooshing—though now with a sort of comical presence—and I sit with Leighton on the stone half-circle surrounding the small body of perpetually churning water. We kick our shoes to the grass and spin on our perches to the water behind us, pulling our synthetic black robes to our knees and sinking our legs calf-deep into the recycling pool.

"Have you decided to stay in LA, or not?"

"No," I tell her, our eyes fixed on the sparkling water. "I don't think I'm going to stay."

"I get to visit you in San Francisco, then. Perfect!"

"Actually ..." I hesitate a moment.

She looks up at me.

"Actually, what?"

"Actually, I have decided that I am going to move to Rome."

She blinks twice.

"Rome, Italy," I reiterate. "*Rome* Rome."

"Of course I know what Rome you're talking about. Give me some credit here."

Leighton knows about Rome. Leighton knows just about everything. Friends call us a *pseudocouple*. We have a lot of fun with that one. I am her *pseudoboyfriend*; we have *pseudofights*; Leighton even *pseudocheated on me*. Twice. The pseudotramp.

"I know you've sort of joked about it before," she continues. "Are you being serious right now?"

"If I'm really going to do it, I feel like now is the time."

Leighton nods her head.

"I think it's a great idea. Why not now? You *have* to move somewhere. You *have* to make a transition."

My eye catches Phil down the edge of the grass, continuing his solitary messaging. Next to him, my parents remain lost in colorful conversation with Leighton's, trying to piece together some sort of truthful completeness from the countless story fragments they have gathered from each of us individually over the years.

"If I can last five or six months there, that will be enough to make it worthwhile, right?"

"Sure. Probably. Long enough to do what, exactly?"

"To really live there. To like ..." I stare back to the twinkling water. "To understand the place like a local. To ... I dunno," I shrug.

We both laugh, partially at my lack of a coherent objective, but also at the mutual understanding that forcing such an emotional goal—an intuition—into a linear statement of reason would be next to impossible.

"Have you told your parents?"

I glance back to Dad, who is making a huge gesture with his arms as he recounts something to Leighton's mom.

"Not yet," I laugh.

Leighton laughs with me and replies, "Oh, man, I thought having my moving-out-of-state conversation was difficult."

Just down the edge of the lawn all four of our parents break into laughter as Dad finishes his story.

"They have no idea …"

TRE

I moved the milk carton in a slow, hypnotizing circle, sending a controlled and evenly distributed stream of white downward. It burst into random dispersion upon hitting countless ridged flakes of cereal.

I sat at the small kitchen table, my back to our clunky gas oven, the open terrace doors just beyond it, and our view across a short section of parking lot to the flat, broad face of another drab 1950s apartment complex.

I spun my spoon between my fingers, encouraging the still-crisp flakes to absorb the thick white liquid surrounding them. Ayden entered, carrying a glass.

"Ciao, Michael. Come stai?"

He passed me and moved to the sink. Ayden's Italian was pretty good, but his English was even better. And he seemed to throw out some easy Italian small talk before continuing our conversations in English as a way of humoring me. And humor me it did.

"Siamo a Roma, sto benissimo!" *We're in Rome, I'm great!* I replied.

Ayden laughed as he filled the glass with water from the sink faucet. He leaned back against the countertop. I continued to stir my cereal.

"How is the thesis going?" I asked.

"Well. It's going well."

Ayden was working on his thesis statement for his master's in criminal law. He had told me something about how the Turkish and Italian justice systems used the same rules or codes, or something of that nature, so he was able to study at an affiliate university here in Rome.

"Have you settled into your room?" he asked.

Unpacking my luggage the first day had taken me a total of twenty minutes. I had no furniture to buy or pictures to put on the walls. So, I assumed settled in I was.

"Yeah. The single bed is a little small for me, but everything seems fine."

The front door clicked once, and Nina came tumbling in with three grocery bags hanging from her fists. Ayden and I watched her intently as she dropped the bags onto the table in front of me and then moved back to the door to slam it shut with her liberated hands.

"I don't understand Italians!" she called to the ceiling.

Ayden drank again from his glass. I brought a spoonful of cereal to my mouth. We looked at each other and grinned.

"What happened this time, Nina?" Ayden offered.

Nina stepped back into the kitchen and began forcefully unloading items into the refrigerator and surrounding cabinets.

"No one here can even figure out how to form a line at the supermarket!"

She reached into one of the plastic bags and pulled out two boxes of pasta, one with each hand, and held them while pausing to elaborate.

"For some reason, the GS decided to only open two lousy registers. And everyone just got off work so there were so many people buying groceries, and instead of doing the normal thing and forming two lines, one at each register, everyone just started piling up in between the two!"

She started shaking her head and talking to the ceiling again. I took a bite of cereal and shared a silent laugh with Ayden. She then turned and placed the boxes of pasta on her shelf in the cupboard and went on.

"So, I kept trying to keep my position but these lousy Italian men and women just kept cutting right in front of me. They just pushed into the group as far up as they could. And I even tried saying something. I'd say, 'Excuse me, I'm standing here, you know,' but they would just ignore me. So I tried in my crap Italian, 'Mi scusi,' but no one would listen. And then when an Italian would say something they would just get into fights with each other."

"That is very typical of Italians," Ayden said to her as she tossed the first empty plastic bag into the cabinet under the sink. "An inability to organize."

"So, they aren't sheep, big deal," I countered.

"They aren't what?" Ayden asked. I had forgotten how careful I had to be with metaphors in this house.

"They aren't victims of a system."

"But we're talking about the supermarket now," Nina fired back at me, "not the evil *man*. C'mon." She was pretty good with English expressions like that—like, *the man*.

"The problem is *trust*," Ayden began, with an emphasizing forward thrust of his water glass on the word *trust*. "As a country, Italy is not unified. As a people, Italians are not unified. They feel they cannot trust Berlusconi—their government. They feel they cannot trust the *carabinieri*—their police. There is no respect for national systems. There is no nationalism."

The words of a true scholar.

"Unless, of course, they win the World Cup," I revised.

"Ha! Yes, yes."

Ayden and Nina both laughed.

"But honestly, they are such self-centered individuals," Nina continued while emptying the second of the three bags.

"Look at the flip side, though," I countered. "Look at how strong the Italian household is. Look at how here friends and family come first—even if it is only because you can't trust a larger system. It places the trust and the worth back on actual people—back locally to your relatives and neighbors who are directly in your life."

"It is admirable, the value of family here," acknowledged Ayden. "But it also means that many Italians will very rarely travel or do business outside of their own city or even neighborhood. There is very little exchange of capital among Italy's separate regions. And it hurts the economy greatly because they don't work together."

"Thank God I work for the United Nations," snickered Nina. "Though being paid in dollars is pretty rotten right now."

I shook my head and dropped my spoon into my bowl.

"Does anyone in this kitchen besides me even want to be here?" I asked, half joking. But honestly, had they even been outside—outside of their bedrooms or offices or the supermarket? This city was spectacular.

"The city center is quite beautiful," admitted Ayden.

Thank you.

"Exactly. The city is beautiful, the language is gorgeous, and the food is great. You guys are focusing on the wrong issues—all your political and economic hogwash." I smiled at Ayden.

"My what?" He batted his eyes.

"Your nonsense!"

He laughed, then finished the last gulp of water and placed his glass on the counter next to the sink.

"Allora, it seems time to get back to work. Ci vediamo dopo, ragazzi."

Ayden left the kitchen, as I fished for the final soggy bites of cereal. Nina pulled the last two items—one jar of tomato sauce and a bar of dark chocolate—from the single remaining bag.

"Aleksia and I were talking about seeing that new Matt Damon movie later tonight. *The Bourne* something. Not *Identity*, but the new one. You can come if you'd like."

God bless Nina, our flat's official social captain.

"I'm going to try and pass out more résumés. But let me know what showing you're going to. Maybe I can meet you there."

She smiled, placed the jar of tomato sauce onto the shelf, and closed the cupboard door. I slurped the last pair of flakes from their milky bath. She then tore open the chocolate bar's wrapper and offered me a piece.

"How is the job hunt going?"

"Pretty badly. Only one place even entertained me with an interview—this cocktail lounge in Campo de' Fiori, called Metro. The owner spent a few years in the States and knew who UCLA was, so he told me I might be able to help out a few days a week."

"That sounds great. When do you start?"

"The problem is that I need these permit-document things." I slid my travel guide across the table and flipped to the notes I had written on its inside cover. "A *Permesso di Soggiorno* and a *Libretto di Idoneità Sanitaria*."

"Ugh," Nina threw her head back. "You have to go all the way to the immigration office for that *Permesso*—all of us at work had to go. That place is a zoo." She bit into a square of chocolate. "What was that other thing?"

"It's this sanitary certificate for working with food and drink. But you can't get it without a work visa."

"So, what are you going to do?"

"I'm going to try to get it anyway. Don't overlook the value of unwavering determination and universal charm," I beamed.

She shook her head.

"Why don't you just teach English?" she laughed. "It would be so much easier."

"I didn't come to Rome to work on my English."

She rolled her eyes and bit off another chunk of chocolate.

"What are you up to tomorrow?" she asked.

"I'll probably explore the center again. There are a couple areas of the city I want to check out. One is like, *Trastevere* or something. Have you been around there?"

"Yeah, it's all right." She curled the torn chocolate wrapper back over the exposed end and slid it into the cupboard behind her. "I can't believe how much you like it here."

"I'd been here before. I knew I loved it."

"Yes, but how long have you been living here? A month?"

"Almost six weeks."

She started out of the kitchen.

"Give it time," she smirked. "I'll let you know about the movie."

Nina disappeared toward her room.

I rose from the table and rinsed my bowl in the sink. I dried my hands on the small towel hanging from the drawer at my waist and then pulled a glass from above the sink. As I began to fill it with water from the tap, Aleksia marched through the kitchen doorway and slumped into the chair opposite from where I had been sitting. She stared at her mobile phone and said nothing. Here, finally, was someone who had to enjoy Italians.

"How is Paolo?" I asked.

"Italians are such idiots!"

Good Lord.

"What did he do?" I asked unenthusiastically.

"He refuses to introduce me to his parents! He met my dad when he was in Rome visiting me, and he met my mom in Norway during the summer, but—I mean, he lives with his parents! Can you believe it? He is thirty-one years old and he still lives with them and we have to sneak around in his car—which is really their car—or hide in my room all the time. I just don't understand Italian men. How do they do it?"

Aleksia seemed to always be in her pajamas, as she was now. There was a certain predictability to her personality.

"I don't know what advice to give you about that. How was class today?"

"I didn't go."

Sort of like that.

"I thought I heard you leave around ten thirty," I said.

My bedroom door shared the wall with the front door and I was able to hear—and in the morning forced to hear—every entrance and exit made by my flatmates.

"Yeah, I got up to go. But I just went shopping instead."

Again, predictable.

"Where'd you go?" I asked.

"Cola di Rienzo."

"Where's that?"

"You know where Via del Corso is in the center?"

"Of course."

"Okay. The Corso runs up and down and at the top of it there is Piazza del Popolo."

"Okay."

"If you go left out of the piazza you take Via Cola di Rienzo."

"And it has better shopping than the Corso?"

"I like them both."

I should have guessed.

"But I think Rienzo is a little more nicer," Aleksia added.

"How are classes going? They are in Italian, right?"

"God, yeah. I can't understand a lot of what the professor is saying. So I go to the computer lab and play on the Internet. And here at home it takes me like an hour to read five pages in my book. I end up just watching movies. I don't know why they let me in, really. I barely know any Italian."

Probably because she had paid the registration.

"Nina said we might watch a movie tonight," I mentioned.

"Yeah," she paused. "I don't really feel like it anymore."

Aleksia's phone let out a high pitched series of digital tones. She looked down at the screen in her palm and then pounded the table with her free hand.

"Ugh!"

I drank some water.

She stood quickly and ran off toward her bedroom.

I placed my glass down onto the counter next to Ayden's and then looked out through the open terrace doors. My damp clothing hung silently from the metal dry rack, soaking in what was left of the late evening sun. Across the way and up one floor an elderly woman waved a single bed sheet rhythmically in the dense Mediterranean air. Below, I heard a motorino kick start, then buzz off into the distance, carrying with it what must have been its two passengers—one male, one female—and the playful Italian tonality of their exchanges.

Io sto benissimo. Io sono a Roma.

Welcome to **Wells Fargo** Online Banking ...

Your statement as of **December 01, 2004** is

Cash Accounts

Account	Account Number	Available Balance
CHECKING	XXX-XXX0385	$3,482.92
SAVINGS	XXX-XXX6608	$100.02

Total $3,582.94

QUATTRO

I stood at the towering black metal gates surrounding the guarded complex. My shoes crunched on the loose gravel at the edge of the barren parking lot as I shifted my weight forward and peered between the lean, metallic bars. From what I could make out at my distance, the entire structure appeared devoid of movement.

The rain was preposterous. Thick, lopsided spheres of liquid—hundreds of thousands of them—came crashing down from the gray sky above and had been doing so relentlessly for the last two hours. They pounded furiously upon the silky synthetic fabric of my compact umbrella, which I had pulled down tightly against my head. The minor protection it was able to provide had valiantly guarded my face and shoulders from the viscous liquid army but my exposed lower body had long since drowned beneath the inescapable hordes of water.

As I stepped back from the fence, I felt my socks diffuse water inside my shoes—a phenomenon I had at first cursed myself for inducing by naively stepping into a seemingly shallow, actually cavernous, puddle while boarding the 477L bus. By this point, I might as well have just dragged myself out of the Mediterranean itself.

I glanced right to the small gold plaque fastened to the lengthy metal rods: *Ufficio Immigrazione*.

I was at the right place. I had to be at the right place. I had just been here three days earlier during the afternoon. A dry afternoon. The afternoon I had first made this wretched hour-long voyage involving both the metro and the bus system, only to find that the single day the office remained open past eleven-thirty in the morning was Thursday, and the segmented gate adjacent to the posted golden plaque, was decisively locked. And so, after I had quietly confirmed on my phone's display that the day of the week was in fact not

Thursday, but Tuesday—I had pretty much completely lost track of what day of the week it was—I had diligently copied down the office's official hours from the official-looking sign affixed to that very official-looking fence.

But as I checked my notes again there under my battered umbrella, and then verified them with the hours posted just below the golden plaque a second time, I still could not locate my misstep.

Ufficio Immigrazione
Via Teofilo Patini (angolo via Salviati)
Zona Tor Cervara

Metro Linea B, fermata 'Rebibbia.' Bus 447L

Lunedì— Venerdì: 8:30–11:30

Giovedì: 15:00–17:00

It was Friday. *Venerdì*. The offices should have been open for another hour and a half. At least, I thought it was Friday. I checked my phone to make sure it was Friday.

Acceptance is an essential trait to surviving Italy—an embracement of individualism over efficiency. And when faced with what could, should, or would elsewhere be done differently, one, assuming this expectant frame of mind, is best simply forcing a smile and muttering an acknowledging and centering, *Oh, Italy*.

I leaned to the fence again, water shifting in my shoes, the front of my umbrella denting inward where it met with the metal rails. I squinted toward the darkened windows and numerous locked doors at the building's lower level.

Baffled still, I pulled my vision back to the gate, to the section through which I theoretically should have been able to enter. I then tracked the path which I theoretically should have been able to follow. It was a labyrinth of poorly connected temporary metal barriers filling the otherwise desolate space between the outer fencing and the building itself. They wound an unnecessarily extensive path—equivalent on a much larger scale to what I assumed a human's digestive track exploited in the body's limited abdominal area—ending at a door much further left than seemed logical.

The door's upper half framed a square glass window where a piece of paper had been fastened from the inside. In large, handwritten block letters were two offensively brief and absurdly uninformative lines.
SIAMO ... CHIUSI.
WE'RE ... CLOSED.
Oh, Italy.

CINQUE

September. Friday. I shuffle towards the back of the small U-Haul, passing my empty bookcase which has been laid on its side. My mattress is pinned between my hands and is slowly being dragged into the last slender available cargo space.

"Careful, Mike. Watch the bookcase," Dad warns me.

"Don't worry; I've got it."

I give the mattress a final inward tug, let out a sharp exhalation, and lean against the back wall of the van.

"Now, how are you going to get out?" Dad grins warily and shakes his head.

A mountain of cardboard boxes, each one labeled in exaggerated black Sharpie, sits at my left. *CDs & DVDs*, *Stereo Wires*, *Kitchen*, *Computer Stuff*. I step up onto the narrow wooden side of the gutted bookshelf.

"Mike, you're going to break something," Dad insists.

I shift the weight of my crouching stance to my left foot as it reaches the plastic of my television set, then quickly back to my right foot as I skip onto a box labeled *Books*.

"Mike!"

"It's just books, man!"

I hop to the metal grating at the van's bumper and then to the ground.

"I was more worried about the TV."

"It's fine. Let's go; last pass."

I lead us back up the set of concrete stairs and into the apartment lobby. We watch the digital display above the elevators count down from fourteen.

"You certainly seem more awake now," Dad says.

"I think today was the first time I've seen seven thirty AM since first-year economics class."

Dad laughs.

"I'm just ready to get out of here," I continue. "We still have the six-hour drive. I can't believe how long this took. What time is it, anyway?"

"Almost noon."

"Unbelievable."

Dad nods.

"That's just how it always seems to go," he adds. "It takes more time than you think it will."

I had calculated two hours for moving the heavy stuff—my bed and bookcase and television and desk and chairs and even clothing. And I had allotted an extra half hour or so for gathering the leftover clutter. But that clutter—that amassing of pens and remote controls and wires and odd or even embarrassing memoirs that I simply could not rationalize parting with—that was what took the real time. An entire extra two hours of real time.

The elevator doors split and we move inside. I hit eleven and lean against the mirrored back wall as the doors seal again.

"You sleep all right on that air mattress?" I ask.

"It was actually okay, but I don't think my stomach agreed with the Mexican food we had for dinner."

"Don't you blame Wahoos!"

"Don't you side with them after I flew down here to help you pack!"

We each smile.

"You want to drive the U-Haul or the Explorer?" I ask.

"I'll take the Explorer."

"Great," I respond sarcastically.

I reach into my pocket and pull out my keys. I slide all three off the metal ring and hand the Explorer key to Dad.

"After this last trip," I continue, "bring it around to where the U-Haul is parked. I have to go turn in these apartment keys, and then I'll meet you back at the cars."

The elevator opens and we start down the long carpeted hallway.

"And by the way," I mention, "if the subwoofer goes out, or anything, after a couple of hours, it's normal. It's just too hot and the amplifier cuts it off until it cools down again."

Dad shakes his head. He does have *AM radio* written across his forehead.

We reach the end of the hall and enter the now barren studio apartment. At our height, eleven floors up, the midday sun comes flooding through each of the two perpendicular walls of windows. The small, undressed corner studio is stunning, exclusively white, and exceptionally bright now that it's empty—devoid of the browns of my furniture and grays of my bedsheets. The sunlight splashes onto the paint, falls on the carpet, saturates even the ceiling.

I move to the bathroom, carrying out my bath towel and shutting the door behind me.

"Bathroom officially finished. Can you hang onto this for me?"

Dad takes the towel in his hands and begins working to evenly drape it over his right arm. I grab a few loose items—some magazines and a spiral notebook—from the opposite corner and cradle them between my left arm and my chest.

Dad stands stationary in the middle of the room, facing the expanse of west Los Angeles and the Pacific Ocean out the series of windows, but his vision seems fixed on the white carpeting at his feet.

"You know when you asked me last night how things were going around the house, now that Phil's gone?" he says.

"Yeah, I remember," I reply, pulling a black GE surge protector from its socket.

"Well." He pauses.

I crisscross the room.

"It's been pretty difficult."

Three loose CD cases.

"How do you mean?"

I move into the kitchen.

Five birthday cards on the counter I should just throw away. Two Sharpies.

"You know how you got to that point with Charlotte—I mean it seemed to us that you got to a point—and I'm not saying I ever did anything as incredibly thoughtful for Mom as you did for Charlotte …"

Dad continues to speak to the vacant main room.

"… But you got to a point where you kept giving and wanted to keep giving but she just didn't want to receive anything from you anymore?"

"That was a really long time ago," I call back from the kitchen.

"I know. But I feel that's sort of where Mom is with me right now," he tells me.

Two picture frames. A sole fork—how did this not get put in the silverware box?

"So, what do you think she wants? Does she want to travel more? More than her Paris trips?"

"No." Dad pauses. "No, I don't think it's traveling." He pauses again. The carpet remains his immediate audience. "Mike, I don't mean to be dropping this all on you right before we go home or anything—and don't say anything to Phil."

"Sure, really, it's fine."

My *Italy Through the Seasons* calendar tacked to the back of the kitchen door—almost forgot that. I angle the door halfway shut and yank loose the calendar.

"Kitchen finished," I announce.

I step into the main room a final time. Dad is still standing there, in the middle of all the white—all the sunlight and all the blankness, illuminated from every angle, staring at the floor.

"So, what does she want then?" I ask again, while making a final visual sweep of the apartment.

I turn to face Dad, my left arm cradling the last of my possessions, my body reading readiness. Today Los Angeles; tomorrow San Francisco. And in two weeks, Rome.

Dad moves his eyes from the floor. Finally. They meet mine.

"I think she may not want a relationship with me anymore."

Welcome.

SEI

I was pacing in the empty hallway just outside the *Unità Sanitaria* offices. Or maybe I should say *office*, because although the hallway I was standing in opened onto four large rooms, three of the four sat exposed, their doors flung open, their naked interiors implying some sort of mass departure at a time long since past.

Centered on the face of the single closed door in front of me was one of those clear binder sheets in which one can slide papers to protect them, or look at while eating ice cream, or simply to give them a greater importance than other unworthy pieces of paper. The clear sheet had been taped to the door horizontally, and inside was a computer printout listing a doctor's name—*Dr. Pellegrino* or *Pettiuci* or something with a *P*, a schedule of hours—*Lunedì* through *Giovedì*, *09:00* to *12:00*, and a list of three bullet points, one of which read *Libretto di Idoneità Sanitaria*.

I had knocked on the door a few minutes ago and a nurse had opened it. She had inquired about my presence, and upon hearing the words *Tessera Sanitaria*, had handed me a clipboard with a short form to fill out before making a finger-twirling hand gesture which seemed to signify she would return later to let me in.

I reviewed the simple form—birth date, address, and a list of *si* or *no* questions. Discernment of most of the questions had proven a challenge, but given that those I had been able to decipher involved grave physical health problems—tubercolosi, febbre tifoide o paratifoide, diarrea e vomito, secrezione dall'orecchio, secrezione dall'occhio, secrezione dal naso—I presumed this was the standard what-are-you-even-doing-here-if-you-have-this-kind-of-problem questionnaire and I circled straight *no*'s across the board. And some really thick circles regarding secretions from my ears, eyes, or nose.

There was another sheet pressed against the back of the nurse's clipboard, a sheet I had brought with me. It was my *Permesso di Soggiorno per Stranieri*.

I had woken up at seven, made the hour-long journey for the third time aboard the metro and bus systems to the *Ufficio Immigrazione*, and this time there was no wrong day, no wrong hour, no cowardly paper taped to the inside of a window, and, thankfully, no rain army. There was, however, a boatload of people—it seemed from all over the world, speaking a myriad of languages.

I had taken a numbered ticket from the kiosk inside and sat patiently in the large, boisterous lobby for my number to appear on the digital display. The display was suspended from the ceiling in the middle of the room and expelled a callous monotone buzz every time a number advanced. Two hours and eighty-seven buzzes later I was at window twelve presenting my passport and traveler's insurance. And two hours after that, I had made it back to the Piramide metro station with my brand-new, sparklingly official, three-month tourism permit to stay.

Cognome	*Gyulai*
Nome	*Michael*
Luogo di Nascita	*California, USA*

I eyed the formal permit number.

N099B756

It was meaty and official looking. The only problem area was at the bottom.

Motivo del Soggiorno, Turismo: Motive of the stay, Tourism
Scadenza 13/01/2005: Valid until January 13, 2005

The permit was irrefutably official, but it also listed in plain sight the fact that I was neither here for the motive of study, which would have required the submission of a student visa, nor for the motive of work, which would have required the submission of a work visa. And the unavoidable truth was that one only needed a *Libretto di Idoneità Sanitaria* to work—work in a restaurant or bar or pizzeria or whichever kind of workplace served food or drink.

But I was feeling cool. I was feeling confident. The legitimate permit, complete with legitimate number, would give this doctor something legitimate to put down in my Libretto—a simple technicality—and I would just have to fudge my motives for needing the Libretto in the first place. If the doctor were to even ask, that is.

I just had to avoid the word *lavoro*, work. If I did not mention the word *work* and the doctor did not inquire about the details, we would move right along through the monotonous formalities. He would make his doctoral signatures where necessary, and I would pay whatever fee was required, and there would be a stamp and a receipt, and I would be gone, Libretto in hand. This was only a doctor's office after all, not an interrogation room.

I heard the muffled sound of two chairs sliding behind the closed door and what sounded like a meeting reaching its conclusion. I pulled myself off the hallway wall, stood up straight, inhaled deeply, and released a rapid exhalation of readiness. The door opened, and a well-dressed, short, middle-aged Italian man with a dusting of grey in his hair animatedly bounced past me and disappeared down the stairwell.

The nurse from before, draped in a white gown, graying roots at her scalp disclosing the true shade of her otherwise dyed-black hair, ushered me inside.

The room was fairly large and sparsely decorated, comprised mainly of two sizeable desks, one flanking the right wall and sitting vacant due to the nurse being occupied, and the second desk perpendicular to the first, paralleling the far wall. At that second desk sat another white-gowned figure, scribbling busily on one of an array of papers. The nurse addressed him.

"Dottore."

He glanced up briefly from his papers and motioned for me to take the chair opposite him. I seated myself and removed the medical form I had filled out from the clipboard, tapping it flush with my Permesso on my thighs. Dottore Pellegrino, or Pettiuci, or whatever it was, penned a final line with an exaggerated swoosh of his thick ballpoint, slid the page to the side of his desk, and then looked up at me.

"Allora, Lei che - --- --- oggi."

Oh, how I hated the formal verb conjugations. I had studied Italian for a number of years but was still far from fluent, and the fact that the kind doctor had addressed me as *Lei*, a sort of Sir, or Madam, reference, meant he would be speaking to me using only very formal phrasing—I was already lost on his opening line. But context can speak volumes, and given that he had started his sentence to me with *allora*, so then, and ended it with *oggi*, today, I assumed he was asking what I needed to have done today. Or what he could do for me today. Or some inquiry into the motivation for why I had just sat down across from him now only eleven minutes before he was supposed to be able to call it a day and go home for his afternoon siesta.

"Cerco una Tessera Sanitaria," I said clearly and confidently. *I'm looking for a Sanitary Card.*

Perhaps having said I was there *to apply* for a Sanitary Card or that I was interested in *being issued* a Sanitary Card would have been more precisely appropriate, but I did not have the vocabulary to formulate those exact phrases, so I instead slid my completed medical form and freshly issued *Permesso di Soggiorno* across the desk between us to imply that I was indeed aware of the requirements and I did in fact know I was in the right place and I would certainly be appreciative if we could have this small but obligatory process completed *oggi*.

He lifted the two sheets from the desk, sat upright in his chair, let out a second *allora*, and began reviewing the medical form. I crossed my hands in my lap and skimmed the room with my eyes.

The décor seemed more appropriate for that of a high school science classroom than a doctor's office. In fact, the flooring and windows and lighting, and just about every intangible feeling the room gave off, articulated the limited budget of a public, government-run operation.

The doctor read over the forms with the casualness of a process executed fifteen times a day for many years running. This wasn't going to be difficult. I could tell.

He then dropped my papers back onto his desk and spoke to me.

"Ma Lei ha un permesso -- ---- motivo di turismo"

That I had understood. *But you, kind Sir, have a permit to stay for the motive of tourism.*

"Sì," I nodded, and smiled widely, in an attempt to deflect his problematic implication with a display of grand delight to be sitting there in Italy, the place I loved oh, so dearly, with him.

"E per quale motivo Lei cerca il Libretto di Idoneità Sanitaria?" *So then why am I, the kind Sir that I am, in search of a Sanitary Card?*

Dottore Pellegrino, or Pettiuci, or whatever it was, appeared to be more of the sleuth than I had so optimistically assumed.

My mind began working out a probable explanation while my mouth tried to vocalize some light non sequiturs in Italian as a stall method. But, of course,

I didn't know any light non sequiturs in Italian and all that came out was an embarrassingly extended "eeeeeehhhhhh ..."

The doctor, astutely deciphering that I had no readied answer, interrupted me after about three seconds of sustained *eeeeeehhhhh*ing.

"Lavoro?" he asked. And, crap. *Lavoro.* Work. The word to avoid at all costs tossed right there onto the playing field with no alternative move in sight. The baldness of the obvious motive, highlighted in such a prominent fashion and exposed by the transparent air of silence which followed, produced a knee-jerk response.

"No!" I exclaimed, following up with a short laugh and painting my face with *are you kidding ... kind Sir?*

I had to think. Quickly. And then translate. Why would I need this Sanitary Card if I was not going to work? It would have to be for something in a restaurant or coffee shop or bar or something like that. Maybe it was something like work but not exactly work. *Lavoro? Not* exactly. What were the requirements for something to be work? You showed up, you did a duty, you got paid. It was pretty simple. I would have to do a duty in some sort of food or beverage serving—

"Allora?"

An impatient sleuth.

"Ho un amico ..." I started. And it was a pretty good start too, I figured, given the circumstances. *I have a friend.* You do not work for friends. You work for bosses.

"L'amico mio ha un bar ..." Oh, this was good. *My friend has a bar.*

"E lui mi ha detto che ... ummm ... che posso aiutare con fare i caffè e con ... eeehh ... con lavare," I made a motion of washing a plate with my hands. "Ma mi ha detto che non può pagarmi soldi." *And my friend told me I could help out a little with coffees or washing things but he couldn't pay me*, obviously.

Wonderful! I kept with it.

"E torno in California a Gennaio ..." Even though I wasn't really planning on returning home in January, I was indeed from California. And who did not like California? "Ma lui mi ha detto che devo prendere questa Tessera Sanitaria." *But he told me that I still must get this sanitary card.* And I sort of made this face like, *what a pain: all these strict government rules and regulations which hamper even the most harmless of gestures between friends.*

The doctor shifted in his chair and took a long breath. My story was decent, and in this specific case, I believed my elementary Italian was helping to create an even more innocent likeness. But something was still lacking in my reasoning. Ultimately, why would I want to make espressos and clean dishes for free in the first place—whether it was for a friend or otherwise?

"E voglio aiutare nel bar perchè voglio praticare il mio Italiano." *And I want to help in the bar because I want to practice my Italian.*

At about the word *praticare* I elongated my already present smile and spread my arms from my sides, palms opened skyward, and tilted my head just slightly as if to say, *Oh, how much I adore your incessantly beautiful language, a language which I will never be able to master but from which even the simplest of phrases that I am able to produce bring me such joy and inspiration that I will forever aspire to improve.* And by the word *Italiano*, I was looking right, across the room to the nurse. She had paused from her work to witness my grand request for a small token of compassion which would allow me passage into an against-all-odds quest to simply try and be a little more like them.

I locked eyes with the nurse. I held my exaggerated smile, steady and firm. This had to be a heartwarming moment for the both of them. And sure enough, a smile then flickered across the face of the nurse—an affectionate, demonstrative smile. And she looked to the doctor across from me and sputtered off a few lines in Italian. And he in turn looked to me, and sighed, and spoke.

"Il suo amico, ha un *bar*?"

"Sì."

"Un *bar* bar?"

I could see what he was getting at. In Italian, *bar* didn't mean *cocktail bar* or *Irish pub*. It meant specifically a *coffee bar* where the majority of items sold were espressos, reheated croissants, and prepackaged gums and candy. He wanted to be sure that I wasn't going to be touching people's dinners or handling unwashed vegetables in a kitchen or preparing raw meats for an afternoon buffet. The sanitary certificate he was about to issue was printed with office markings traceable to him personally and he was doing his best to ensure there would be the lowest possible risk of someone being sent to the hospital after ingesting something improperly prepared by the little, overly-eager, aspiring young Italian-language student sitting in the chair across his desk. He was trying to cover his ass. And, I guess he was also performing his honest civic duty to the fraction of anonymous Roman citizens who would end up as clients at wherever it was I would be lending my hand.

"Sì, un bar." I assured him.

He pushed back from his desk for a second and opened a drawer beyond my view. He pulled forth a small, thin, orange paper booklet and placed it on the desk. As he moved to close the drawer, I worked to read the cover of the booklet upside down.

Libretto di Idoneità Sanitaria.

My God—it had worked.

He opened the booklet's first small page and skipped to the middle—to a line I would later recognize as the type of work intended by the booklet's holder. He penned in all-capital letters large enough for even me to read from the opposite side of the desk:

B-A-R

"Lei mi fa vedere le mani?"

I lifted my hands and dangled them before him like a begging puppy. He examined each for a moment.

"Giri."

Not a word I knew. He spun his pen in a circle at my finger tips. I rotated my hands. After an equally brief exam of my palms he let out a *va bene* and returned to filling in the numerous other blank lines of the small booklet. He then worked through a series of three rubber stamps, flipping back and forth among four of the booklet's pages, stamping over designated squares, stamping over his own signatures, stamping dates and times.

He placed the libretto underneath my medical form and permesso and pulled a new sheet of paper from an organizer atop his desk. It was long and thin and had the universal € symbol of a bill to be paid at the post office. He filled in the Euro denomination, 25,82. He then spun his wrist and gazed at his watch.

"Lei ha cinque minuti," and he handed me the receipt. *Five minutes.*

I stood quickly and resolutely made my way to the door. Once to the stairwell, I broke into a frantic run, bouncing down three steps at a time and then sprinting through the vacant lobby between an assembly of motorinos parked outside.

The post office was only a few blocks down the street and, luck undeniably already on my side, the line there was nonexistent. I moved to the first teller and passed her the receipt. I shoveled money from my pockets onto the metal counter—a crumpled ten-Euro bill, an equally wrinkled five, and then numerous one- and two-Euro coins. At twenty-six Euro she ran the paper through a machine to her left, tore the sheet on its dotted line, and handed me the payment stub with my eighteen cents change.

I scurried back to the sidewalk and retraced my sprint from the Unità Sanitaria. Again I sliced between the motorinos into the lobby and lunged up the echoing stairwell. As I reached the second storey, I pulled my phone from my jacket pocket and checked the time: 12:02.

I stepped through the open door and turned to the nurse. I threw my arms wide, winced my face, and clenched my teeth.

"Due minuti troppo?" I asked her regrettably. *Two minutes too late?* Well, *two minutes too much*, is what I said, because I couldn't think how to say *too late*.

She appeared amused at my slight loss of breath. And probably at my graceless Italian phrasing as well. She folded her arms on her desk and glanced at her watch. She then looked back at me and inhaled deeply, displaying an obviously overstated pensiveness, and clearly mimicked concern. She spoke.

"Dia, ce l'hai fatto!" *C'mon, you made it!*

I had made it! I stepped across the room and handed the payment stub to the doctor. He thanked me, placed the small square of paper into a drawer by his stomach, and then slid my *Permesso di Soggiorno* and *Libretto di Idoneità Sanitaria* across his desk to me.

I reached down and collected my two pristine Italian documents from Doctor P.

I smiled, said my best *grazie mille*, and started back toward the door. The nurse watched me from her desk, arms folded atop her papers, face fixed in a grin ad infinitum.

"Grazie mille!" I waved to her.

"Ciao, bellino," she waved back.

And that, my kind Sirs and Madams, is the prevailing power of universal charm.

SETTE

I dragged my heels leisurely as I ambled down one of the countless gravel paths of the Villa Borghese, scattering discreet waves of pebbles with each step. The dense ceiling of leaves extending endlessly into the distance sliced the midafternoon sun into a thousand slanted blades. There was a cautionary coolness to the temperature—though I would make it through the rest of the day in only a pair of slacks and a thin, long-sleeved shirt, the weather was changing, and I would have to start dressing more appropriately.

The colossal villa provided remarkable solace—not that I was in any particular need of solace. I still got off on all the buzz and bustle of urban life found in the paved thoroughfares and cluttered piazzas of the city center. But it was a nice reminder that such relief was there if ever required—that via a short subway ride to the northern edge of the city I could completely isolate myself from all the dashing Vespas and rumbling buses and towering buildings and international tour groups and streetlights and crosswalks and pavement and … well, just about everything that attracted me to big cities in the first place—that intense accumulation of civilized human development and creation.

This reminder had been inspired by an e-mail I had received two days previously. Leighton had gushed over her own rediscovery of Central Park, now from the perspective of a New York citizen, and how nice it was to have a sectioned-off region right smack-dab in the middle of the otherwise entirely concrete island of Manhattan which was wholly dedicated to trees, streams, grass, birds, squirrels, ponds, and, above all else, space.

I was unsure whether she was as content to backpocket Central Park as I was the Villa Borghese—as quick to place its value, not on the delight felt to escape the city, but on the diving back in afterwards. Regardless, her point of highlighting the contrast and her appreciation for it was indeed valid. And I was truly grateful that Rome's city center was surrounded by dozens of villas, perhaps not all as large as the reigning Villa Borghese in which I was meandering, but dozens of little reminders still of just how slowly life can, and did, and elsewhere does, move.

In a moment of spontaneity I cut off the gravel trail and between a sparse break in the low-lying brush bordering it. My shoes hushed upon hitting the delicate emerald grass. It was sprinkled with moisture and delicately polished the rubber edges of my sneakers.

It did not surprise me that Mom wanted to shift to a more independent lifestyle. My initial gut reaction—which had probably lasted the mere fifteen minutes from the moment Dad had disclosed their situation to me in my emptied apartment to the instant I thrust the pedal of our rented U-Haul to its carpeted floorboard and merged barreling onto the I-5 freeway—had been a trite, masochistic, *Oh, I never would have imagined it could be happening to my parents—to me!* But that was total nonsense.

Dad had spent four months living on an exotic beach after college before transferring cross-county to San Francisco. Mom had grown up between Chicago and Florida, chased some boy to foreign country in her mid-twenties, and then endeavored the cross-county trek herself to the unknown land of California. More recently, Phil had skipped across the entire United States to attend the University of Miami, and I ... well, it was evident what I was up to. I will just highlight the fact that it involved crossing a continent, an ocean, nine time zones, two layovers and a customs check.

Of course Mom wanted to flex her newfound freedom after being anchored, in the interests of Phil and me, to a steady school system and fixed social network for the last sixteen years. Maybe if there had been some unified family unit she would have been breaking away from I might have been more concerned. But there was not. It was each of our individual independences which categorized all our family members. We were strong and self-sufficient people with individual passions and goals. If Mom *had not* been trying to take off after her own bottled-up ambitions she would not have been a Gyulai.

The only problem was that when you talk about personal ambitions within a relationship as intimate as a two-decade-and-running marriage, then you are talking about brushing against and bumping around another person's independent ambitions. And to alleviate that friction, you use compromise. But if those ambitions grow large enough, or build to the level they must have by now with Mom, that bump can become a push—intended or not.

I had sensed Dad's controlled, yet present, distress in his delivery of the news. But then we had been separated by a car length for six hours traveling up I-5, and our brief fast-food pit stops involving bottomless root beer and chicken fajita pitas simply had not felt like the appropriate venue to continue such a dialogue. And then my ten days at home had been left diced into erratic acts of preparation for my move, and Mom had always been somewhere nearby.

But the fact was that Dad knew their marriage far better than I ever would and he, together with Mom, would decide what was best for them. And the always-independently connected Gyulais would move forward. Besides, at the current moment I had my own issues to be addressing, like how on earth one would find one's way out of this mammoth backyard named the Villa Borghese.

I walked toward the sun, figuring that if I kept heading west I would eventually hit the villa's border with the city center. I added a touch more stride to my step, having obtained enough calm and quiet for the day—probably enough for the month.

Within five minutes I had reached a short stone wall and the conclusion of the leafed ceiling. The villa ended at a surprisingly high altitude and I paused for a moment to gaze out across the expanse of the Eternal City—a textured plane of browns and aged pastels, terracotta roofing, and marble spires. The structures rose and fell upon the seven subtle hills beneath them, overlapping one another in a delicate series of rolls leading to the ultimate horizon line, at which point the holy crown of St. Peter's Cathedral, Michelangelo's dome, made the city's final and supreme heavenly thrust skyward.

A short set of stairs to my left trickled down to a narrow winding road which ran parallel to the villa's edge. The road was lined by a stone barricade, beyond which a grassy hill slid steeply downward into the perimeter of city structures at its base. I descended the short set of steps and began along the road on its far side, searching for an additional westward route.

For nearly ten minutes I followed the road's subtle bends and curves as it maintained its hug on the green lip of the Villa Borghese. One of those ridiculous single-seating, three-wheeled motorcars went buzzing by in the opposite direction, the uncovered back section containing a pair of rakes and a hedge trimmer which rattled in heated competition with the vehicle's small engine.

I then spotted what appeared to be an open piazza in the distance. It was centered by an obelisk and its single back wall comprised of a church façade. As I continued toward it, the hill to my right abruptly ran into a tall building, of which I was at roof level. As I passed the building, I peered down over the chest-high barricade and spotted a deep, open-air passageway through which streamed hundreds of tiny people. Further ahead, the pathway's end seemed to open into a large square complete with palm trees, horse buggies, and passing currents of individuals.

I reached the original piazza before me and spotted a break in the wall to my right, which had shortly ago transformed from stone to marble. I directed myself toward the opening, and as I was about to place my foot onto the first of a wide, arching series of stairs, the sudden recognition of where I was spread out below me.

I was standing at the top of the Spanish Steps.

Hordes of Italian teenagers littered the immaculate marble staircase. Some isolated themselves in pairs, casual body movements directed exclusively between each other. An occasional kiss, a persistent physical touch, everything performed with the most intimate of conduct in a most public of settings. Others crowded in parties of five or ten, the focus of the group darting rapidly between its members, half of whom held their backs to the gushing oval fountain, and hordes of people at the base of the stairs. Frequent smiles and laughter lit their faces, which were otherwise shaded by the latest in designer eyewear. Everyone gestured with the utmost animation and greatest insistence at what must have been the most trivial of verbal exchanges.

Past the fountain, to the distance opposite, ran Via dei Condotti, awash in sophisticated shoppers. The most respected names in fashion—Versace, Prada, Dior, Fendi, Bulgari—lined the avenue walls as it faded toward Via del Corso.

Only in a city such as this could one have such an unreasonably high probability of accidentally stumbling upon such splendor. The Spanish Steps, the Trevi Fountain, Piazza Navona, Piazza Venezia, the Coliseum, the Pantheon—the list went on and on. One moment you would find yourself pacing down some nondescript backstreet—the third which you could have sworn you passed down just moments before—mild agitation produced by your disoriented state diluting your initial hopefulness, the sensation of expectation having fully receded back into your now unguarded soul, and then—BAM—one of these artistic architectural triumphs pounced right on top of you.

Leighton was right. Thank God for the parks.

OTTO

It was late, and the rest of the apartment had gone to bed over an hour ago. I pushed onwards, however, casually strumming my acoustic guitar atop my bed, using these final hours in search of the right finger pattern or chord change or vocal harmony to act as the creative seed for a future song.

Writing music is a tantalizing task. The reality of the matter is that everything you could possibly need is sitting right there in front of you. Every possible note and every possible combination of notes must be played out on the six strings lining the wooden neck of the guitar, openly positioned in full, plain sight. It's not like staring at a blank page before a term paper, or a naked canvas and set of watercolors. The guitar has set limits and rules, a finite mathematical way in which the notes can be arranged. And those melodies and those chord changes, they hide there on the neck of the guitar, waiting for you to uncover them.

There are times I just stare at the strings and the marked wood below them, and I think how extraordinary it is that there is a progression in there that I will one day discover, and then a song I will write around that progression, and soon there will be an entire musical composition I will learn to play by heart. And every time I pickup a guitar thereafter, I will see that song's patterns and spot that song's changes in the physical construction of the fret board itself. But right now, for the life of me, I just can't see them.

Tonight—as had happened on the previous fruitless occasions where I had pulled my guitar out from under my small single bed and tried exposing myself to inspiration—I had found nothing. Instead, I simply stared into the cherry-stained wood and ran my fingers along its curved body.

The customs official at the airport had looked at me as though I was crazy when I had claimed the cumbersome instrument case at the airport. But that was a look I had gotten used to in the final weeks leading up to my flight.

Whether they had expressed it subliminally or explicitly, most everyone had presumed I had gone straight out of my mind—that I was crazy.

But this had not been the lunatic, asylum-certifiable type of madness. This had not been *that* definition of crazy. This was the good *crazy*—that same crazy used to define the first mobile phone that took digital photographs, or had been used to describe the first television broadcast from the moon. This was the kind of crazy employed by the less-inspired and apathetic, for the designs they would have never even dreamt possible. And so, in this case, I was entirely comfortable with my assumed classification as absurd.

My phone, on the end table next to me, began to chime. I slid my guitar to the bedsheets and reached for it.

>*Caller ID Unavailable.*

I answered.

"Pronto."

Nothing.

"Pronto," I repeated.

"... Mike?"

"Who is this?"

"Mike, you didn't sound like you."

"Who is this?"

"It's Leighton. I bought a new phone card just for you."

"Leighton!" I remembered the hour and lowered my voice. "What time is it over there?" I asked, guessing to myself the exact difference.

"It's like five something. I wanted to say happy belated Christmas."

"You, too. How was home?"

"I could only stay for three days before I had to fly back to New York, so that was really frustrating. But home was so nice, Mike. It was so nice. Did you talk to your family?"

"My parents, yeah. They called me, and we talked for a little while."

Leighton paused on the other line.

"Did you read the e-mail I sent you last week?"

"I did read it. I just haven't been back to the Internet place yet."

She sighed.

"Mike, I don't want to go to work tomorrow."

Leighton was struggling in New York. She seemed to be growing bipolar regarding both the city and her work. The novelty of an urgent company meeting or first foot of winter snow still succeeded in sending her into a state of exhilaration. But the tedious days in between—which far outnumbered those of innovation—left her increasingly emotional, nostalgic, and lonely.

Anyone could build a social group—even a life, at that—in a large city as sizeable as New York, but there would always remain the impression that you are only a tiny piece of a larger, much more overpowering system. That, in fact, was the exact reason why I was drawn to big cities myself—that feeling of anonymity. Every day felt as if I were crashing a big party thrown by a host unknown. I found this exhilarating and even liberating. But I also acknowledged the flip side: feeling lost in a maddening house party where each room was alien and every face foreign.

"It's just hard to have no one from my rooted past around me," Leighton started. "There is no one to bridge past concepts of home and comfort and stability with this new place."

"You just need to give it some time," I encouraged. "You need to keep planting your own stories around the city—give meaning to what is now just anonymous stretches of pavement."

There was silence.

"Does that make sense?" I asked.

"Yeah. I guess so. It's just ..." she hesitated. "I don't know, Mike."

"I'm sure you're already doing it—New York is just such a big place. But think of one year from now. You'll have all these events that have happened to you—and I'm not talking big stuff. Little things—an absurd argument you had with your boyfriend on some street corner at four in the morning, the pizza place that charged you six bucks for a piece of cold veggie combo composed of two mushrooms and three olives, the stretch of sidewalk you camped out on at six in the morning for theater tickets. As those things happen—and they will happen on their own as long as you get out there—a map of Manhattan will change from the elusive diagram of street names it is now, to a personal record of your memories there. You'll become part of the city itself. And then you'll be a piece of the system that in turn makes another new twenty-two-year-old girl feel lonely when she moves out from the West Coast."

There was silence on the other end of the line, but I could feel her smile. This was one of the reasons Leighton loved me.

"Mike. I miss you."

BEEP, BEEP, BEEP.

I pulled the phone from my ear and looked at the display.

>*+390668359367 Unknown Contact—Accept Call?*

I moved it back to my ear.

"Leighton, sorry, I have this other call. I'll e-mail you soon, I promise. You're all right, aren't you?"

"Yeah, I'm all right."

"Good, I'm glad you called."

"Me too. Bye, Mike."

"Bye."

I quickly pulled the phone from my head and pressed the small black button corresponding with *Accept Call*. I then switched hands and placed the mobile to my opposite ear.

"Pronto?"

"Hi, is this Michael?"

"Yes, speaking."

"Hi, this is Dario, from Metro."

Intriguing. He continued, "Hassan told me you came by earlier this week and that you have your documents in order?"

"I got them. The permit and the certificate—I have them both."

"Good. We've had a lot of buzz surrounding our New Year's Eve event. I know this is last-minute but would you be available to come in, say, ten o'clock?"

"Sure. Yes. Definitely."

"You don't have plans?"

Nina had invited me to something.

"Nothing I'll regret, no," I told him.

"All right, ten o'clock and bring your Tessera Sanitaria. I was thinking fifty Euro for the night, most likely until four or five in the morning, plus whatever tips you make."

"That sounds fair." I really had no idea what was fair, but I also didn't care.

"And wear all black."

"Will do."

"See you tomorrow, then."

"See you tomorrow!"

NOVE

I entered Campo de' Fiori at quarter to ten. The piazza was already anarchic. Teenagers and young adults of countless nationalities swamped the piazza. Some worked at opening cheap bottles of wine, others at breaking them. Thick clusters of individuals swelled at the entrances to each of the numerous bars lining the square, waiting anxiously to be let inside the already bursting nightclubs.

I moved swiftly through the crowds, steadily making my way toward the large umbrellas covering Metro's outdoor seating. To my left, there was a sudden small scattering of five or six mischievous-looking kids. Their pants slid down past their buttocks as they fled, a single hand reaching back to clench a baggy back pocket, the other occupied with a cigarette or bottle of beer.

One of them collided with the black tote bag I had slung over my shoulder. He stumbled, and then a chain of small rapid explosions fired from the emptied space of cobblestone where the kids had been huddled moments before. The quick flashes of white, red, and orange lit the faces of the startled bystanders who then began to cheer and clap at the deviant fireworks display.

I passed under the outdoor umbrellas of Metro and pushed my way down the center lane of tables scattered about the cobblestone at the club's entrance. Customers were everywhere, yet only a handful were seated, the rest wandering the alleyways between the tables.

I spotted a waitress at the far table closest to the wall of the piazza. She stacked empty martini and pint glasses onto her tray. She looked fatigued and expelled a hard exhale as she emptied a beer bottle into a planter.

I pushed toward the entrance and was met by a barrier of people, their backs to my face. Deep, booming bass rhythms pounded through the large double doors ahead. Hints of the repetitive higher melodies were muffled by the glass and obscurely floated into the space around us.

At the front of the small crowd I spotted a doorman dressed in a charcoal sport coat. He held a demanding precence. His eyes narrowed as he returned my stare.

"Lavori?" he called huskily over the heads of eager onlookers.

"Sì!" I called back, nodding assertively.

He stepped from his perch at the door and began motioning for the crowd to part.

"Fatelo entrare, raga'," he ordered. "Fatelo entra.'"

I looked to the ground as I entered the club, biting my lip to restrain the broad smile breaking across my face.

Inside, the dance music was deafening, and the boisterous clientele screamed into each other's ears. I was unable to make out a single table, as a dense, wall-to-wall sea of people churned in front of me.

I sensed someone behind me and quickly turned, nearly knocking to the floor the entire tray of glasses the waitress from outside had gathered. She yelped and swung the tray to her side just in time.

"*Sorry!* Err, scusami!"

She giggled graciously as she regained her composure. Her jet-black hair was fixed into a tidy bun. Her skin was smooth and caramel, her nose distinctly Roman, her eyes wide and dark. She appeared quite comfortable displaying her well-endowed figure; her ample cleavage seemed barely contained by her dark Metro V-neck top.

"Lavori con noi stasera?" she yelled over the music.

"Sì," I yelled back.

"Mi chiamo Isabella."

She thought for a moment about extending her hand from her tray but quickly opted for a simple head nod, so as to maintain her grip on the precarious arrangement of glasses.

"Io mi chiamo Michael. Mike, se preferisci." I nodded back.

"Piacere, Mike!" And Isabella disappeared into the stirring bodies, toward the bar.

I spotted Dario along the left wall, at the register. He was on the customer side of the glass counter, yelling something to Hassan at his post opposite. I made my way to them, Hassan noticing me first and pointing his chin in my direction. Dario looked back over his shoulder.

"Good, you're here," he said. "We were supposed to have a third bartender tonight, but the unreliable fuck didn't show and has his phone off."

"Where do you want me?"

Dario reached over the counter and grabbed a small black apron.

"Here, put this on."

He pressed it to my chest and began guiding me away from the counter.

"I want you to get behind the bar and try your best to keep things moving. Clear the dirty glasses, refill the ice, clean the tins—just keep it going for the bartenders."

"Okay."

"You want to throw your bag at the deejay booth?" Dario asked as we began pushing through the first layer of screaming patrons.

"That would be great," I called back.

The place was a madhouse. It wasn't that large of a club, and with each slow, extended step forward, the pressure of bodies became greater, the music pounded even more heavily, and the crazed atmosphere grew exponentially more fanatical.

By the middle of our journey across the main floor my bag was repeatedly anchoring on other customers as I fought past them, battling to keep up with Dario. Everyone's skin was tinted an eerie pale green which radiated from the surrounding Plexiglas walls.

Dario cut toward the bar—finally at its end—and the deejay booth just behind it. I wrestled with my bag a final time and broke into the tight space at the end of the illuminated counter.

"Calum, socialize after I'm done paying you, man," Dario snapped to the deejay. He shook his head and leaned to the ear of the attractive brunette in stilettos and a short black skirt who was blocking our narrow passageway forward. She listened intently, then covered her mouth and bashfully stepped past us and back onto the crowded floor.

Dario climbed behind the bar and motioned for my bag. I slid it off my shoulder and handed it to him.

"You have your Tessera Sanitaria in here, right?" he asked.

"Yeah. And a jacket for later. And an umbrella and a few other things."

"Let's see the certificate."

I unzipped the bag, suspended in front of me from Dario's hands, and dug out my small, orange *Libretto di Idoneità Sanitaria*.

"Here." I handed it to him.

He passed my bag to the deejay, and then fingered through the first three or four pages of the Libretto.

"How'd you convince them to issue it?"

"I guess my Italian is good enough to persuade a doctor," I laughed.

He did not.

"I want you to remember," he closed the small booklet and looked up at me, "If you try to pull anything tonight, I have this." He slid my Tessera Sanitaria into the back pocket of his jeans. "Hassan is in charge of everything at the register. If he tells me you gave anyone—and I don't care who they are or how hot she is—if anyone gets a drink without paying, the first thing I do is fire you. The second thing I do is call the police."

I nodded and timidly looked away, working to gather the strings of my black apron to tie around my waist.

"Mariano!" Dario called down the bar.

One of the bartenders—the shorter of the two, with curly black hair—looked over to us. He had a blender pitcher in his hand and was in the middle of pouring its contents into a pair of tall glasses which had chocolate syrup spiraled up their insides. In front of him, the ocean of clients splashed onto the counter, extending hands waving Euro bills, frantic faces begging for eye contact.

"Questo ragazzo qua," Dario continued to him while pointing at me, "Ci sta --- ------- ---sera. Spiegaglielo tutto che ---- ----." *This kid is here ... evening ... explain everything to him that ...*

The blasting music made it harder than normal to make out the Italian.

The bartender nodded and went back to emptying his blender into the glasses. Dario turned to me.

"Mariano will take you from here."

He shot an advisory eye at the deejay and then dropped past me back into the swarm of customers. I worked to finish tying the strings of my apron behind my back.

"Can you believe that?"

I looked up at the deejay.

"He wants me to wait until five in the morning to talk to these girls. You see how much ass is in the place right now?"

"Yeah," was all I could think of.

"Sei l'Americano?" a voice spoke to my left.

I looked. The bartender was standing at my side. He was a good eight inches shorter than I was.

"Sì, mi chiamo Mike," I replied.

He patted me on the shoulder and reached for a key hanging on the wall beside the deejay.

"Sono Mariano, piacere. Vieni con me un ------ a vedere -- ---------." Mariano spoke incredibly fast. Thankfully, his lines were fairly basic. His name was Mariano and I would be going with him to see something.

I followed him back onto the floor and into the crowd. Just beyond the bar's end the tightly packed invasion reached its limit and the final back room, lined with a set of couches and another stretch of illuminated Plexiglas walling, was surprisingly desolate.

Mariano gestured with both his hands toward the back of the club as we walked. His left motioned toward a set of flapping double doors, his right toward a low-lit stairwell.

"Di là sta la cucina che l'usiamo solo di giorno, e qua giù -- l'abbiamo i bagni e il ---------." Through the slim double doors was the kitchen which they only used during the daytime. And down the stairs in the direction we were heading were the bathrooms and something else I had not understood.

"Giù c'è cosa?" I yelled over the music and shook my head.

"Il magazzino!" he screamed back.

Magazzino. Not a word I knew.

We descended the staircase, which doubled back on itself halfway down, and then stepped past a line of men and women waiting awkwardly in front of two bathroom doors. There was a grey access door just beyond the restrooms into which Mariano guided the large silver key. He spun it twice and the door fell open.

Fluorescent lighting lit a long, stale corridor lined with metal shelving. We moved towards the rear, past a wall of peanuts and potato chips. To the left, an oversized refrigerator, with a large black handle and digital temperature readout, hummed throughout the otherwise quiet underground space. Beyond the snack food, we passed stacked kegs of beer and sealed cartons of Coca-Cola, Sprite, Fanta, and an array of other drink labels I could not recognize.

Magazzino. *Storeroom.*

At the end of the walkway—which must have extended the entire length of the club above—was the collection of alcohol. Mariano began waving his hands left and right at the walls of bottles.

"-- --- ci sono i whiskey che -- ---- ------ a parte del rum che --- ---- ----. Qua in mezzo --------- -- vodka, gin, ed i liquori. Ovviamente non c'è bisogno -- ------ ----- che -- --------- oggi ma ------- benissimo per noi se - -------- il più ------ possibile." I was missing half the words Mariano was telling me. He just spoke so quickly. But I figured I could not have been that lost.

The whiskey was over there on the top shelf, the rum was on the bottom, mixed in the middle was the rest of the stuff—vodkas, gins, and liquors.

"E poi di qua ci stanno i -----. Sai cambiarli?"

I stared at him silently, hoping his question was only there to segue into further explanation. But he waited for me to answer him. And I had no idea what he was asking me.

"So fare cosa?" I finally repeated.

"I fusti. Sai cambiarli?"

Fusti. What on earth was a *fusto*? I smiled and forced a laugh. I understood he was asking if I knew how to change a *fusto* but I simply had no idea what a *fusto* was.

"Ma tu parli Italiano?"

I took initial offense at the question. But it was fleeting, and embarrassment quickly permeated my mental state.

"Man, do not to worry," Mariano then began in English, "I have been to London to work in a bar for six month."

His accent was garbled, but intelligible.

"Ma voglio imparare l'Italiano," I insisted.

"We learn you Italian another day. Today I explain to change the keg of beer."

Fusto. *Keg*. They were right at his feet; I should have guessed that.

He crouched over one of the five metal cylinders. Plastic tubing sprouted from each of their centers and ran into a hole in the wall behind them. Next to the hole, a set of three pressure gauges measured the levels of the adjacent gas tanks. I leaned over Mariano's shoulder and watched him grip a small green clutch where the plastic tube met the metal keg.

"First you make *up*, then *turn*."

He jerked the tab upwards and then yanked it to the right. It came loose and he held it up to me.

"Then you put the new keg. But this one is still," he paused, "filled?"

"Still full."

"Still full," he repeated.

He placed the connecter back into the keg.

"First you *turn*, then you make *down*."

He twisted the tab back into place and shoved the handle downwards, locking it.

"Okay?" he smiled at me.

"Okay."

"Now we go to the party."

We sped back to the end of the storeroom and locked the door behind us. We climbed the stairwell, and I followed him to the bar. We stepped behind it and found Dario at Mariano's bar station.

"Dove ----- siete andati?" he yelled to Mariano. He then looked across to me.

"Where did he take you?"

"The macasino," I replied.

"The magazzino?" he corrected, as his eyes shot back to Mariano.

They argued for a few heated seconds. I pretended not to listen.

Dario made a final conclusive statement and then pushed past us. Mariano turned to me.

"He says I explain that another time. Now we work."

I nodded. "Where do you want me?" I asked.

"Remain at the sinks."

He pointed to the main bar station. Just left of the main bartender, where the glass counter made its large, arched beginning, sat a pair of circular sinks. I started toward them.

The space behind the bar was exceptionally tight, no wider than the aisle of a passenger plane. To the right ran three glass shelves of a back bar. I gazed at the numerous bottles as I passed, able to recognize only a scattered few—Jack Daniel's, Malibu, Baileys, Peach Tree.

I reached the sinks and for the first time turned to face the mob of swarming clients. The bar took on a new dimension, spacious and rarefied. I was a good foot and a half above the crowd opposite me. I felt extraordinary, emphasized, important. I caught the eye of a woman just in front of me. She started screaming something at me. Then the man next to her began shaking a twenty-Euro bill toward my face. He started screaming too. I quickly looked down to the sinks at my waist.

There were two white dishwashing baskets, one in each sink. Each basket was partially filled with a confusion of dirty glasses. Between the glasses lay pieces of random garnish—a wedge of orange, a pair of cherries, a cluster of mint leaves. I looked to my knees below for a washing machine but found only a shelf with various cleaning supplies and packets of iced tea mix.

"O!"

I turned. The second bartender—the tall one with the shaved head—pointed his knife back in Mariano's direction.

"La lavatrice è la giù," he told me. I followed the direction of the blade and spotted a small red and white speed washer built into the wall between where I was standing and where Mariano worked. I nodded and gripped one of the white baskets with my fingers. The bartender stepped to me and motioned for me to stop.

"Devono stare pieni prima," he instructed. *They must be full first.*

I released the basket and worked to fill it with dirty glasses from the space of counter before me.

"E ----- quella altra merda," he added. I had to do something with shit. *The other shit* to be precise. I looked up to him with uncertainty.

"Do you speak English?" I asked.

He stared at me for a moment, perplexed. Then he speared an orange wedge with his knife and held it to my nose.

"Togli questa merda qua." I guessed that was a *no* to the English. And the *other shit* was the leftover garnish I had to remove.

The nameless bartender stepped back to his station, less than three feet away from me, and I began fishing out the alcohol-saturated lemons, oranges, limes, and cherries. I then lifted the basket and took the two steps to the speed washer. I balanced the basket on my thigh and carefully opened the square metal door. I slid the basket inside, closed the door, and eyed the three grey buttons above.

The first button was stamped with an image of a circle enclosing a dash. I assumed it meant power. The second was a small clock. Probably the timed cycle. The third was a series of dashes forming a V. I had no idea what that could possibly mean. I went with the clock.

Nothing. I pressed it again. The adjacent orange light remained unlit. From what I could tell, the machine made no sound. I held my knees and squinted at the machine. Suddenly a hand thrust into view and a finger jammed the clock button inward.

"One and two and three," he counted. It was Mariano. The machine hissed as it started its cycle, and Mariano released the button.

"And it is more easy to open first the machine, then to bring the cestino," he said to me.

Cestino. *Basket.* And open the washer door first.

"Got it," I nodded.

I filled another basket, removed the previous one from the machine, and loaded the new one in its place. I grabbed a pair of steaming glasses from the first basket and turned to the back bar. The music pounded relentlessly in my ears from the speakers above.

In front of me were three tiers of green illuminated shelving. Upon the first sat pint glasses, tops down. The second shelf held daiquiri glasses and the third, martini. I rapidly slid the clean glasses in my hands to their respective shelves.

I turned back to the sinks and found Isabella unloading a tray of bottles and dirty stemware onto the countertop. I smiled at her and began sorting them into the sink.

A second girl appeared at the bar, also adorned in a Metro shirt and carrying a tray of empty glasses. She and Isabella exchanged words over the music. They rolled their eyes and made overstated gestures of elbowing people in their sides and explosions with their arms. Isabella's eyes darted to mine and then back to the other waitress. She said something to her and pointed at me. The waitress leaned into the counter and I bent down to meet her.

"Ciao, Mike, mi chiamo Carmen," she yelled into my ear.

She had thick, wavy black hair which fell past her neck and off her shoulders. She had a rounded nose and wide cheeks which dimpled as she smiled at me. She wore a dark undershirt, creating a more conservative view than Isabella's relaxed display of skin.

"Carmen? Di dove sei?" I asked.

"Peru! Sei americano, giusto?"

"Sì."

A Peruvian. Rome seemed like an odd place for relocation. But what did I know about Peru or Peruvians.

They turned and sank back into the mob.

Over an hour must have passed before I developed a comfortable rhythm—fill a basket with glasses, exchange it with the one in the machine, and stack the clean glasses in their appropriate areas. I focused on the music and blocked out the crowds constantly vying for my attention at the counter in front of me.

Every few minutes Mariano or the other bartender would slam a mixing tin onto the space next to the sink. I had committed the taboo act of cleaning the first pair with soap. "Rovina il gusto dei cocktail," the bartender had told me. *That ruins the taste of the cocktails.* But after that initial misstep I had been swift with the simple rinsing, and raced to place them back onto the rubber bar mats at the heads of their bar stations as they worked.

As my routine gathered momentum, I began closing the washer door with a flip of my foot, and rinsing tins with one hand while the other continued to organize dirty glasses. I found a bag of cocktail straws behind the iced tea under the sink and proceeded to jam them into the depleting supply at each bartender's station.

"Scusa." The second, tall bartender appeared at my side. He was holding two glasses of champagne.

"Sì?" I asked, forcing the last fistful of straws into the holder at his workstation.

He extended one of the glasses towards me, and I took it in my hand.

"Come ti chiami?" he asked.

"Mike," I responded.

"Roberto, piacere."

We shook with our free hands.

"Senti, Mike," he looked at his watch, "mancano ancora un paio di minuti. Metti il prosecco a parte fino a ------." *Listen, Mike, still a few minutes left. Put the prosecco to the side until ...*

I thanked him and began searching for a sheltered space of counter. The music lowered, and Calum's voice amplified throughout the club.

"Due minuti! Two minutes until two thousand five, ragazzi! Siete pronti?"

The room filled with whistling and applause. Then the music rose back to its previous ear-splitting level.

"Mike!"

I looked left down the bar. The plastic pitcher of Mariano's blender was in midair, its arcing path having just reached its pinnacle, its trajectory heading straight for my stomach. I spun my body, sending a splash of champagne across the sleeve of my shirt. My free right hand met the pitcher's large plastic handle as it fell into me. I guided it into a controlled fall past my chest, an extension of its natural descent, before swinging it back up to my chest. I spun to Mariano, my body open, champagne dripping off my left hand, his dirty blender in my right, and yelled to him.

"How about a little more warning next time?"

"That was great, man!" he clapped.

I dipped my head in a mock bow and then placed my champagne glass onto the counter beside me. I rinsed the pitcher, stepped back to Mariano's station, and dropped it atop the blender's metal base.

"That was really something to special," he smiled.

I grinned and started back up the narrow aisle.

"Mike!" Mariano's voice called from behind.

"What!" I twirled to him.

His two metal tins collided with my chest, sending a wave of ice and alcohol crashing across my neck. I seized one of the tins between my body and right forearm. The second went clanging to the floor below.

"It is okay! We will practice more that one!"

This guy was ridiculous. I picked up the tin from the ground. Roberto was watching me over his shoulder, smiling and shaking his head. I heard Mariano call to him up the bar.

"Cosa!"

Roberto yelled back, "Sei uno stronzo!"

I didn't know what *stronzo* meant but assumed it was a playful insult. Mariano made a quick rebuttal, unintelligible to me, and the two laughed and returned to work.

Just as I finished rinsing Mariano's tins, Calum's voice returned over the speaker system.

"Thirty seconds everybody! Trenta secondi!"

I moved down the bar to Mariano's station again and placed the tins onto his bar mat. He was crouched at the small fridge below. The double doors were open, and he was rummaging inside. He looked up at me and waved me down to him.

"What can I help you with?" I asked as I squatted to fridge level beside him in the tight walkway.

"Twenty seconds!" Calum's voice blared overhead. "Venti secondi, ragazzi!"

"Listen," Mariano started as he pulled a carton of orange juice from the small refrigerator. "I must to tell you something."

"Sure, what it is?"

He twisted the blue plastic cap from the carton's top and threw it to the floor behind him.

"It is really a pleasure to work with you. Truly." He closed the metal doors of the fridge, and we sat motionless for a moment, ducked in the aisle below counter level.

"Thank you, Mariano. It's a pleasure for me as well."

"You are very much help for us tonight. Really."

"Good," I smiled.

"Ten seconds! Dieci! Nove!" Calum began the final countdown.

"Now go get your prosecco, motherfucker!" Mariano snapped and sprang upright.

I stood myself and quickly paced back to the sinks to grab my champagne. The entire room began to count in unison.

"Sei! Cinque! Quattro!"

I raised my glass to Roberto who raised his in return. We turned and saluted Mariano, also holding his sparkling prosecco to the sky.

"Tre! Due! Uno!"

The sea of people tilted their heads to the ceiling and screamed: "Buon anno!"

Couples began to kiss; others cheered. James Brown ripped across the speakers. Everyone started to bounce up and down and mouthed the lyrics in an overly enunciated fashion: "I feel gud, new fat I could!"

I spotted Isabella and Carmen at the front corner of the club. They were jumping to the music themselves, their own prosecco glasses in hand. They waved to me. I raised my glass, then placed it to my lips and gulped down the sparkling prosecco.

It was midnight in Rome.

By two in the morning the scene had reached its frenzied apex. The entire club seemed inebriated, affectionate, uninhibited, and playful. I continually moved glass after glass into the baskets and through the washer, Mariano sending an airborne blender or mixing tin in my direction every few minutes.

I glanced to Roberto. He worked seamlessly with the bottles and juices and glasses surrounding him. It must have felt incredible to be a bartender, especially on a night such as this. I flipped my gaze down the bar to Mariano. He gripped one of the beer taps and was dancing as the golden liquid streamed into a pint glass held in his opposite hand.

Suddenly the glass exploded with white foam, sending a shower of suds into the crowd pressed against the bar.

"Mike!" he screamed without even glancing in my direction. I wiped my wet hands on my back pockets and raced to him.

"Mike. Can you do for me a very great favor?" he asked.

"Of course. Tell me."

"You need to change the keg. The beer of Carlsberg."

"Okay."

"You remember how to make the change?"

"I think so, yeah."

"Good. Go!"

I stepped past him and sprinted to the end of the bar. I stepped to the floor and began pushing through the crowd in front of me.

"Mike!"

The voice had been barely audible over the music. I turned back to the bar. Mariano was raised on his toes, his hands cupped over his mouth.

"La ------!" he screamed.

"The what?" I yelled back.

"La chiave!"

He gestured as if starting a car. Shit! *The key.* I fought back to the deejay booth and found Calum dangling the silver key toward me. I raced to the stairwell and through the grey access door. The music faded to a muffled bass line, the mammoth refrigerator steadily hummed as I skipped past it. At the back of the storeroom I found the keg stamped *Carlsberg* and gripped the plastic tab of the connecter.

What the hell had it been—up and then turn, or turn and then up? I yanked the tab right. It immediately broke loose in my hand, and a mist of beer shot across my face, accompanied by the piercing sound of rapidly escaping pressure. I jolted upright and cursed as I cleaned the beer from my eyes with my shirt.

I found a new keg behind me and dragged its unexpected weight across the tiled flooring. I removed the rubber seal from its top, reset the tab of the connector, and pushed the two together, making sure to first twist the connector into place before depressing the tab. Yellow liquid streamed into the plastic tubing and I hurried back to the door. I climbed the stairs and the deep electronic music pulsated back into audible focus.

I emerged from the stairwell and began through the back room towards the bar. Against the wall opposite the couches I noticed a girl. Her figure was petite and her skin fair. She had platinum-blonde hair—almost white—pulled into a ponytail behind her head. Her arms were crossed and she stared at the mass of outrageous customers. Her eyes skipped to mine as I passed.

"Ciao," she waved loosely.

I stopped. I wanted to look and see if there was anyone behind me but I could sense there was no one.

She smiled.

"Ciao," I stepped to her. "Mi chiamo Mike."

"Skye, piacere."

We shook hands. What kind of name was Skye?

"Di dove sei?" I asked her.

"Islanda."
"Iceland?"
"Sì."

That explained the obligatory Nordic hair. She glanced toward the crowd again.

"Che casino," she muttered. *What a mess.*

She rolled her eyes and looked back at me.

"Sei Americano, giusto?"

It seemed everyone could tell.

"Sì."

"Da quale parte?"

"California. Los Angeles."

Her delicate lips widened and a smile of intrigue lit her face.

"Conosci qualcuno di famosa?" *Do you know anyone famous?*

Her expressions were spirited and sparkling with emotion. Her eyes were large and light, either blue or green, it was hard to tell in the darkness of the club.

"No, non conosco nessuno famoso."

She shrugged and looked back toward the main room. Then her arms fell to her sides, exposing a small embroidered *Metro* across the left side of her shirt.

"Wait, you work here?" I asked, forgetting the conversation's Italian precedent.

"Sì. Purtroppo." *Unfortunately.*

"You can understand English?"

"Of course I can."

"You speak it too? Didn't you hear my terrible accent?"

"It was cute."

I stood silent.

"Allora," she began, "Dovremmo tornare a lavorare." *We better get back to work.* She pulled herself off the wall and started back toward the bar. I trailed her and then forced my way up behind the counter.

"The hell were you doing down there for so long?" Calum asked, his headphones clutched between his shoulder and right ear.

"Nothing, changing a keg," I replied as I fixed the key onto the wall next to him. Calum focused on something over my shoulder and then grinned down at me. I glanced backwards. Skye's radiant hair acted like a beacon, signaling the position of her modest figure as it fought through the ocean of dark bodies. I looked back to Calum.

"Careful, man," he told me, "I'm pretty sure she's taken."

I stepped back down the aisle, past Mariano and to the sinks. Hassan had disappeared from his post at the register. Roberto spotted me and pointed frantically to a pair of tins. I grabbed them and began rinsing, but before I could finish Mariano was at my side screaming fanatically.

"Quick, come here! Very quick!"

He grabbed my belt and dragged me from the sinks, around the pyramid back bar, directly behind Roberto, who continued to work diligently for the relentless customers at the counter. From our position practically pressed against the wall of bottles, we were hidden from the view of the main room. Mariano held one hand on my shoulder, instructing me not to move, and shot rapid glances around the corner and back down the length of the club. I looked again toward the vacant register.

"Mariano, where is Hassan?"

"I don't know, man. I don't know where he went to," he replied without looking at me, continuing his cautious looks around the edge of the pyramid back bar.

Mariano's hand dropped from my back and I leaned in behind him, following his gaze to the back of the crowded floor. At the bar's end, past Mariano's vacant workstation and across from the deejay booth, I could see Dario talking to an older man in a suit. The man propped a small briefcase on the glass counter next to him. He looked official, authoritative, legal. He looked like a cop.

Mariano spun past me, pulling us both completely out of sight.

My first night and the cops show up! In a way I should have guessed it; New Years Eve must have been one of the most policed nights of the year. Of course there were going to be cops everywhere. What major city in the world would not have their largest police force on duty for New Year's Eve? Maybe my Tessera Sanitaria could get me off the hook. Maybe they would not ask to see a work visa.

Mariano wrapped an arm around my waist.

"Do not to move!" he called from behind.

Fuck this. I could hop over the bar. I could hop over the bar and drop into the crowd and disappear. I wasn't wearing anything Metro-branded; I was simply dressed in black. I could hop over right beside Roberto and skip straight out the front doors. I couldn't be deported, not yet. It was too soon to be deported.

I heard the shifting of bottles behind me and felt a fist press into the small of my back. Mariano's other hand moved from my waist to my forehead. He pulled backward and my vision shot to the ceiling.

"Open your mouth!" he screamed.

What the fuck was going on?

"Your mouth, it is opened?"

"Yes!" I screamed skyward, mouth gaping.

The concise pressure on my back vanished. The black and white label of Jack Daniel's glided into view. The spout of the bottle centered just below my nose and a stream of aromatic brown liquid fell from its metal tip and splashed off my tongue, filling the inside of my open mouth.

Suddenly the stream was cut, the bottle disappeared, and Mariano skipped around me and back toward his station. I dropped my head, winced, and swallowed. Then I slowly stepped back to the sinks, wiping the corners of my mouth with my shirtsleeve, and gazed down the length of the bar.

Hassan was sliding past Mariano, who was already back to mixing something in the pair of metal tins on his bar mat. He adjusted his belt as he moved toward me, drying his hands on the thighs of his jeans. Beyond him, still at the end of the bar, Dario and the older man smiled and lightly kissed the air around each other's cheeks. The man then slid his briefcase off the countertop and pushed back into the crowd. He waved over his shoulder at Dario, who smiled and nodded in friendly acknowledgment.

I looked back at Roberto. He was grinning at me while he worked.

"Siamo ----- di cazzo," he called to me.

He and Mariano were *what*?

"Siete cosa?" I asked.

Roberto slid two cocktails off his bar mat to a pair of customers. He then stepped next to me and placed a hand on my shoulder.

"Lui," he pointed to Mariano, "È una testa di cazzo. Ed io," he pointed to himself, "sono una testa di cazzo. Tutti noi due semo teste di cazzo." *Mariano is a dickhead. And I am a dickhead. Both of us are dickheads.*

Mariano noticed our conversation and skipped back up the aisle.

"What does Roberto tell you?"

"He says you're a dickhead."

Mariano shrugged. "È la verità." He smiled and turned to leave.

"Wait! What happened with the cop?"

Mariano turned back toward me, confused. "What cop?"

"The one speaking with Dario!"

"There is no polizotto. There is the boss of the property."

"Mariano!" Hassan's voice came thundering from the register. "Che fai!" He jammed his finger first at Mariano, then to the abandoned bar station.

"Quanto ti amo, Hassan." Mariano blew a kiss across the backbar and then raced back to his position.

I looked backward to Roberto. He was shaking his head.

"Scusaci, Mike."

"No, no," I insisted. "Mi piace molto lavorare con voi!" *I really like working with you guys!*

He smiled and patted the back of my neck.

"Sei uno bravo."

It must not have been until five thirty that we finally succeeded in clearing out the last rowdy customers. With the club empty and the stark white house lights ignited, the expanse of leftover disorder provided a discouraging sight for our worn-out bodies. Isabella and Carmen had reluctantly begun stacking the tables and chairs on the outdoor cobblestone, while Skye began to sweep and mop the floor inside. Roberto and Mariano wrapped leftover fruit in cellophane and jammed their plastic speed bottles of fruit juices into the fridges. I was assigned to trash duty and worked to carry the bursting waste bags to the piazza outside.

The cobblestone was littered with broken glass—greens and purples, sparkling and transparent. Disparate individuals, some in pairs, a scattered few alone, slowly crossed the open square. Stacks of black garbage bags anchored the foundations of each lamppost, the glossy plastic lit from above by a dim yellow light. Tattered staff appeared from the open doors of the numerous bars lining the piazza and added individual bottles or cardboard boxes to the established piles.

My hands on my hips, I watched my warm breath mist off the cool morning air. A young couple stumbled past me. They held each other as they walked, giggling hysterically. My thumbs ran the line of my apron tied at my waist.

I felt like I had taken part in something exclusive and elite, like I had slipped my way into the backstage of an event for which I had not gained actual authorization. I might have been playing a part at the beginning of the night, but was it not a simple fact that by the night's end, over seven hours later, I was no longer acting but was indeed *doing*—doing a job alongside Mariano and Roberto, doing a job which complimented those done by Carmen and Isabella and Skye, the six of us serving the hundreds of outsiders that should have included me.

I turned and began to cross the now-vacant cobblestone leading to Metro's double doors. Inside I could see Mariano and Roberto talking to Dario across the counter. They shot quick glances through the glass toward me as they spoke.

As I entered, Mariano and Roberto dispersed to their stations and Dario called me to the bar next to him.

"How did you feel the night went?" he asked.

"Well. Really well. You seem to have a great staff here."

He reached into his front pocket and extracted a meaty sandwich of Euro bills.

"Roberto said you really helped them out tonight." He turned to Roberto, who was wiping down the metal workspace at his station. "Roberto, che dici?"

Roberto stood upright and stepped to us.

"Lavora bene, lavora veloce, lavora preciso. È un grande, Dario." *He works well, he works fast, he works precisely. He's great, Dario.*

Roberto turned to me and extended his arm.

"Grande, Mike. Grande," he said as our hands locked.

Roberto moved back to his cleaning. Dario peeled three blue twenty-Euro bills from the outmost edge of the bundle and placed them onto the glass countertop between us.

"I'm going to give you sixty Euro for tonight instead of fifty. How does that sound?"

"Tremendous. Thank you."

I slid the bills off the counter and into my left pocket.

"Now," he continued, "do you have another position in the city?"

"No, at the moment I don't really have anything else lin—"

"Then here is what I'd like to do," he interrupted. "You'll come in at ten Thursday, Friday, and Saturday nights to help Roberto and Mariano behind the bar. For each shift, which is essentially a half shift, you'll get twenty Euro plus whatever tips you divide between yourselves."

I nodded, as if reviewing the proposal and its details in my head, but in actuality only to suppress what would have been an embarrassingly excited outburst.

"Great," I replied.

"Good. So we will hang onto your sanitary certificate; I'll file it alongside the others, and how about this first Thursday you come in at six instead of ten so the guys can show you a few things when the atmosphere is a bit calmer."

"Thursday at six."

We shook.

"You may want to see if Roberto or Mariano need anything else, but as far as I'm concerned you're free to go."

I moved to the deejay booth to find my bag. Calum was seated at the couches of the back room, lounging alongside a pair of young girls. I untied my apron, placed it into the handbag, and pulled my leather jacket from inside.

"Mariano, do you need me to do anything else?" I asked as I approached him.

"No man, we have finished, you are free to go away. I will see you next week?"

"Ci vediamo Giovedì," I confirmed, and zipped my jacket to my neck.

"Ciao, Roberto!" I called across to him; his body was hunched low to the metal workspace he had just cleaned. He looked to be counting money and grabbed a handful of bills.

"Ecco, Mike."

He spread the colorful currency across the glossy green counter in front of me. I looked up at him.

"Che cos'è?" I asked.

He smiled at me.

"Tips," he said and then moved back to his sorting.

I counted the money and moved it to my pocket along with the sixty Euro from Dario. Roberto had slid me thirty more Euro. I had made ninety Euro tonight. Ninety Euro cash, in my left pant pocket.

I waved to Hassan at the cash register. He waved back silently. At the front doors, Isabella and Carmen had changed into their street clothes and were exchanging drags off a single shared cigarette as they conversed. Skye stood to the side by herself, staring intently down at her phone. Isabella was the first to notice me.

"Ciao, Mike!"

She reached behind me with one hand, the other delicately fingering the slowly burning cigarette, and pulled me toward her. We kissed cheeks and smiled. I turned to Carmen.

"Piacere, Mike!" she said to me.

"È stato un piacere, Carmen," I smiled.

We embraced lightly and tapped cheeks as well. I turned to Skye. She continued to stare fixedly at her phone.

"Do you work on Thursday, Skye?" I asked her right cheek. She looked up at me. Now, under the white house lights, her wide eyes shined a stunning and sparkling sapphire.

"Yes, yes I do," she smiled politely.

"I'll see you Thursday, then."

I leaned down to her and gently pressed my skin to hers. I then stepped to the door and turned to face the entirety of the club as I pushed backwards to the piazza. In the distance Calum laughed with the two girls on the back couches. At the bar, Roberto was handing Mariano his tips; exaggerated gestures accompanied their enthusiastic discussion. To my immediate right, Carmen and Isabella fired rapidly in Italian, interjecting giggles and amplified body movements into their sentences. And to my left, the increasingly alluring Skye focused again on the mobile phone in her hand. What a perfect night.

I spotted Dario at the register speaking with Hassan.

"Bye Dario!" I called to him.

He looked up at me from behind the register and waved.

"I'll see you Thursday, Mark."

Almost perfect.

Welcome to **Wells Fargo** Online Banking ...

Your statement as of **January 01, 2005** is

Cash Accounts

Account	Account Number	Available Balance
CHECKING	XXX-XXX0385	$2,375.41
SAVINGS	XXX-XXX6608	$100.02

Total $2,475.43

DIECI

"So you found a job, Michael?"

I lifted my head as much as I could, my body hunched over, my hands tying the laces of my left boot. It was Ayden.

"It's only part-time, though," I replied as I pulled myself upright.

"But it's a start, no?"

"It is a start. Tonight I have to be there at six for training, but normally it'll be ten until closing at two."

"I am very excited for you. Do you think you will be able to extend your stay?"

It was a dangerously enticing possibility. Dad had e-mailed earlier in the week to let me know everything had gone smoothly with moving my flight. But now that I could be earning Euro, my budget situation suddenly brightened.

I would never make nearly enough from three days a week at Metro to sustain my expenses, but I now felt confident in making it to April. And if I could somehow make it another two months past April, I would be pushing through spring and into summer, undoubtedly Rome's busiest season. It was a possibility that Dario would hire me full-time if I could prove myself by then.

One year? Could I make it an entire year? The boy who moved to Italy with enough U.S. dollars to last him five months and turned it into a year. Rome through the seasons. All four. Back to back to back to back. What a sight it would be. Who would compose my social group come summer? Which cafés would we frequent? The thoughts engulfed me; the daydreams swallowed me whole.

"It's too early to start thinking about that, Ayden," I smiled. "Vediamo. Vediamo." I slid my gloves over my hands, and made my way out to the street.

The commute to Metro would be simple in calculation, yet unpredictable in execution. The 23 bus line ran straight from the Piramide subway station north along the Tiber River, and dropped me at the Ponte Sisto. From there it was another five minutes on foot through a series of winding side streets to Campo de' Fiori. The problem was that the bus system in Rome defined erratic. A line that was supposed to run every eight minutes arrived every half hour, two busses at the same time, leapfrogging stops along their route. Being car-less, motorino-less, and therefore at the mercy of public transportation, I had no choice but to allow at least forty-five minutes to make what should be a fifteen-minute trip.

Tonight, however, the bus dropped me opposite the Ponte Sisto over half an hour before I had to be at Metro. I took the short remaining walk leisurely, soaking in the details of the anonymous backstreets I hoped would soon become my most familiar. They were typical of the narrow, winding, cobblestone charm I loved about Rome—that gritty urban canvas splashed with the contrasting colorful appeal of children playing soccer in the street and cooks adorned in stained white aprons smoking cigarettes at the steps of modest bakeries and pizzerias.

Even the cobblestones themselves amazed me. Someone, an actual person—probably a team of people—must have laid each fragment of these streets by hand. What a tedious and all-consuming task to perform. What a way to construct a city. A time before Mack trucks, before asphalt and steamrollers, hardhats, and walkie-talkies. A city built by bare hands—the hands of its residents.

I entered Campo de' Fiori and paused to take in the flamboyant scene before me. The piazza was top-heavy, the majority of its weight amassed at the square's northern end opposite Metro—a small fountain, a newspaper kiosk, and two enormous flower vending posts—which I could only assume was a cheap gimmick based on Campo de' Fiori's literal meaning, *Field of Flowers*. Anchoring all the action was a large statue of Giordano Bruno, who had been burned at that very location in 1600 for contesting the Church's geocentric universe theory.

I glanced at my phone. Twenty till.

Riding the high of how my newfound workplace provided me an excuse to parade into the historic center come dusk, I decided to skip across to Piazza Navona to see if the God-awful carnival they had set up for the winter holiday season had been taken down yet.

I moved north across the main Corso Vittorio Emanuele II and rode a current of pedestrians into a tight alleyway, beyond which our collective flow dissipated into the southern end of Piazza Navona. I cringed in disapproval at the sight before me.

The carnival devastated the piazza. Borromini's immaculate Church of San Agnese was drowned in a neon rainbow of fluorescent lighting. Bernini's Fountain of Four Rivers sat smothered by the distasteful distractions of a target range, milk-bottle challenge, two water-gun-propelled horse-race booths, one gargantuan merry-go-round, and endless mountains of stuffed animals. It was so contrived—a fleeting façade concealing the humbling permanence of the piazza below.

Ten till. I made my way back towards the Campo. This time I opted not to jaywalk the major Corso Vittorio Emanuele II, instead respectably stopping at the sight of the little yellow walking man turned red with caution. The traffic whizzed by. I stared down at my shoes. It had been cold the past week and it seemed to be getting colder as January gathered steam. I slid my gloved hands into my jacket pockets.

When I looked up again, little walking man was adorned in bright green, already motioning for us to cross. The congestion of people previously at my back swept me into the intersection. I stumbled forward, taking quick, choppy steps to avoid the couple whose heels I was riding. I gathered myself and evened the pace with the meandering twosome.

I took a quick read on the young pair locked arm-in-arm in front of me. He wore a grey beanie; a matching scarf lined the collar of his brown leather jacket. His jeans looked fashionable, most likely a wash sold at Diesel or Energie. She wore a cherry-red hat, her blond hair—almost white—poured out the back and down her neck. A long manila coat draped past her knees and a multi-shaded mix of greens sewn into …

Hair blonde? Almost white?

Skye! I slid sideways through the crowd, strategically beginning a large, sweeping arch as I reached the opposite curb and entered a short, narrow alleyway. My eyes fixed on the girl, the validity of her presumed identity still uncertain, the side of her face blocked by the brim of her scarlet hat and the shoulder of her male companion.

The alleyway opened into the vast piazza of the Campo. They were heading straight for Metro. It had to be Skye, being walked to work. They reached Metro's outdoor seating. Twenty feet behind them I pulled my mobile phone from my pocket, placed it to my head and began a fake conversation.

"Hmm. What? Uh-huh. Ahh."

They turned to face each other. It was Skye, all right.

"Ahah. Forse alle dieci." I liked to throw in some Italian here and there for extra effect.

Skye and the young man exchanged words. She raised on her toes.

"When? Mmhmm. Sounds good."

She playfully crumpled her nose and leaned toward him.

"Sure, I will see you tomorrow then."

They kissed.

"Fuck!"

UNDICI

"One and two and three and four and one." I cut the flow of liquid with a twist of my wrist.

"Nice close, man! Much better."

Mariano had filled an empty bottle of Absolut vodka with water and plugged its spout with the customary metal pour. Each one count, he had explained, theoretically equaled one-quarter ounce of liquid—that is, if you had counted and opened and closed the flow of the metal pour accurately. A four count therefore equaled one ounce, or a shot glass.

"Now pour in three-quarter ounce more," he told me.

I lined the metal tip to the open tin and swung the bottle upright.

"One and two and three." I swept the bottle down again. Mariano turned to the backbar and grabbed a pair of shot glasses. He placed them onto the bar mat next to the tin.

"Pour them," he instructed.

I took the tin in my hand and filled the first shot glass. I mimed nervous eyes to him and slowly began to fill the second. The level of water in the second shot glass reached just below rim. I tilted the tin completely perpendicular to the counter and shook the final drops from inside.

"Fucking great, man!" he applauded.

Mariano took the two shot glasses and emptied them to the floor.

"We go again."

His knuckles rubbed his cheeks as he contemplated the new ounce combination.

"How long have you been a bartender?" I asked.

He smiled, "Since I am fourteen years old."

"What made you start?"

He gazed into space as he buffered his explanation. "First I needed a job I can do at night so I can go to the university."

"You go to university?"

"Of course, man. I am only twenty years old."

"What do you study?"

"Ehh," he rubbed his chin. "I do not know how to say in English."

"Try in Italian."

"Biologia molecolare."

"Molecular biology? You study molecular biology?"

"Oh, it is the same." I could see him repeating the English in his head.

"Is it strange to you that I study this thing?"

"Yes. I mean, I have only known you a short time. But I would not have guessed."

He nodded and appeared pleased at that fact.

"I want to discover how the parts of the universe work," he said. "To me it is fascinating."

"Of course," I agreed.

"Everything," he continued, "is made of the same. Of the cells."

"Right."

"But some cells, they make this glass." He held one of the two shot glasses to my nose. "And other cells, they make you." He put a finger to my chest.

"And bartending?" I asked.

"And bartending is a work of the night for my study, but it is also a work of the world." His arms opened from his body.

"It is a work you can do anywhere on the earth. I told you I have been to London for six month to work in a bar?"

"Yeah, you did tell me that."

"I would very much like to go to Australia next summer. Or maybe to New York."

"Bartending is a job you can travel with," I reiterated.

"Esatto."

"I think that is what excited me about bartending too. It is a job of the night and a skill I could travel anywhere with."

"Wait, now," he raised a solitary finger. "You are not a bartender, *yet*. One ounce and one quarter! Go!"

I laughed and lined my bottle up to the tin. I swung it upright and began to count.

"One and two and three and—"

"Che cazzo fate!" Hassan's husky, accented voice came rumbling towards us from the head of the bar. *What the fuck are you guys doing?*

"È solo acqua, Hassan!" Mariano called back to him.

"Basta con i scherzi, Mariano. Basta!"

"È acqua!" he insisted.

Mariano leaned to me as I quickly flipped the tin to the edge of his barmat alongside the other.

"What a motherfucker," he whispered. "We practice again later."

I moved back to the sinks. Hassan sank to his seat on the heavyweight trash can next to the register. I could feel his stare on my back as I carefully placed the three empty glasses from the counter in front of me into the baskets at my waist.

Skye emerged from the crowd in front of me, slapping her tray on the bar and placing one elbow alongside it. She spoke to no one.

"Che palle."

Two days had passed since I had seen her with her boyfriend. I hadn't mentioned anything to her, but had rather waited a few minutes before walking into Metro and greeting her as if it were the first time I had seen her that day.

I watched her intently as she pulled a packet of matches from her apron and lit one of the numerous white tea candles scattered across the bar. Her lips puckered and she extinguished the match with a soft exhalation. She then brought the extinguished head to her mouth and sealed her lips around its wooden base. Slowly, she drew her hand away, the match still clenched between her thumb and index finger, its sulfur top having disappeared.

She flicked the remaining stick onto the counter and lifted the candle delicately over the back of her opposite hand. She tilted it forward, initiating a slow drip of translucent fluid. The liquid wax fell to her skin, solidifying to white almost instantaneously.

She glanced at me. My eyes darted away. But too late.

"Raccontami qualcosa di bella." *Tell me something nice.*

I leaned down to her. "In inglese?" I asked.

"No. Dai. In Italiano."

"Umm, okay. Umm, due anni ..."

A table of patrons stood to leave and Skye hurried off to clear their dirty glasses as they paid.

Soon the house lights were on and the customers were being ushered to the piazza. The girls dragged the tables, chairs, and giant umbrellas in from outside. I whittled away at the stacks of dirty glasses in front of me while Roberto and Mariano packaged their leftover fruit in plastic wrap and wiped down the mini-fridges below their workstations.

Downstairs, I neatly folded my shirt inside my apron and placed them on the top shelf of the anonymous locker in front of me. As I began climbing back up the stairs, I could hear a clutter of conversation in the now-vacant club.

I reached the top of the stairwell and eyed the group—Roberto, Mariano, Carmen, Skye, and Isabella—in the middle of the empty main room. Isabella spotted me emerging from the darkness.

"Mikey! Vieni con noi?"

"Dove andate?" I asked.

"Si chiama Seven Eleven, a Piazza Cavour." They were going to a bar called Seven Eleven, which was north of Metro in the opposite direction from my apartment in Piramide. I forced my eyes to pan left and right across everyone's faces, but they caught only on Skye's. I spoke hesitantly.

"Ma chi va? Abito a Piramide, è al ..." I couldn't remember how to say *opposite direction*, so my clenched fist did the talking, my protruding thumb jerking back over my left shoulder.

"Tutti di noi. Vieni," Isabella insisted.

Again I tried to keep my eyes moving though they stopped repeatedly on Skye, standing mute. In my silence I hunted for a confirmation that *everyone is going* did not mean *almost everyone is going*, and *almost everyone is going* did not mean *everyone except for Skye is going*.

"Mi-key! Mi-key!" Isabella chanted.

I should have gone, regardless. I needed to build experiences outside of Metro which would bond me to the established team. And it would challenge my Italian to be in such a social environment.

"Mi-key! Mi-key!"

I had a lot to thank Isabella for. Every time I had walked into Metro she had appeared enthusiastic to see me. She took the lead on the kiss hello and good-bye. And tonight, had I sensed the slightest bit of doubt in her voice that I was not truly wanted wherever we were going, I would have sheepishly told them I simply could not go and would have begun my long, cold walk home alone. But Isabella persisted.

UNDICI

"Okay, okay!" I answered, finally. "Ci vengo." And we all exited to the quiet cobblestone.

We reached Seven Eleven at quarter past three. The surrounding streets were empty, cars asleep in their spaces lining the curbs. We stood in a circle at the hood of Mariano's car, our ears able to make out the muffled sound of beats in four/four time and a mass of chatter in the club below.

Roberto appeared from around the corner, helmet in hand, and Isabella and Carmen shouted in playful Italian to him.

We descended a short set of stairs into the dim lounge below. Deep electronic music filled the previously blank space around us. A lava lamp of cigarette smoke morphed continually along the ceiling. The décor was cluttered—a red Budweiser surfboard propped next to an inflated beach ball above the bar counter, Guinness and Carlsberg posters slapped onto the wood and stone walls. The eclectic decor appeared to get the job done, however, as the small underground club was full, even now, pushing three thirty in the morning.

We crowded around a dark wooden table toward the back of the room. I sat sandwiched between Carmen and Isabella. They were speaking Italian right through me. I couldn't understand anything they were saying. To my left, past Isabella, Roberto and Mariano continued a conversation that had started at the door. I glanced right, past Carmen, and watched Skye reading over the one-page menu, her tiny figure slouched in the booth in a way that made her look like a curious twelve year old examining a chart on insects.

A waitress appeared in front of us and placed six shots of an unknown alcohol onto the table. She then took our drink requests and disappeared into the crowd of dancers. I had no idea who had ordered the shots, but we all toasted and tossed them down our throats.

A few moments later the waitress appeared again and placed our cocktails onto the table. Italian was flying all over the place. I pulled off my Long Island and continued to watch Skye. She was quietly playing with her phone and sipping her drink through a single black straw. Carmen still blocked her from me. To my left, Isabella had now joined in conversation with Mariano and Roberto.

"Che fai a Roma?"

What?

"Uh, cosa?" I responded to Carmen's question. It was so unexpected, being completely engaged in my world of Skye observation and all.

"Perchè sei venuto a Roma?" *Why did you come to Rome.*

"Ho finito università e ... umm ... ho portato tutto i ... i miei soldi e la mia chitarra qua perché amo Roma." I was done with university and I had brought all my money and my guitar to Rome and I loved the city. That summed up enough for this basic conversation. Without diving into the whole "legacy of Rome" spiel.

"Mio marito suona la chitarra! Lui suona in tre gruppi qua. Hai un gruppo?" I could have sworn *marito* meant *husband*.

"Wait, quanti anni hai? Hai un marito?"

"Venti due. Lui non è proprio mio marito—siamo quasi sposati." *Quasi married?* Was I translating this right?

Roberto and Mariano announced to the table that they were heading to the bar. Isabella clapped and bounced in her seat. She slid out of the booth with them and started toward the front of the club. She grabbed Carmen's hand across the table as she passed.

"Balla con me!" she exclaimed. *Dance with me!*

Carmen smiled and looked to Skye. Skye stood to let Carmen pass, then returned to her seat as the two girls headed for the deejay area.

The music blared from every angle. The table was now suddenly mute. I observed the abruptly evacuated seats, from left to right: four winter coats, three purses, me, one abandoned rum and Coke, Skye.

Say something.

"So, what are you doing here in Rome?" A for effort. D minus for originality.

Skye looked at me and smiled. There was something about her—something unique beyond the physical that drew me to her. She didn't seem necessarily scholarly or secretly tortured or anything, but there were layers she was not letting out at the surface.

"I finished high school," she told me, "and wanted to live somewhere in Italy, so I came to Rome."

"High school? How old are you?"

"Twenty-one. In Iceland you finish high school when you are twenty and I lost a year when I studied abroad."

"Where did you study abroad? Florence?"

"Ha! No, Sardegna."

"The island? How strange!"

"I didn't have a choice, really. You are assigned a location by the government."

"Isn't everyone in Sardegna really short?"

Skye laughed and looked away for a second. "Yes! Some of them are shorter than I am!"

I smiled.

"What are you doing here besides working at Metro?" I asked.

"I am in a class. A theater class. I like to act."

"Really? I took theater for three years when I was studying." Studying in high school. American high school. But I would let her decide during which part of my academic career those three years had occurred. Skye's eyes enlarged to twice their normal size.

"Are you an actor?"

Did she want me to be?

"I just did it for fun" I answered. "But, you know, it's actually been really helpful."

She smiled enthusiastically. I slid to the empty space beside her where Carmen had been sitting.

"After you have sat in front of an audience of fifty people and improvised a five-minute sketch about a brown paper bag, it makes everything else seem so much easier—like talking to someone's parents or to your boss at work." Or to an attractive Icelandic girl at a bar in Rome. Skye nodded in an exaggerated fashion. Her passion for theater explained her animated character. But there was something more going on—something quirky and eccentric. Maybe the wax dripping and match eating had been symptoms. But there was something deeper that had shaped these peculiar mannerisms. What was it?

"So you studied Italian for a year in Sardegna. When did you study English?"

Skye looked confused and sipped the last of her cocktail.

"I never studied English. I mean, we had some in grade school but we always had English on the television and watched movies in English."

"That is really impressive."

She shrugged and picked up the menu again. It was yellow, laminated, and consisted of only one single-sided page.

"Is your boyfriend Italian?" Now, why would I have brought that up?

"Yes, he is from Rome."

"And what does he do?" Of course. To size him up a little. Very mature of me.

"He works in a bank."

Idon'tcareIloveworkinginabar.

"How did you two meet?"

"His bank is on the same street where I live so we kept running into each other and then—well, then he was my boyfriend!"

She looked back at the menu. She hummed and rolled her fingers across her lips. What was it?

Carmen appeared at the table. She stretched her arm towards me, fingers flickering, and spoke.

"Puoi darmi la borsa?" I heard the words clearly but didn't understand them. I looked down and left in the direction her hand was flailing. The three purses. Of course, *can you hand me my purse?* I picked one up at random and gave her a questioning face.

"No, quell'altra nera là!" I put black purse option one back on the seat and handed her black purse option two. Carmen pulled out her wallet, tore a ten-Euro bill from the zipped side pocket, shoved the wallet into the bag again, and handed it back to me across the table.

"Grazie, Mike!"

"No problem."

I placed the purse alongside the two others and returned to Skye, still next to me, still reading the menu—the same yellow, laminated, single-paged menu. She seemed to be concentrating so hard on her next drink decision. Her eyebrows rose and fell, then rose again—higher—as her eyes morphed from squint to shock. What was it?

"Skye. You've been looking at that menu for five minutes now. What's the deal?"

She laughed and hid her face up to her forehead behind the laminated cocktail list. Then she let it drop to the table and smiled at me.

"I am dyslexic."

Bingo.

"Really? You can't, like, memorize everything backwards?" I asked.

"It's not backwards. It's scrambled"

That had not been my proudest suggestion.

Skye continued, "Sometimes it is hard here in Italy because they think if you are dyslexic you are mentally handicapped or something. They think you can't do other things like ... like drive a car or ... or sing."

I wanted to tell Skye she didn't need Italy's approval. She had learned a third language and could barely read a grammar book. Or a dictionary. How did she read her scripts for theater class? How must the world look from behind her eyes?

My mind began to wander. The creative possibilities in such a relationship would be endless. Without e-mail or post-it notes, I would have to discover new, novel ways to convey ideas, to say I would be late for dinner tonight, to say I love you. We would be the envy of all other aged couples watching us in astonishment as I leaned in close and gently read to her the menu at restaurants and our grocery lists at the supermarket.

She picked up the menu again and looked to me.

"Can you help me read this?"

Of course, Skye.

She pointed to a word crammed into a list of cocktail ingredients.

"Triplesec," I read, "Yeah, that's a hard one."

A really hard one, Skye. Don't let it get to you.

"What is that?" she asked.

"It's an orange-flavored liquor. They, like, grind up orange peel to flavor it."

"Oh. Well, what are you drinking?"

I laughed and leaned away for a second.

"I'm drinking a Long Island, but I don't think you want to drink one of these."

Long Islands were for men. Big, strong, protective men.

"No, I want one. I drink," she pounded the table, "to get drunk!"

"I like the way you think, Skye." I tapped my index finger at my temple. "I like the way you think. I'll get this round, wait right here."

I rose and slid onto the narrow dance floor which led past the deejay booth and to the bar. I fought through the outer layer of dancers, their eyes sealed, hair and appendages flying outwards sporadically. I pushed forward, slowly rubbing against the anonymous bodies, my feet planting at any angle possible so as to keep the forward advancement.

Isabella appeared at my shoulder. She tugged at my shirt and I swayed with her a few times before smiling politely and then pressing onwards.

I then felt a pinch on my left cheek and turned my head. Carmen drew back her hand and smiled at me as she pulled from her cocktail and slithered to the music. Didn't she have a quasi-marito?

I broke through the final tier of bodies and wedged myself between two couples at the bar. The single female bartender was a few feet to the right, taking orders from a mob of Italians. A finger tapped my shoulder.

"Mariano, hey," I turned my head to acknowledge him.

"How are you doing motherfucker?"

"Good, just getting a drink."

"I want you to meet Francesco. He used to work with us at Metro too."

I turned completely from the bar. Mariano introduced me to Francesco: average height, spiky brown hair, standing with Roberto.

"Piacere," I said.

"Piacere."

We shook. The four of us sat silent for a moment.

"Che fai a Roma?" Francesco asked me.

I couldn't explain it again.

"Niente di che," I replied.

I was doing everything, Francesco, everything. And at the moment, I was trying to buy a drink for a young woman who, as of three minutes ago, had infatuated me completely. So, if he could kindly go dance with Isabella or Carmen, who were apparently in need of partners on the dance floor, or get the attention of the bartender behind me, it would be much appreciated.

"Lavora con noi un paio di giorni a settimana," Mariano took over.

"Come bartender?" Francesco asked him.

"Come barback. È bravo comunque, molto bravo."

I leaned to Mariano's ear. "I'm going to get a drink, okay?"

He nodded. As I turned back to the bar, Skye emerged from the crowd behind me.

"Hey. Umm, I was just …" I leaned to the counter. The bartender was serving the group of customers to the right again.

Skye smiled and joined me at the bar.

"Listen, sorry this is taking so long. I just can't get the bartender's attention."

The bartender swapped three finished cocktails for a handful of cash and began to cross toward the register. I raised a finger and opened my mouth. The bartender's eyes drifted across my face and then stopped on Skye.

"Dimmi."

"Prendiamo due Long Island," Skye replied.

She nodded and moved to a stack of clean glasses. Skye turned to me.

"You can get the next round."

The bartender slid us our drinks and I tried to pay her, but she had formed some coalition with Skye and thus refused my money. Skye took her glass from the counter and stepped back.

"I am going to the bathroom."

"All right, I'll be here."

Skye then turned and stepped away, the amoeba of dancers absorbing her tiny figure. Roberto appeared at my shoulder. He said something to me, but I couldn't hear it over the music.

"Cosa?" I screamed.

He repeated the comment, this time louder and directly into my right ear. I heard him but didn't understand. I pulled back and laughed and sipped my cocktail. He laughed and drank as well.

I stood in silence at the bar with Roberto for what must have been half an hour. My phone displayed the early morning hour: 4:27 AM.

The mob of dancers had been slowly disintegrating and the Isabella-and-Carmen dance party moved to where we were standing. Isabella pulled me between them. I smiled and bounced and pumped my empty cocktail glass toward the ceiling. I slowed for a moment to sip from my straw even though my drink had been finished for a good ten minutes. Plastic in mouth, I glanced behind me at the bar. Mariano had taken my position next to Roberto. Francesco was nowhere to be seen. I shuffled to face the opposite direction, my feet taking short, broken steps to avoid the two pair of female feet. Then I spotted her.

Skye was across the room back at the table. Her head was down, buried in her arms. Her only company was the four coats and three purses.

"I have to go." I slipped out from between Carmen and Isabella and moved across the cavernous room to the table. I slid into the booth next to Skye and placed my hand on her back. Her head rose from the hardwood, her blond bangs a frazzled mess, her eyes searching for orientation.

"Hey, there," I whispered. "I told you that you didn't want a Long Island."

She smiled and closed her eyes again.

"Che ora è?"

"It's almost five. Listen, where do you live?"

"Vicino alla Piazza Santa Maria Maggiore."

That was east across town, near Termini station.

"The metro should be starting again soon. If you can make it, I'll walk you to the nearest stop and we can take the subway home together."

She smiled, nodded an appreciative nod, and placed her head back into her arms. Isabella and Carmen appeared in front of us and began collecting their bags and zipping their coats. Roberto and Mariano followed and gathered their things from below the table. I leaned to Skye, told her it was time to go, and we both stood. She pulled a thick beanie over her head, gathered her purse and jacket, and we trailed the rest of the group across the room to the stairs. The music muffled, the smoke cleared, and we emerged back to the still-sleeping side street.

There was a tornado of kisses good-bye. Mariano pulled me aside.

"You don't need to go in my car, man?"

"I'm going to walk with Skye."

"Are you sure?"

"It's a short walk to the metro. I'm sure."

Skye stood on the wall playing with her phone.

"Okay, you take good care to her," Isabella nodded. "Take good care!"

The group climbed into Mariano's tiny vehicle. It shuddered alive and then disappeared southbound under the yellow streetlamp lighting. I turned to Skye and we started off in the opposite direction.

"Okay, there is a metro stop at Piazza del Popolo," I started. "I think Via Cola di Rienzo is up this way. It should run straight into Popolo."

I was pretty sure I had seen Rienzo on the taxi ride in. I had looked it up on my map at home after Aleksia had mentioned she liked to shop there. It was definitely in this area.

The frigid air seemed to have awakened Skye. She became jittery, and moved at lightening pace along the sidewalk.

"It's cold, huh? Aren't you freezing?" she asked.

"It is cold, but I'm not too bad myself. I think the alcohol is helping me a bit."

"I'm freezing."

We stopped at the next dark intersection. The streets were narrow, the buildings tall and dim. Every direction looked the same. Skye looked at me.

"Do you know which way to go?"

"I'm pretty sure it's this way."

I took a definitive step in the direction I presumed was north.

A taxi appeared from behind. Skye hailed it. The driver rolled down his window and Skye spoke to him.

"Scusi, dov'è Via Cola ... Cola ...?"

"Via Cola di Rienzo," I interjected.

"Cola di Rienzo? Vai sempre diritto," he pointed in a trajectory perpendicular to the one in which I was taking us. "Poi, al secondo incrocio girate a destra."

I didn't see the point of first heading west, then north, and ultimately backtracking east on Rienzo. But Skye thanked the man and began to tread off in the direction he had pointed. I quickly shot after her.

"What did he say? To go which way?" she asked.

"He said go straight and then right. Right at that next intersection there."

The blocks were short and our pace was rapid.

"Which way is right?" Skye asked.

"Destra," I translated.

She looked over to me as we continued to scurry along.

"Which way is that?"

Right. Destra. To the right. A destra. What did she mean, which way is right?

Skye's face appeared suddenly withdrawn in reaction to my confused look. I forced a laugh and swung my arm in a long curve to display which way we would turn. By then we had reached the intersection and we wrapped around its corner. As we continued, slightly slurred English began pouring from Skye's mouth.

"I don't understand why you are at Metro. Do you like it there?"

"Yeah. I mean, I'm not really making any money. But I'm happy to have met some young Italians and they all seem very accepting of me."

We hit a main intersection and I searched the stone wall of the corner building for a street name. I found one two floors up etched into a granite plaque.

Via Cola di Rienzo.

"Rienzo!" I announced. "I think if we head about five minutes this way we should reach Popolo."

We began down the wide, unoccupied walkway. Our pace was steady but less frantic now that we had achieved orientation.

"You really think they are being nice to you?"

"It seems to me like they are," I laughed. "Do you think otherwise?"

Skye shot me a cautious look.

"You have to be careful. Really careful. I'm just telling you this because I think you are a good guy and you are new. They will tell you they are your friends but really they are just jealous and they go and talk about you behind your back. I'm just warning you. They are stupid, Italians. All of them are stupid."

I knew Skye was speaking in a fit of impassioned tipsiness and tried not to take her suggestions and accusations seriously.

I spotted Piazza del Popolo ahead in the distance. Infused with confidence, I skipped from the next curb, spinning in midair before landing on the first stripe of the proceeding crosswalk. I continued backwards, facing Skye head on, legs seamlessly shifting into reverse. I reflected for a moment on what she had said—her opinion that all Italians were in some way stupid.

"Isn't your boyfriend Italian?"

What a setup. Skye stopped in her tracks. Her arm shot from her side, her stance widened as if preparing for an impact. Her finger pointed directly toward my chest as I faced her. Her eyebrows rose, her eyes enlarged. This was going to be good.

"And he's stupid!"

I let out a boisterous laugh, my head tilting skyward, my body spinning back to about-face.

"What is your apartment like?"

She let out a groan and then started a detailed critique of her shared flat. The rest of Rome remained silent. Maybe it was the fact that we were both foreigners, maybe it was the fact that we conversed in English, maybe it was the fact that we had both had a fair amount to drink, but I sensed something in my interaction with Skye—a comfort, a relaxed attitude—that I had not sensed in the others. I listened to her describe the absurdness of her living situation.

"And we aren't allowed to use the kitchen even though everything works just fine. Our landlady will come by and see dirty dishes in the sink and start going crazy at us!"

"You have a perfectly functional kitchen and no one is supposed to touch it? That's stupid."

Stupid had officially become the word of the night.

"Yeah, but I … I only pay two hundred eighty a month."

"Two eighty!" I exclaimed in genuine astonishment. "How is that possible? How big is your room?"

We continued down the empty thoroughfare, the details of Piazza del Popolo materializing one final block ahead of us.

"My room is really tiny and it's not even connected to the rest of the apartment. I have to use a separate key if I want to go to the bathroom at night or anything."

"Your landlady is out of her mind."

"Everyone in this country is crazy."

UNDICI

We stopped at the metro entrance at the northern end of Piazza del Popolo, about to submerge into the caverns of recycled air and fluorescent lighting. Skye fished her phone from her bag, dialed a number, and placed it to her head.

"Ciao, amore ... no, sono a Piazza del Popolo. Prendo il metro."

I could hear a voice on the other line firing rapidly.

"Dai! Niente succederà, sto con un collega!" she insisted.

Skye spoke Italian impressively well and the next thirty to forty seconds were filled with dialogue so hurried I understood only the tone. And it was one of irritation.

She abruptly hung up and immediately took to the stairs.

"'Ugh, you are going to be robbed, you are going to be hurt, let me come get you,'" she said in a mocking whisper.

We navigated the underground labyrinth, nearing the station's main lobby. She spoke. I laughed. I spoke. She smiled. We focused on one another exclusively; moving within a bubble of intimacy. We passed the turnstiles without losing a step, opting instead for the gateless entrance alongside the ticket booth which was reserved for monthly ticket holders.

I could make out the blue of her irises better in this light; Metro was so dark all the time. We pushed forward when—

"Signori, biglietti, per favore." Checking tickets at 5:30 in the morning in a vacant metro station. This young man had to be out of his mind. I pulled my Gennaio pass from my wallet.

"Ecco il mio," I offered.

But the young uniformed man was already talking with Skye. Apparently, she didn't have a ticket. Young Officer Man pointed to me.

"Forse il suo ragazzo può pagare per te." *Maybe your boyfriend can pay for you.*

I wished Young Officer Man were a bellhop so I could have tipped him fifty Euros for his erroneous assumption.

"No, lui non è il mio ragazzo," Skye corrected.

The officer suddenly relaxed his aggressive stance.

Skye sifted through her bag, her gloved hand returning with a one-Euro coin. She handed it to him, sputtering off a short line in Italian. Young Officer Man smiled and bounced away toward the ticket machines.

She was unbelievable.

The station was lifeless. Then, from seemingly nowhere, another Young Officer Man appeared in front of us. This one was more boyish in appearance and spoke in poor English only to Skye.

"You was going just to get on the tren without to buy the ticket?"

"No, no. Mi scusi. L'ho dimenticato. Forse ho bevuto troppo sta sera," she responded, smiling a bashful smile of impenetrable defense. Boyish Young Officer Man appeared delighted at the sound of her fluency. And probably also her comment that she'd had too much to drink. He set his cap back a few inches on his head, inviting more casual conversation. He hadn't looked at me once.

"Ma di dove sei?" he asked her.

"Vengo dall'Islanda."

Original Young Officer Man returned with a ticket and we both apologized greatly for the confusion and headed down the escalators to the platform. Our train was waiting, doors open, and we made a short sprint inside.

The train accelerated into the dark underground tunnels. Our bodies counterbalanced the shifting momentum as we stood centered in the empty car, sharing one of the numerous red metal poles rooted to the floor of the carriage.

At Termini I guided us flawlessly up the various escalators and through numerous corridors as we zigzagged our way to the B-line platform. As the train approached, I placed my hand lightly on the small of her back and guided her between the opening double doors.

Skye told me she never took the subway. I pointed to the map above the window, explaining how she would get off at Cavour, whereas I would take the line the three additional stops to Piramide. She swayed with the train as it barreled southbound. I rocked with her.

Now, facing her under the stark light of the subway car, I was able to look more closely at her dress. She had on the manila coat from the Piazza Navona incident. It had a fine embroidery of vines crawling along its left pocket. Her scarf was an explosion of orange fringe sprouting from an indiscernible central line. I had seen nothing like it. An oversized beanie covered her head, the excess at the top folding backward ever so slightly. Its design shifted through multiple hues of green, capping in a dark olive. Her purse was a psychedelic bull's-eye, uneven rings of pastels radiating outwards from the brown background.

"Skye ..."

"Yes?"

"I love your style."

She smiled. Bigger. Then tugged at her coat. "I dress for myself, you know. I don't dress for what other people think or anything."

The loudspeaker interrupted, "Cavour. Prossima fermata, Colosseo"

The train decelerated, wheels squealing, before halting abruptly inside the stale-smelling Cavour station.

"This is you," I spoke softly.

The doors beside us opened with a depressurizing hiss.

"Dario told me I can return to working mornings now that the holidays have passed. But he still wants me to work the night on Thursdays."

Thursday. Five full days. It felt a lifetime away.

"I'll see you Thursday, then," I smiled.

"Sì, ci vediamo giovedì." Skye leaned to me, our cheeks brushed, lips kissing the air around each ear. She stepped off the train and onto the underground platform. She glanced right and then began walking away.

I wanted to walk her home. I wanted to keep talking. I wanted to walk her all the way to Iceland. To California. I pondered hopping off the train after her.

The doors hissed in preparation, then rattled closed.

I followed the line of windows in the direction Skye had walked.

The train lurched forward.

There she was, taking resolute strides in the same direction as the train. Then she halted. The train steadily crept forward, slowly gathering momentum. Skye's head shot to a sign on the wall, confused. She flung her arms vibrantly to the sky and twirled on her toes—a ballet of exasperation. She then marched off in the opposite direction, quickly disappearing as the train reached full acceleration.

What a creature. Inversions embodied; hopeless and dazzling.

I gazed back to the train's cabin, taking it in for the first time. Five or six scattered bodies dotted the blue plastic seating. Most appeared to be asleep under the harsh artificial lighting. Two had their heads propped against their respective windows, their necks rolling to and fro in motion with the train. The absence of dialogue was deafening.

An Arabic man sat nearest to me, about five feet away. He was awake, but his face sagged with fatigue, the bags under his eyes melting down to his prominent cheekbones. It was then that I became conscious of the fact that I still had a foolish smile plastered across my face. The man stared at me, his body shifting back and forth ever so slightly.

You look ridiculous, Michael.
I know.
You better be careful.

DODICI

Thursday. I was counting down the days until Thursday. Three days had passed since I had left Skye at the Cavour metro station. Three days of pacing in my bedroom and replaying the night repeatedly in my head. Three days of sitting idle at my desk or lying mute on my bed analyzing each detail and every word that I could remember being exchanged throughout that evening. Three days of ever-growing anticipation as the hours passed, one by one, one more of twenty four, crawling forward at their grueling pace until I could claim one day closer to a new interaction.

My mind ached for something new to work with. The little information I had obtained had been playing on repeat for nearly seventy-two hours. On my fifteenth trip to the refrigerator that afternoon, at which point I discovered for the fifteenth time that still no strawberry Yoplait had materialized on my shelf inside, I decided that something had to be done.

I grabbed my sport coat and slid it over the long-sleeved thermal I had worn both to bed and around the house since Sunday. I hurriedly threw on a pair of jeans and shoved my wallet, keys, and phone into my pockets. I swiped my sunglasses from my nightstand and broke for the front door.

I careened down the single flight of stairs, through the parking lots, and onto Via Matteucci, where I spotted the 716 line in the distance, rounding the far corner, and beginning toward me.

I skipped through the crosswalk, a firmly extended hand displaying my unyielding objective of crossing whether the oncoming traffic willed it or not. The cars had no choice but to let me pass and I hailed and boarded the bus.

It hissed, rattled, and squealed its way onto Via Ostiense, past the pyramid, and up Via Marmorata. At the final stop before the Tiber River I sprang from the center double doors and, now on foot, dodged traffic once again as I doubled back across the main avenue and into the tighter roadways of Testaccio.

At the foot of the Church Santa Maradonna, I cut through a scattering of abandoned motorinos and ducked into a small Internet café. A young Indonesian girl directed me to PC14 and I sat patiently as the computer started up. I then loaded Internet Explorer and rested the pads of my fingers softly on the jet black keys.

The problem I was having was clear. It was a lack of information. And whenever I was having a problem with lack of information, there was one place that consistently held resolve. My fingers moved swiftly across the keyboard.

w-w-w-.-g-o-o-g-l-e-.-c-o-m
Enter

The primary colors of the Google logo loaded onto the screen. I placed my cursor in the *search* field box.

Icelandic stereotypes
Enter

I scanned the page of results. The first ten links appeared to be government statistics—population, geographical location, that sort of thing. I clicked to page two.

Xenophobe's Guide to the Icelanders

I closed my eyes for a moment and concentrated on the blackness.

Skye.

I envisioned her face, her soft features, her radiant eyes.

Skye, I know you're in here.
Mike?
Skye, there you are.
Mike, hi! I thought I wasn't seeing you until Thursday.
I know, but I need to talk to you. I need to know more about you.
Right now?
Right now.
All right, then. What do you want to know?
I want to know about Iceland. I want to know about where you grew up—what it was like and what you were like. Can you meet me in, say, five minutes?
Sure. Just tell me where.
Here. Right here. Coffee and an afternoon stroll right here in my mind.

I gently opened my eyes and clicked the link. The page loaded.

The Xenophobe's Guide to the Icelanders by Richard Sale: A guide to understanding the Icelanders, which takes an insightful, humorous look at their character and values.

A menu on the left of the page displayed tens of other nationality choices—Aussies, Dutch, Germans, Irish, even Californians. I scrolled down and found a selection of extracts from the book on Icelanders.
Mike? I'm here.
Great, Skye. Let's get started.
I recited the first passage aloud in my head:

> The Icelanders have style. They suffer a climate that is best described as miserable, but they don't allow it to get in the way of wearing the trendiest garb. If this decrees open-toed sandals, then that is what they will wear, even if the snow is four feet deep.

Is everyone as liberal with their dress in Iceland as you are?
Not every single person, but on the whole, yes. Here in Italy they think fashion is important too. That is one thing I really like about Italy.
That's something I love about Italy, too.
I moved to the next quotation.

> Art is shared among the population rather than being maintained by an elite. Whereas in Britain it is often assumed that scientists do not understand the arts and vice versa, in Iceland it is taken for granted that everyone is interested in art.

It must have been easy for you to pursue theater within such a supportive community.
Is it not like that in California?
It is better in California than in other parts of the United States, but, really, if you are an artist, you can be looked at as the bottom rung of the social ladder. Unless you find commercial success, at which point you are admired.
That sounds backward. You would love Iceland. You should visit with me the next time I make a trip home.
That would be wonderful.
The final of the three extracts followed.

> The Vikings who settled Iceland in 870 were folk who could not tolerate the order imposed on their Scandinavian homelands by the king who had unified the countries. That independence is still an Icelandic characteristic: the Icelander is an individualist and an adventurer.

We both know that is true.

I never thought of myself as individualist or nonconformist. I just think I'm a strong person.

I think you are too. I think the way you've grown up—the Icelandic culture, the dyslexia, the theater—it has all made you who you are. They all compound one another. They all add to your strength.

Is that just a nice way of saying I'm an eccentric loner?

Of course not. I love everything that makes you you. I want to know more about your dyslexia.

Okay. When will I see you next?

How about ten minutes? We'll meet again right here. Dinner and a movie.

Okay!

I backtracked to the blank Google search page. I pulled my hands from the keyboard and cracked my knuckles. I stretched my neck left, then right, and then focused back on the screen.

Facts on dyslexia

Enter

Five results down the first page I found a promising link.

The Dyslexia Institute: Recognizing Dyslexia

I clicked the link and the page loaded. Blue headings and black text on a yellow backdrop composed the majority of the site.

Centered on the opening page was an image, a scan of a child's drawing. A caption above the illustration read, *"One in twenty five," by Lawrence Cockrill, age 11, Winner in a Dyslexia Institute "As I See It" competition.*

Ciao, Mike!

Come sit down and look at this with me.

The drawing was done in black and white, a bird's-eye perspective of twenty-five students seated at their desks in a classroom. Each of the twenty-five appeared busy with pen and paper, except for a single student at the center. He sat outlined in blue—the illustration's only coloring—his two hands locked under his chin, his eyes fixed down on the work before him. His face read unrest and anxiety.

Was it hard for you?

Was what hard?

School, the early years, before you knew what was going on.

You know I'm independent. I never needed babysitting.

But at first. Was it difficult at first?

No. Well. Yes. Yes, it was a bit ... trying.

Did you ever feel like giving up? Like taking a different route entirely?

No, never. I finish what I start.

I scrolled down the page, past a writing sample and a succession of quotations. I reached a series of bullet points.

> *Dyslexia Checklist*
> *If the answer to most of the following questions is Yes it would be wise to seek advice:*
>
> - *Does s/he have particular difficulty with reading or spelling?*
> - *Does s/he put figures or letters the wrong way e.g,. 15 for 51, 6 for 9, b for d, was for saw?*
> - *Does s/he have a poor concentration span for reading and writing?*
> - *Does s/he confuse left and right?*

Skye! Skye, I'm so sorry. I should have been more understanding when we were walking from Seven Eleven and you asked me to tell you which direction was right. I had no idea.

I knew you didn't understand. It's okay, really. I've gotten used to it.

But I don't want to be what you are used to. I want to be different. I want to be better.

I know you do, that's why I like you so much.

I scrolled down again. The page listed a series of common problems with dyslexic students: difficulty in copying accurately, poor handwriting, trouble remembering a list of instructions. Nothing seemed relevant. I scrolled further.

> *Some common strengths*
> *You may be surprised that:*
>
> - *S/he has a good visual eye*
> - *S/he's artistic and skillful with her/his hands*
> - *S/he's practical*
> - *S/he's got a fantastic imagination*

This is you. This is how you see the world, with novelty and inspiration. And this is how I see Rome. And I want you here with me. I want you in my Rome. I want your added imagination and brilliance to set this city ablaze.

This city is cold at times, its people seem distant and forbidding.

Skye, I am not. Listen to me, I am not and never will be.
I believe you.
So then what do you say, Skye?
So then, what do you say?

TREDICI

I checked my phone a final time as I entered the Campo. It was quarter to ten on Thursday, finally Thursday. I crossed the glowing piazza and made my way to Metro's double glass doors.

Inside, the scene was relaxed. I changed downstairs into my Metro fatigues and prepared to join the rest of the staff in random acts of tidiness and preparation for the night rush.

"Ciao, Roberto. Come stai?" I called out as I hopped up behind the bar. He reached for my hand and we shook.

"Bene. Tutto posto, Mike?" he asked.

"Siamo a Roma, sto benissimo."

Roberto smiled and turned back to slicing limes on his black cutting board.

"C'è qualcosa per me da fare?" I inquired, looking for a way to help.

"Mi prendi un apriscatole dalla cucina?" *Apriscatole*. Not a word I knew.

"Un ap-ree-cosa?" I asked him. Roberto held up a metal can of coconut mix and made a winding gesture at its top.

"Ap-ri-sca-to-le," he enunciated, each syllable timed with a twist of his hand.

"Lo prendo subito."

I pieced together the request as I made my way toward the end of the bar.

Cucina was the easy part. He wanted something from the kitchen. *Aprire* was a verb that meant *to open*. He was holding a can, but I could have sworn *scatole* meant *boxes*. It must have also been a generic term for containers, in this case a can. Apriscatole. *Can opener*.

I pushed into the kitchen and then froze. Skye was two feet in front of me, searching for something. It was just the two of us. She looked up at me.

"Mi serve una penna. C'è l'hai tu per caso?" I knew I didn't have a pen for her but I slapped my thighs at my pant pockets anyway.

"Mi dispiace, ma no," I replied, my face reading great pain and regret.

I joined her search for a pen, obviously circling the miniature kitchen. There clearly was not going to be a pen in with the salad bowls. Nor in the silverware racks. But there we were, alone. My senses were on overload.

A stack of plates slid on a metal counter. A handful of spoons chimed as they were pulled out of and then placed back into their plastic container. Then silence.

Nothing more was said for the remainder of the fruitless search. In some cases, nothing can be a good thing. There is the nothing that is full of somethings: the nothing composed of tension, fumbles, and a shared acknowledgement that both parties want to say something but have temporarily found that their language circuitry clogged.

This nothing, however, did not feel like the something nothing. I was tense. I fumbled foolishly around the kitchen. I wanted to say something but could not unclog my circuitry. And as I watched her search—immersed, precise, lips fixed—I recognized that I was transmitting on a one-way frequency.

Worse, I realized that I had just lost a battle of intrigue to a piece of ink-filled plastic. If, right then, the distance between Skye and I had been split by, say, a Pilot Fine 0.99mm—a superior writing utensil, mind you, but a writing utensil nonetheless—Skye's scope of attention would have never expanded beyond the pen. It would have stopped her in her tracks. She would have centered all attention on the Pilot. The Pilot alone would have made her happy. She would have grasped the pen in her hand and exited the kitchen content, leaving me mute and humiliated.

I snapped back to the moment, suddenly conscious of the fact that I had been going through the same bucket of fifteen spoons for far too long. I wished I could sneak in a sniff at my armpits to see if the blatant stench of desire was as obvious as I feared. But then, in some sort of twisted, merciful consolation, it appeared as if I had proven so uninteresting to Skye that she didn't even send a glance my way to notice my restlessness. Instead, she promptly gave up her search and punched back out the kitchen doors without a word.

I watched the flapping of the doors slow to a crawl, my right hand still buried in the spoon container.

No pen, no conversation, no good-bye. Nothing. And not the good kind.

I leaned against the metal island in the center of the room and stared toward the ceiling.

Silence.

My vision dropped back to the kitchen doors, now motionless, and then continued to my feet. My chest expanded, inhaling the stale kitchen air, then collapsed in an extended sigh.

Silence.

What the hell had I come back here for, anyway?

QUATTORDICI

A cool winter breeze swept across my ears and the back of my neck. The blunt, square buildings rising from the Piazza di Trevi framed the crisp blue sky above.

People were everywhere—European and American, children and grandparents, couples and tour groups. They peppered the tiered white marble seating radiating outwards from the glittering aqua pool of the piazza's centerpiece. Some climbed the wide center set of stairs; others descended. Still more wandered the grey cobblestone lane at the water's edge. Street vendors armed with bubble guns or flashing pins or bouquets of roses moved carelessly between the continually replenishing assembly of prospective customers.

Dwarfing everything and everyone, bursting forth from the northern wall of the humbly sized square, swelled the Trevi Fountain itself. Neptune stood centered between three pairs of multi-sized marble pillars. He was framed by a mammoth façade, also marble, which rose above the roofline of the building to which it was affixed. At Neptune's feet ran a broadening cascade of fountains, the third emptying an arched sheet of white water into the colossal main pool below. To both his left and right a pair of Tritons wrestled with two winged horses, the scene's extreme fervor trapped in the frozen stone. Fanning from the three central figures, across the entirety of the fountain's northern half, spread an amoeba of jagged unfinished marble. Countless runs of water careened off the figures' coarse faces. The perpetual sound of crashing water blended with the steady hum of human voices to fill the piazza with that vibrant buzz only Rome seemed able to craft so effortlessly.

I was on the far side of the fountain, leaning against the uppermost metal railing, gazing down onto the lively sight below. Directly ahead, a family was staging a photograph on the polished marble trim surrounding the shallow bath. The father directed the wife and two young girls to lean together, further, then to hold still.

To their right I noticed a couple. They were young, probably seventeen or eighteen. He was tall, dressed in a plain white T-shirt, a beige visor, loose tan shorts, and sandals. She had her dirty blond hair pulled back, her short-sleeved, red-and-black-striped top cut low in front; her hands dug into the pockets of her white cargo shorts. The pair appeared unaffected by the frigid winter air. They smiled and brushed against one another with a sunny casualness.

There is a phenomenon that happens to me, a visual mind trick. I call it *Back to the Future* vision. It was in the second film of that trilogy where Marty returned to the site of the plot-pivotal dance from the first film, and, from across the parking lot, he spotted his younger self playing out the actions from the original episode. He watched, captivated, as his past self repeated the exact motions from the previous trip directly before him. That is the best way I can describe the vividness of what happens to me.

I knew that Charlotte, with whom I had made my first trip to Italy back when we were together, could not have been there at the water's edge below me. But the more timeless, permanent, and unchanged the setting, the more vividly the scenes manifested themselves. And I could see the two of us with stunning clarity, playing out the final afternoon of our Italian vacation together beneath the blazing midsummer sun of four years ago.

An aged, peculiar-looking man approached us at the fountain's edge, one slow step at a time. His tattered brown suit hung loosely on his boney frame; a worn fedora hat shaded his face, his wooden cane clacked along the cobblestone. I could remember his toothless smile, his leathery, sun-beaten skin. I watched our faces smile politely as he began to speak to us in broken English.

The legend of the Trevi, he had told us, was one of the city and one of love—*d'amore*—he had reiterated with a fluttering fall of his free hand. Tossing a single coin over one's shoulder and into the fountain's churning waters ensured a speedy return *a Roma*. But the tossing of two coins would not only guarantee a speedy return to the Eternal City, but also the promise of falling in love upon that return.

The man lifted his cap and modestly bowed in conclusion. Charlotte and I laughed and began sifting through our pockets. He then slowly moved away from us and into the denser crowds toward the center of the fountain.

I continued to watch us from my perch. In our palms, we fingered the largest lire coins we could find and counted down from three. Our backs facing the shallow rippling water, we flung our hands to the sky and our bronze coins took to the air. Charlotte spun to watch them fall and spotted the three small splashes where there should have been only two. She hit me in the shoulder and my guilty face matched my playfully hollow excuse.

I blinked, and we were gone. The family next to where I had seen us huddled around their father's digital camera to view the photos he had taken moments before. My eyes lifted to the rugged marble beyond them. Rough streams of water tumbled down their crude faces, staining the white to brown where they spilled.

My eyes lifted higher, to the more furious of the two winged horses. The triton fought with its bit, struggling at the animal's weight as it bucked the two of them backwards.

My vision moved higher still and met Neptune. A commanding hand cast downwards in the direction of the thrashing creatures at his feet, his dominant figure orchestrated the scene. I fixed on his resilient marble eyes.

You owe me.

QUINDICI

"Mannaggia," Roberto muttered.

I looked to him over my shoulder as I cleaned the mint from an emptied Mojito. He had a bottle of Jameson whiskey in his hand, searching for a vacant space of illuminated shelving.

"Che c'è?" I inquired.

I had decided to make a conscious effort to practice more Italian and found myself venturing into unknown sentences with him, headlights off, pedal to the floor, far more frequently.

"No c'è posto per un'altra bottiglia," he replied. *There's no space for another bottle.*

Roberto had been busy reorganizing the collection of bottles on his backbar. And I had absorbed his comment fast enough to allow an opportune window for a naturally-timed response.

"Mmm … Forse Mariano … ummm … può … mmm … rompere qualcosa per te." I had crept through that delivery. But I was ecstatic I had said everything correctly the first time through. And damn, *Maybe Mariano can break something for you*, that was pretty funny.

Roberto's face cracked at the eyes and mouth. He let out a wheezy laugh, halting his search as he placed his free hand on my shoulder. He dropped his head, still laughing, in amusement.

Mariano, the little firecracker that he had turned out to be, had recently been given a lecture by both Hassan and Dario. At the same time. For about half an hour straight. The lecture was apparently nothing new; he needed to stop being so disorderly; he needed to make sure his trash made it to the nearest trash can; he needed to respect them when they asked him to reprioritize what he was doing. But the fact that he had broken an entire bottle of high-quality rum while attempting an overly exaggerated, behind-the-back toss to himself had really sent them over the edge.

Roberto called Mariano over to recount my observation and the events which had led up to it. Mariano shook his head, his face wearing a sheepish grin, and then told me to go fuck myself. But in a loving way.

I returned to facing the sinks and surveyed the few scattered customers, feeling confident from my successful escapade into second-language humor. Roberto joined me at the counter, crossing his arms at his chest. We each took a deep breath, reviewing the mingling crowd, double-checking that there was nothing immediate to attend to.

Despite my difficulty communicating with him, Roberto's respected presence was comforting at Metro and provided a nice balance to Mariano's scatterbrained antics. And when the club really packed out, our teamwork behind the bar had become extraordinary. It must have been a show to be seen from the other side of that bar: Mariano tossing blenders and tins and bottles of beer to me at the sinks with minimal warning, me flipping the washer door shut with a kick of my foot and darting around Roberto to refill his ice or replace his straws as he poured colorful cocktails and affixed exotic fruits to the glasses.

Isabella passed us, dropping off two empty coffee cups and a half-empty bottle of Ferrarelle sparkling water. Carmen followed moments later, smiling at me and placing two martini glasses onto the counter.

I reached first for the cups, casually placing them in one of the baskets. Roberto, arms still crossed, head lightly bobbing to the beat of the music, continued to wait on call next to me. I took the Ferrarelle bottle in my hand, poured the remainder of the sparkling water into the sink, and then placed the bottle into the small trash bin next to me.

"No, Mike. Aspetta."

"Cosa?"

"Non buttiamo quelle bottiglie. Le mettiamo qua, nel cestino." Apparently we didn't throw away the empty Ferrarelle bottles, but rather placed them back into the red plastic bin in which they arrived.

I pulled the bottle from the trash. Roberto returned to staring ahead, arms crossed. I ran tap water over the bottle with one hand, sloppily attempting to rinse it off. My motions read a cool casualness. Then Roberto spoke in his low, full-bodied Roberto voice.

"Skye -- - ----------."

The last two—or maybe it was three—words had been completely scrambled by the sound of Skye's name. It had come straight out of nowhere. Skye was off tonight. I would not see her until next Thursday.

"Hai sentito?" Roberto asked.

Had I heard what?

"Non ho capito. Dimmi un'altra volta," I asked him. *Tell me again.*

"Lei ha smesso," he rearticulated. *Ha smesso.* I recognized the phrase, but my brain was still recovering from the minor circuitry blow. *Smesso.* That was the past participle of *Smettere.* It was irregular. For some reason I associated this verb with Roberto. Why? I still held the empty Ferrarelle bottle in my left hand. Had Skye done something with a bottle? *Smettere.* I really had to improve my Italian. Wait. Ah, yes. Roberto had used this verb all the time my first weekend at Metro. He had made a New Year's resolution to stop smoking cigarettes. Ho smesso fumare. *I quit smoking.* Smettere. *To quit.* Skye ha smesso. *Skye quit.*

Skye quit.

Welcome to **Wells Fargo** Online Banking …

Your statement as of **February 01, 2005** is

Cash Accounts

Account	Account Number	Available Balance
CHECKING	XXX-XXX0385	$1,544.81
SAVINGS	XXX-XXX6608	$100.02

Total $1,644.83

SEDICI

I pushed through the double glass doors of La Galleria, the massive structure along Via del Corso which housed a small but famous collection of clothing shops, and inhaled the brisk winter air outside. Sensing I had exited alone, I turned back to see Aleksia still inside, her newly acquired second shopping bag in hand, fondling a scarf from a pile of discounted sale items.

"Aleksia! You already have two bags' worth of new stuff."

She heard me but refused visual or verbal acknowledgement. Instead, she placed the scarf back on top of the pile and slowly made her way out the doors herself, her visual line remaining on the markdown heap as if to say, *I'm sorry, I have to leave you now, but not because I want to.*

She turned to me and let out a melancholy whimper.

"I thought you did good today," I assured her.

"The stuff is okay." She looked up at me. "Your coat is really nice, though."

I had not wanted to spend the additional Euro, but at the hours I had been getting out of Metro, the temperatures had become unbearable.

"Let's keep heading up the Corso," I proposed.

Aleksia replied with an unenthusiastic but accepting okay and began to shuffle her Ugg-clad feet as we moved forward, both mentally and physically, from her mediocre shopping performance thus far.

The Corso was overrun with pedestrians and nearly all vehicle traffic had been diverted off the main boulevard for the afternoon. A few scattered taxis could be seen, their white and black *taxi* signs flashing in and out of view as they fought sluggishly through the swarms of post-holiday-sale shoppers.

We strolled northbound, Aleksia scoping for prospective fruitful shops which could save the afternoon's outing. I took in a deep breath and probed my back right molar with my tongue.

"I ave his uhn ooth," I started, before realizing it was nearly impossible to understand what I was trying to say with my tongue shoved to the back of my throat.

"I have this one tooth," I began again, "that gives off these little pulses of pain every once in a while."

"Really? Does it hurt a lot?"

"Not really. It's not a sharp pain. I had this little head cold a few days ago and it seemed to start with that, but now the cold seems to be gone, yet this pain in my tooth still comes and goes."

"Maybe you have a hole," she replied.

"A what?"

"A hole in your tooth."

I wasn't sure what a hole in my tooth would feel like but I assumed it would be far more painful than what I was experiencing. Then I understood what she was trying to say.

"You mean a cavity."

"A what?"

Exactly. This was a perfect example of the most unexpected linguistic challenges I seemed to be finding myself in as of late—working to patch up communication efforts with a Norwegian design student in regard to tooth decay. The differences in vocabulary were proving far less romantic than I had envisioned.

"We call them cavities, and I guess it could be that. I've never had one."

"You call them what?" she crumpled her forehead.

Language is a funny thing. If you were to look up the formal definitions of *hole* and *cavity*, you would see that they mean pretty much the same thing. Yet for some reason the society in which I had grown up in had chosen *cavity* to also mean *decayed area of a tooth*. And I had been hit over the head so relentlessly with this usage of the word that *cavity* had lost nearly all initial meaning, and all visuals associated with the word now consisted of dentist chairs and small power tools and gold fillings. *Holes* were something different. When was the last time you overheard two children playing on the beach exclaim in anticipation, "Let's go dig a giant *cavity* in the sand!" A line like that doesn't even seem to make sense.

"Cavities. That's what we call them."

"You never got a single hole in your teeth?"

Apparently we were sticking with *hole*.

"No, have you?"

Aleksia covered her mouth, giggled, and looked toward the pavement as we walked. She must have had at least four. I would not have been surprised if her hole count bordered on double digits.

Aleksia's cell phone began to ring and she stopped in the middle of the crowded boulevard to begin a lengthy search of her purse. She handed me her two shopping bags as her hunt required both hands working together in an effort that nearly tore apart her purse's seamed stitching. She spotted the chiming mobile and struck with her left hand. Her purse then dropped to her side and she put the phone to her ear.

"Pronto? ... Ciao, Paolo! Are you here already?"

I fumbled with her bulky shopping bags.

"We are still on Via del Corso—I'll come back and meet you."

As she hung up I outstretched my left arm, her bags dangling from my flattened palm.

"Here you go," I offered.

"Are you sure you don't want to walk back with me?" she asked.

"I think I'm going to finish these last few blocks to Piazza del Popolo."

"Okay, well thanks for coming shopping with me." She spoke with a self-conscious grin as she eyed the two bursting garment bags in her hands and then the vacancy in mine.

We kissed cheeks and Aleksia headed south down the Corso, back in the direction from which we had come. I watched her disappear into the crisscross of pedestrians. I then turned north and eyed Piazza del Popolo the two short blocks ahead.

The sky exuded only the purest of blues through which the sun had tracked a low arch, radiating just enough warmth to keep the winter air from biting my fingers and nose. It was nearing six o'clock and the shadows steadily engulfed the buildings lining the Corso—the darkness beginning to flood the narrow alleyways which branched off from the main street.

I passed a group of street musicians; the worn look of their instruments a fitting match to their prematurely aged faces. I had grown convinced that Rome housed an underground street performance training ring in which eager foreigners were strapped with a cheap acoustic guitar or used accordion and coached on one of two mandatory pieces: "Somewhere Over the Rainbow" or "The Girl from Ipanema." I hummed along with the latter as I entered Piazza del Popolo.

The structures surrounding the oval piazza threw a single monstrous shadow diagonally across the cobbled ground. The eastern half of the piazza basked in its remaining half hour of sunlight while the western end prepared for the assuredly frigid night ahead.

At the center of the piazza, extending just high enough to emerge from the rising shade and gasp final breaths of illumination, stood the obelisk of Pharaoh Ramses II. Brown, solid, stone, and wrapped in hieroglyphics, this particular obelisk was some three thousand and two hundred years old.

Thirteen such stone giants sat strategically placed about Rome. They had lain buried, forgotten and untouched, for centuries after the fall of the Roman Empire, before being unearthed during the Renaissance and given to that period's Christian rulers, the popes. The popes happily topped the towering monuments with crucifixes and placed one at each major location around the capital—the Spanish steps, the Vatican, the Pantheon, and so on.

During the rule of ancient Rome, the obelisks had provided a top prize to conquering rulers. The inscribed apexes of stone had stood for the divinity and immortality of the Egyptian pharaohs and then, in turn, the divinity and immortality of the overpowering Roman Empire.

And there I stood admiring the irony of it all—the fact that the obelisks themselves had outlived both empires. I was amused at the almost irritated look of that particular obelisk—the forced goody-goody Christian crown it had been adorned with some twenty centuries after its Egyptian conception provided a laughable contrast to its hieroglyphically tattooed body. The dissimilarity seemed to create the knowing self-consciousness of a teenager whose mom had insisted on dressing him for his first day of high school. *When can I take this stupid thing off,* it seemed to say in regard to its crucifix cap. As if the Church's fate would ultimately prove any different than that of the obelisk's previous possessors.

My eyes fell back to the piazza. A pair of travertine fountains anchored the center of both the western and eastern walls which enclosed the large oval square. At each wall's end sat a relief portraying one of the four seasons. I began walking toward the western wall, and exited via autumn.

I rubbed my back right molar with my tongue again. Maybe it was a cavity. How long could one wait out the pain of a cavity? Would I be able to see a dentist in Italy? Would I be forced back to the States over tooth decay? Could the pain become that bad?

As I began down the wide sidewalk of Via Cola di Rienzo I began to feel quite preoccupied by that molar. The thought was humiliating—being driven home from a foreign nation over an oral complication that carried implications of inadequate flossing and eating too many m&ms. I was not supposed to go out like that. I was supposed to go out in adventure and glory—something like an undercover document check at Metro or a run-in with border officials on a train into Switzerland.

How would I explain to my fiancée in seven years that yes, I had lived in Rome, but I was forced back to the United States because I had developed a cavity? The scenario was almost painful. There was supposed to be a big police chase or a tense game of cat and mouse with airport officials. Whatever it was going to be, it would be monumental and irreplicable—an unassailable ending to a volume from the tales of a young man abroad which would render speechless houseguests and grandchildren alike. But a cavity? It was almost as absurd as the police-chase scenario.

As I continued along Via Cola di Rienzo, my eye caught a woman emerging from a small side street and entering a crosswalk in front of me. She appeared to be in her late twenties, obviously Italian, and indisputably striking.

She had on dark, stylish blue jeans which tucked into her calf-high black boots. Her short winter jacket started just above her beltline, exposing a sliver of torso, then hugged her from waist to bust, where the zipper resigned and the jacket released into a wide V framing the olive skin surrounding her collarbone. The V then arched into a massively thick, fur-lined hood which cradled portions of her sleek black hair, the remainder spilling out in a display which exuded a fiery carelessness.

As we approached each other my eyes fixed on hers. She gazed back, the distance between us lessening, a mutual awareness unmistakably acknowledged. I held my stare, attempting to mask my intimidation with reverse intimidation.

Suddenly her arms lunged outwards and her hair tossed across her cheeks as her head was thrown downward. Her right leg held an extended position behind her body as if her boot had affixed itself to the ground. She hopped once backward on her free left foot and straightened herself. She then bent to her right ankle and began tugging at it violently.

Slightly stunned and definitely confused, I halted at the edge of the crosswalk and stood motionless about five feet from the woman, observing her as she attempted to free the heel of her right boot which had become wedged between a pair of ancient cobblestones. I thought about lending a hand. But any possible visualization of that situation just did not play well in my mind, so I instead tried to smile in an empathetic manner, even though the stunning Italian female had every ounce of focus directed toward her own foot.

With a final, violent tug the boot slipped free and the woman shot upright. She then wiped the hair from her face and broke into a frantic pace past me while adjusting her purse on her shoulder. I held my discarded smile as she faded toward the Piazza del Popolo. Then I shook my head and snickered—maybe at the way I had just witnessed such complex sophistication from such a beautiful creature transformed into clunky simplicity by a misstep and a pair of stones, or maybe at my own ridiculous and completely directionless vibe-throwing exhibition.

I glanced back to the spot in the cobblestone where the incident had occurred and then curiously gazed across the short intersection lying ahead of me.

I knew this crosswalk.

I took a pair of cautious steps forward, peering down the squat alleyway to my left, double-checking its validity in the fading daylight.

I recalled Skye's animated expressions, her slightly slurred criticisms. I saw myself laugh with her as I skipped from the opposite curb and spun in midair before landing on the first stripe of the crosswalk. *Back to the Future* vision.

I felt a small pulse of euphoria as I stood on that cobblestone, centered between those portly and faded white stripes, realizing that a spot on my map of Rome tucked tightly between the pages of my travel guide back at my apartment had just transformed. To the west, Saint Peter's Cathedral. To the east, Piazza del Popolo. And splitting the distance between them, the sleeping crosswalk I had passed through with Skye at five thirty in the morning after our outing at Seven Eleven. I had taken a small piece of Rome which meant nothing to everyone else and had made it my own. I was giving meaning to pavement.

DICIASSETTE

Nina cut the burner at the stovetop, wrapped a towel around her hand, and carried the boiling kettle to the table.

"Here you are." She carefully filled my mug with the piping hot water. I took one of the small tea packets and dipped it into the steaming liquid.

"How are things back in the Netherlands?" I asked her. She poured her own mug and then sat down at the table across from me.

"They're good for the most part. It is becoming difficult with Luuk, though. We have been away from each other for so long."

"How long has it been now?"

"Almost a year."

We gently blew across the surface of our tea.

"I've decided not to ask for an extension on my contract, so I will be moving back in April. That makes things a bit easier for us."

"That's when my flight is too."

"I'm sure you'll find some way to stay longer."

"Maybe."

"Why maybe? I have to return to the Netherlands to finish my master's. Why do you want to leave all of a sudden?"

"Sixty Euro a week won't carry me forever."

"Oh, c'mon now. If you want to stay, you'll find a way."

Nina sipped her tea.

"So tell me, what's going on with that nice Icelandic girl at work?" she asked.

I shook my head.

"She quit a couple weeks ago."

"She quit?"

"Well, she quit or got fired or something. I didn't ask the details."

"That must take away a little of the excitement now, huh?"

"Seriously," I nodded, "it's like she'd become even more exciting than working behind the bar." I pointed a finger playfully at Nina. "Leave it to a girl to make a lifelong aspiration feel *blah*."

She laughed and sat back in her chair.

I did not mean to say it was Skye's fault that I had been somewhat melancholy at Metro since she had left. I also did not mean to say that women were evil or trouble or any other stereotypical comment regarding relationships with the opposite sex. What I meant was: leave it to human nature; leave it to that overpowering connection our emotions make on their own accord which in one swift blow shatters all sensible reasoning regarding a situation. That was what I meant.

"So when will you get to see her now?" Nina asked.

"I don't have a way of seeing her now."

"Can't you ask someone at work for her number?"

"She disassociated herself from the other staff. I don't know if that was a mutual decision or not, but it seemed apparent."

"I'm sure someone there has it. And you should get it from them."

I winced. I really didn't want to ask around at Metro.

"Listen," Nina started. "If it was me who had been fired, I would be very happy if someone called to see how I was doing."

Thank God for Nina.

"Now I must be off to bed." She downed the last of her tea. "But it was nice talking with you."

She stood and carried her empty mug to the sink.

"You are going to drink that, right?" she pointed to my untouched tea.

"Yeah, of course. Thanks." I quickly brought it to my lips.

"Goodnight, Mike."

Nina left the kitchen and disappeared down the hallway toward her room.

The apartment was quiet. I could hear Ayden rapidly typing on his laptop inside his bedroom. I sipped on my tea and stared at the blackness outside the terrace doors.

Skye. What is it you want me to do?

...

Talk to me.

Mike, I'm lost.

Skye, where are you?

I don't know what to do anymore. Rome is too unkind.

Your boyfriend, is he helping you?

I told you, he's stupid! I'm suffocating in this world, in this closet of a room, in this apartment where I can't even cook for myself. And now I've lost my job. I'm ready to give up on this place.

Skye, no. I'm coming. I'm coming to find you.

DICIOTTO

"Can you take this to the kitchen for me?" Mariano asked. He was holding half of a pineapple.

"Sure, one second."

Metro's house lights were on, and everyone was diligently working at cleaning their stations. I placed the final pair of steaming glasses on the shelf behind me and walked the narrow aisle toward Mariano.

"And do not to forget to put the ..." he paused. "Pellicola?" I thought that meant *movie*. I shook my head.

"The plastic," he reiterated.

"Oh, the *film*."

Pellicola. *Film*. Tricky.

I passed him, pineapple in hand, and started past the deejay booth. Calum called me to the console where he was packing his headphones into his record case.

"What's up, Calum?"

He folded a small square of white paper in half and placed it on the counter between us.

"I'm telling you, though, I already tried to hit that, and she's a bitch."

I slid the paper into my left pocket.

"Right, thanks anyway."

I continued my way toward the back of the club. Dario had allowed a group of four or five girls to sit along the couches at the back room as we cleaned. The girls were young, spoke in English, and had been showing up regularly on Thursday nights.

I heard one of them ask Dario for my name as I strode past them. He told her, but I pretended not to hear what was going on.

I slowed my pace at the narrow kitchen entrance and pushed through the wooden double flaps. Then I froze.

Isabella worked to shield Carmen, who had tears streaming down her cheeks.

Isabella tried to explain to me what had happened. It was something about a table that had not paid their bill. Or maybe they had but not completely. Or maybe there was a computer error. It wasn't very clear. What was clear was that Carmen had gotten a lashing from Hassan and forty Euro—just about her entire night's pay—was going to be taken from her.

I made my way back out to the bar. Roberto was dividing up the tips. I wanted to ask him if we at the bar could help the waitresses cover lost tables on the floor. He looked up at me, my face reading the start of a question. The Italian would not come. He smiled.

"Vuoi un passaggio?" Roberto asked. *Would you like a ride?*

"Sarebbe benissimo," I nodded.

He slid two stacks of coins across the counter to me.

"Roberto, dai—basta!" I insisted he stop giving his tip money to me.

"Prendili. Ti servono di più," he held firm.

The six or so Euro did add to my trivial nightly salary. I wished I could thank him more articulately.

Roberto looked me up and down, still adorned in my Metro fatigues. He made a motion of opening a box. Wait, no. Changing my shirt. Yes, I had to change downstairs.

"Sì, sì. Un attimo solo," and I sprinted past him and to the stairwell.

Downstairs, I entered the storeroom and reached for my bag, tearing my jeans from inside. I kicked off my shoes and let my black work slacks drop to my feet, my mobile phone and wallet still inside their pockets. I slipped into my jeans, stuffed the slacks into my bag, and grabbed my coat.

Coat over my shoulder, black bag in hand, I reached for the door. It hurled inwards.

Mariano. He slammed the door behind him and with the key locked us inside.

"Listen. Can you make me a big favor?" he said, speaking as fast as his English would allow him.

"Tell me what it is."

"Can we use your bog to put somefings in?"

"My what?"

"Your bog." He pointed to my right hand.

"Oh, my *bag*. Yeah, that's fine, but Roberto is waiting for me, so be quick."

Mariano already seemed to be moving in overdrive. He snagged the bag from my hand, sprinted to the back of the stockroom, and started shifting through the bottles of liquor, every few seconds placing one on the floor beside him. I walked toward him down the narrow corridor.

"Mariano. What are you doing?"

"Do you want somefing? Here, this is very good rum. You can keep this one."

"Mariano. Tell me what is going on."

"They have taken our money for too many times. This may be our last night here."

"Whose last night?"

"Everyone—me, Isabella, Carmen. I don't know about Roberto."

"Mariano …" was all that came to me.

He began to stuff the selected bottles into my small tote bag, padding them with my work clothing.

"They want for me to pay for glahsess. They want Carmen to pay for the bill."

He compressed his packing with two open palms, then zipped the bag closed and held it to me.

"Let's go. We walk outside and we divide them at my car."

"Mariano, there is no way I'm carrying that bag past Dario and Hassan."

"Why fucking not? I cannot to carry your bag. It would look too strange."

"You're the one with the fucking problem, not me!"

"So you are with them? With Dario and Hassan?"

"No, I'm not with them, I just—"

"Then you are with us."

"Mariano, it's not that simp—"

He slammed the bag into my chest and started toward the door.

I could not afford this risk. I could not quit. I needed this job—this chance to prove myself as a hard worker, as an honest worker. Someone would take a stock check. Someone would notice things were gone and they would ask me because I would still be there. I did not want to lie. I did not lie to people's faces.

We climbed the stairs. The weight of the bottles tugged at the straps of my bag, which in turn pulled the skin of my palm. The bag was too dense. It felt so obvious. We reached the top of the stairs and started along the couches through the back room. I looked toward the exit at the front of the club. Dario and Hassan were conversing with Isabella and Carmen. They were blocking both glass doors. This was absurd.

Whose side was I on anyway? Who should I have trusted more? Dario? Hassan? Both of them may have liked me as an employee, but that did not mean they gave a shit about my life. Why would they?

Did Mariano give a shit? Was that relationship worth it? He and the whole staff had been very welcoming, but at the end of the day I was not Italian, I could not speak Italian, and I had known them for a month. None of our relationships had been tested. We went out together because we were physically put in the same place every weekend night. But would they still be there if things were not so convenient?

The weight of the bottles bore down on the skin of my palm. As we reached the front of the club, Dario paused his conversation with Carmen and Isabella to open one of the doors for us. The sweat in my palm soaked the rough, synthetic fibers of the bag's strap. I feared even the lightest clink of glass on glass. It was dead silent. It felt so obvious.

"Good night, Dario," I said, neglecting to make eye contact.

"Good night, Mike."

We took ten steps along the Campo's wall. Then Mariano stopped, appearing to set up camp.

"What are we doing? We have to get the fuck out of here Mariano!" I pleaded in a raspy whisper.

"We must to wait for the girls."

"Here? We wait here with a bag full of stolen liquor ten steps from where we stole it?"

Roberto. I had completely forgotten about Roberto. He was nowhere in sight.

"Mariano, where is Roberto? Do you know? I told him I would change and come right out."

"I don't know, man. Do you see him here? I don't see him here."

"He was supposed to give me a ride home."

"Where do you live? Piramide?"

"Yeah, but—"

"I'll give you a ride home, man. Do not to worry."

Mariano inched back towards Metro's doors, concentrating intently on the hushed discourse inside.

"Thank you, but listen, I still need to call him. I feel bad."

I reached into my jean pockets for my phone. Empty. I had left everything in my work pants which were in my bag. I crouched and grabbed the zipper.

"What are you doing!" Mariano exclaimed under his breath. "Are you fucking mad? Not here!"

"I need to call him. Can you call him for me?"

Mariano shook his head and looked the opposite direction.

"Mariano, can you call him, please?"

He pulled his cell phone from his jacket pocket and held it out to me, his face still looking the opposite direction.

"Can't you call him? I won't know what to say in Italian," I said.

"No, you need to call. I can't."

"Why not?"

"Roberto and I ..." he trailed off.

"You what?"

"We had a lot of words a few days past. We are not speaking to him and to me."

I took the phone from his hand and dialed Roberto. He picked up after two rings.

"Cosa?"

"Roberto, sono Mike,"

I wanted to apologize for disappearing. I wanted to say I was unsure what was going on but he should not wait up for me—in case he had been waiting—and emphasize that I was not upset that he left as it had been fair of him and I still appreciated his initial offer.

"Umm ... tu ... uhh ... tu vai?" *Are you leaving?*

Pathetic.

"Sì, mo sto al moto. Sono andato via quattro, cinque minuti fa." *I'm at my motorcycle now. I left four or five minutes ago.*

"Okay, bene. Umm ... Non mi aspettare. Mmm ... Mariano mi porta alla casa mia."

"Okay, ciao Mike."

Goddamn my worthless Italian.

I returned to the world immediate. Dark. Freezing. Mariano had disappeared.

I took my bag and tucked it back into the shadow of the closed storefront adjacent to Metro. The door we had exited through was still propped open. Voices, many at a time, bled from the interior. I peered around the corner. Dario was gone. I leaned in further.

At the end of the club stood Mariano, Isabella, and Carmen, arms practically interlocked. Hassan was behind the bar, at its end, waving his arms in fury, screaming from his post ten inches above them. An unlit cigarette jerked violently up and down as it hung clenched between his lips. Carmen, Isabella, and Mariano looked ready to quit, every one of them, all together. Force Metro to scramble for new staff. Do some damage as they went down.

I walked back to my bag, tore open the zipper, and retrieved my phone from inside. Three fifteen in the morning. It was freezing out here.

I glanced out across the empty piazza. My eyes met the back of Giordano Bruno, immortalized in bronze, his shoulders slouching slightly as he hugged his book with both arms.

If they all quit, you will be able to work more shifts and make more Euro, like you want.

I don't want that, not like this.

What are you saying? This was your dream—to work at a bar in the center of Rome. This has exceeded your every expectation.

All the right words were there—*work, bar, Rome.*

I shook my head and turned away. It was fucking freezing. My jaw chattered. It never got this cold in California.

California. There was a thought. I wondered where I would go if I could teleport back to my driveway, hop inside my car, and turn the key. Maybe just across town to a friend's. A *real* friend. Someone who gave a shit.

I must have stood there for a good forty-five minutes. Finally, the threesome streamed from Metro's doors, led by a singing Mariano. He marched right past me, lost in song, leading Isabella and Carmen out of the piazza in the direction of his car.

I grabbed my bag and darted after him.

"Wha—" I started but then had to clear my throat. "What happened?"

"Is okay, Michael. We work for a while more," he told me, still smiling and singing between sentences.

"So everything's okay?"

"Do not you worry about it. I still take you to your home."

A milliliter of relief fell from an eyedropper into a swimming pool of uncertainty. A glass of water thrown on a house fire.

We reached Mariano's car, and the four of us crowded into the miniature vehicle. He punched it into gear and we took off in an unfamiliar direction.

"Michael, are you in a 'urry?"

"Am I in a hurry? No, why?"
"I stop to buy some joint, okay?"
"Do what you want."

We flew across Rome, stopping for no one, no light, no vehicle. We sped along the Tiber, quickly reaching the base of the Ponte Testaccio where I had seen Mariano buy weed once before. This time the sellers were not there, and we pushed on into the heart of Testaccio.

The streets there were busy, alive with young Italian clubhoppers en route. Mariano invented a parking spot before scraping ten Euro off the dash and disappearing. Isabella and Carmen were absorbed in conversation behind me.

Five minutes later Mariano was back, still with no weed. He started the car and turned to me as he reversed.

"Michael, are you in a 'urry?" he grinned.
"No, Mariano."
"Good, because we go to the place of a friend."

We wound out of Testaccio. The roads changed from cobblestone to asphalt. They widened to multiple lanes. Soon we were on a freeway.

"Michael! Give to me my bottle!" Mariano announced.

I unzipped my duffle bag and sifted through our spoils, unwrapping alcohol from pant legs and shirtsleeves. Mariano hit his tape deck with his fist. Tinny techno beats began to trickle from the four miniature speakers mounted inside the car doors. His finger thrust toward the volume controls, rapidly stabbing at the plus symbol.

"Dove cazzo è il mio capello di babbo natale?" I could have sworn he had just asked where his Santa Claus hat was.

And then a furry red and white cap came flying from the backseat. Isabella had broken conversation with Carmen for just a moment to throw it at him. Mariano pulled it over his head with one hand and then hit at his temple. Four red plastic stars studded along its fuzzy white rim began to flash sporadically. This kid was out of his mind.

I offered him his bottle of rum.
"No! Drank!" he yelled.
"Drink?"
"Yes! Drink! Tonight we celebrate victory against Metro!"

I took a swig. It was rough. I passed it to the girls in the back seat.
"Thank you, Mikey!" Isabella smiled.

I watched out the passenger window. Beyond the blur of the guardrail a star field of city lights gradually shifted as we sped along. I had absolutely no idea where we were.

"You know, Mike. I was thinking you was a poof."

"What is a poof?"

"You know. We call it to someone who does the men in the ass."

I stared blankly at him.

"I mean, is okay with me if you are; I have no problem with those types."

Jesus, he was being serious.

"No. No, Mariano, I'm not gay."

"Okay, okay …"

"You and I approach women and relationships differently," I started.

I would never get what I wanted across to him. And even if the words made sense, he would never understand the concept.

"Where is my bottle!" he suddenly screamed.

Carmen handed the liquor to me over my shoulder, and I handed it to Mariano across the stick shift.

"Thank you, Michael. You are the best …"

Thank you, Mariano. Please don't drink too much while you drive the four of us around the freeway.

"… fucking poof."

We suddenly pulled onto an off-ramp, spiraling a toilet flush of an exit, round and round, before we were expelled into an intersection. We seemed to turn at every traffic signal. Left, left, right, left, right, right again, left. The electronica continued to flow seamlessly from the stereo.

Soon we were speeding down suburban corridors lined with squat parking lots and tall apartment complexes. Mariano spun the wheel and we veered into a lot. He cut the engine, grabbed the ten Euro from the dash again, and disappeared toward the apartment's entrance. Carmen and Isabella finished a thought and then sat quietly behind me. The music had died with the engine.

Isabella let out a wispy "Mmmmikey," almost as an afterthought, while staring out her window down the row of sleeping vehicles. I turned back to them and tried to lighten the mood—to lighten my mood.

"Non lasciatemi mai, ragazze!" *Don't you ever leave me, girls!*

Isabella responded.

"È come dicono. *One for all, and all for one.*"

I tried to laugh. I didn't feel any better. I was sitting in the car with them, but I knew I was not part of the *all* she spoke of. I didn't blame them for that. Isabella, who I now faced, continued.

"You know ... uh ... Carmen ... uh ... is like my best, best, best friend." She hastily spit out the sentence fragments as they finished buffering in her head. "Tonight I ... uh ... was ready to quit with her if they ... uh ... made her to pay."

"But don't you like working at Metro?" I asked.

"No. I mean, I like ... uh ... the staff. But Dario and Hassan, they ... uh ... they do not know how to act with us. It is not a place you ... uh ... you can stay for long times."

"How have you stayed for so long? It's been over a year since they opened, right?"

"Yes. No one else has ... uh ... stayed. I stay because I just ... uh ... tell Hassan *okay!*" she laughed. "Okay—and then I make the face when I turn away. But when they ... uh ... do like tonight. And what they do with Skye—"

"What did they do with Skye?'

"No one say you?"

"No, tell me." *Please.*

"Some people asked Hassan if there ... uh ... was gloves, because one of them had forgot gloves, and Hassan asked if we had ... uh ... saw gloves. I said no. Carmen said no. And Skye said she did see, but ... uh ... now they are gone. And Hassan said she must ... uh ... pay five Euro for the gloves. And they fight. And Hassan said she ... uh ... gets no money tonight, and fuck you, and never come back."

Fuck him, that fake carnival fuck. That was what he was—just as tasteless and offensive as that insulting carnival in Piazza Navona, leeching off Rome, plaguing her streets, preying off her treasures.

Suddenly Mariano was opening the driver's side door. He tossed a bag of weed into my lap and fell into his seat. He was on his mobile.

"Sì, sì Isabella sta qui con noi. No! Non andia—vaffanculo!"

He threw the phone recklessly to the backseat. Isabella picked it up from her lap and began playfully talking to whoever was on the other line. Mariano turned to me.

"This is my friend, Davide. He is out on cocaine and has a ..." One arm sprang up from his side at a forty-five degree angle and held rigid.

"Erection?" I cringed.

"Yes, and he want to fuck Isabella, and she want to fuck him."

Something Mariano overheard in Isabella's conversation set him off and he leaned into the back seat and began screaming.

"No! No! Vaffanculo! Dai! Andiamo da me!"

He twisted forward again, shoved his key into the ignition and gunned the gas. The car rattled as we dropped from the curb and back into the motionless residential street.

Soon we were on the freeway again, Mariano's Santa hat still twinkling atop his head, flat electronic music floating throughout the car's interior. Isabella continued to flirt with Davide over the phone.

The bottle of rum passed repeatedly between Carmen and me. My head was beginning to feel disjointed from my body. We seemed to approach every car too fast, too closely. Headlights left colorful spots in my visual field which morphed through browns and yellows before fading to black.

It must have been close to four in the morning by the time we were back in Rome's cobblestone center, near Prati. I had seen the Vatican but had lost orientation soon after. The car was stopped on a quiet side street, and Carmen was climbing out of the back seat and kissing us all goodnight. Her door closed and then we were moving again.

Five minutes later we were all exiting the car, in front of a building I did not recognize.

"Welcome to my home, motherfucker," Mariano called over the car as I gathered myself.

We took the elevator to the fourth floor and watched him struggle with his keys at the door. The fluorescent hallway lighting hurt my eyes. We entered his apartment.

Mariano's studio had apparently belonged to his grandmother, and her influence remained in the old furniture and rosy wallpaper. The single main room was small. I took a seat at the circular table in the left corner of the room, while Isabella sat on the bed across from me. Mariano turned on only his desk lamp, leaving most of the room in obscuring blackness. I spotted a bong atop his short bookcase. It was being used as a bookend for his biology material. Mariano pulled a paperback from the shelf below and handed it to me.

"I was thinking maybe you translate for me to Italian." *A Grower's Guide to Marijuana.*

"The entire book?"

"Maybe I tell you certain pages."

I flipped through the book. It was full of diagrams of illegal plants suspended among homemade piping systems. Figure 1.3, Figure 4.7. It read like a textbook.

"You make me copies of specific pages and we will see," I told him.

There was a knock on the door and Mariano let Davide in. He was short and slim like Mariano and had spiky brown hair. His eyes darted erratically around the room. I introduced myself, and the conversation became exclusively Italian. I was unable to follow anything anyone was saying.

Davide pulled a small bag of hash from his jacket pocket and began rolling a joint. Mariano turned to me and spoke in English.

"Why do you not smoke with us?"

"I don't do that anymore."

"You makes me feel like we are children and you are too old for our stupid games."

That was correct.

"Listen," I began, "do you remember what you said about my jacket last week? About this jacket?"

I pulled at the unbuttoned right breast of the black winter coat I had purchased with Aleksia on the Corso.

"You said you liked it," I continued. "And you asked me how much it had cost. When I told you it cost almost one hundred Euro, what did you ask me?"

"I am sorry. I do not understand what you tell me."

"You asked me if I knew how much Metro pays me."

"I do not follow you."

"Mariano, you buy a bag of weed every week. I buy a new jacket every three months. It is the same money. I used to smoke when I was younger. Now that I am older I just use that money differently."

I made a scale with my hands and balanced them to clarify. He seemed to comprehend.

I had done my share of smoking when there were no term papers to write, no bills to pay, no such thing as wasted time. That was the beauty of adolescence. You had all the time in the world to try these things. Your responsibilities ended at finishing your geometry homework and taking the trash cans to the end of the driveway—axe that first one come the three-month summer break. It was a safety net of limited liability. The world was a room lined with pillows.

"But you have not paid for the weed! I have pay for you!"

I should have seen that one coming. I cast a final plea.

"Really, I never liked joints. A bong is smoother."

Mariano grinned. He hopped to his bookshelf and pulled the bong from its top. His biology books went tumbling to the floor. He cursed in Italian, but left them sprawled across the hardwood as he stepped toward me and placed the bong in my hands.

As Mariano packed the weed I examined my two remaining options. I could take a final and most likely abrasive stand against the three smokers in the room, two of which were my co-workers. Or I could simply take a rip off this bong, leave Davide and Mariano content, and simply wait out the remainder of the evening—morning—whatever it currently was.

I placed my mouth to the plastic rim and Mariano sparked the lighter. I sucked for about fifteen seconds, knowing if this hit was not satisfactory he would insist I do it again. The space inside the blue plastic tubing filled murky white. How I hated smoke—in my clothes; in my lungs. I removed my thumb from the vent and inhaled. I held my breath, pulled my mouth from the bong's rim, leaned back in my chair, and then expelled a dragon's exhalation toward the ceiling.

"Grande!" Davide applauded.

Mariano laughed in amazement and shook my hand.

"You really aren't a fucking poof!"

The weed hit me quickly. My eyes and head tightened.

I slowly spun a glass of stolen rum with my right hand. Had I been doing this for a few seconds or a few minutes?

Davide and Mariano had rolled another joint and were conversing in Italian with Isabella. I didn't even try to follow. Then Davide said something which seemed focused in my direction.

"What?" I tried to gather social footing.

"He says this is the first time he sees an American," Mariano answered.

Davide laughed and shook his head while rapidly speaking to Mariano.

"Okay, well, not the first time he *sees* one, but to meet one."

"And how is it?" I turned to Davide, "Com'è?"

Davide spoke through Mariano.

"He says you are truly nice and a good man."

Davide then asked me a few questions, continuing to speak through Mariano. Were there bidets in America?

No.

Then how did Americans keep their asses from smelling like shit all the time?

I didn't know.

Is the weed better in northern California or southern California?

Northern.

And the cocaine?

I didn't know.

Do people tell me all the time I look like Indiana Jones?

No. Never.

The conversation faded as THC and sleepiness assumed control of our functionality. My vision drifted aimlessly along the bookshelves of the opposite wall. A second bong I had missed before operated as another bookend on the lower shelf. The face of a wicked-looking clown painted dead center on the bong's shaft stared back at me.

This is exactly where you wanted to be—a local's apartment in Rome, with two Italian coworkers and a new Roman friend. And to them you are representing California—the entire United States. A global exchange performed face to face.

Why do I feel like I am regressing? Why do I feel I am stumbling backwards? Why am I drunk and high when I now have bills to pay and a budget to keep? The pillows have been replaced with concrete. The liabilities are my own.

My eyes searched the floor around my seat. A beat-up acoustic guitar sat propped against the wall behind me. I pulled it to my lap and held it against my chest, searching for stability in a room growing exceedingly alien with each passing minute.

"Suoni?" Davide asked.

"Yeah. I mean, sì."

"Suonaci una cosa."

Davide was lying next to Isabella on Mariano's bed. I was talking to his nostrils. He took a drag off a joint and then passed it back to Mariano, who was sprawled across the small sofa.

"Yes. Play to us something," Mariano said, speaking quietly to the ceiling before drawing off the joint himself.

I began lightly strumming a song I had written three years ago. It was a melancholy acoustic piece. The notes floated across the apartment.

Mariano and Davide shut their eyes, absorbing each chord change, their joint now slowly burning in the ashtray at the edge of the bed.

For three minutes the apartment was void of human voice. The music splashed color—crimson and sapphire—into the black of the room's far corners and doorways. I closed my eyes and followed the notes back to California; back to my dorm room at UCLA where I had first stumbled upon the minor chord change; back to my bedroom in Northern California where I had built the song's structure; back to my studio apartment in Los Angeles, eleven floors above it all, where I had recorded the final version into my computer. My dorm room was warm, my bedroom comfortable, my studio bright. For three minutes Mariano's apartment was warm and comfortable and bright as well.

I struck the closing chord, a climactic explosion of fireworks erupting in our heads. Then the sustain of the notes faded, leaving emptiness, and we returned to Mariano's dark one-room apartment in Rome. It was silent for almost a minute.

"Who was that? I know that song," Mariano whispered.

"That was me. My song. I wrote it."

Mariano's head rolled on the sofa, his eyes opened for the first time, ever so slightly.

"Really? You are serious?"

"Yes."

His head rolled back, his eyes closed again.

"You have some talent for the guitar."

"Thank you."

There were thirty seconds of silence.

"And now I must to take a piss!"

Mariano hopped to his feet, stumbled for a second, and then dragged himself off through the far doorway. I sat in my chair, guitar in hand, across from Isabella and Davide on the bed.

Davide placed his right hand on Isabella's leg.

I began to strum slow, random chords.

Isabella rolled to her side, Davide met her, and they started to kiss.

I was invisible.

I watched them, began to feel voyeuristic, and so stared toward the floor. I continued to strum the old beat-up guitar. I tried again to follow the notes, but this time they took me to dark high school gatherings. Ted Robinson's house. Everyone was wasted. Matt Downing was making out with Lauren Anderson next to me on the couch. Right next to me, as I strummed Ted's guitar. Eric Blackman's house. Whitney Mulberry was with Eric in his parents' guest room cheating on her boyfriend. No one cared. Everyone was high and drunk. I had searched for comfort in his younger brother's guitar which I had brought into the living room.

Mariano returned. He saw Isabella and Davide and began clapping his hands.

"Okay! Andiamo! Da tuo, Davide!"

He was kicking them out. I put the guitar back against the wall and stood with them. Mariano looked at me and then mentioned something to Davide. They seemed to start arguing over who would take me home.

"Okay, okay!" Mariano turned to me. "Let's go; I take you."

Mariano fumbled with his keys. We exited. No one closed the door so I backtracked, closed it myself, and then caught up to them in the stairwell. Outside, the sun was beginning to rise. We all kissed good-bye, and Isabella and Davide headed off toward Davide's car while Mariano and I climbed into his.

Luckily, the streets were empty; fitting for a Sunday morning at quarter to seven. Once we reached the familiar Via Ostiense, I quietly directed us to my apartment. I thanked Mariano for the ride, unzipped my bag, and placed the second bottle of rum and single bottle of white wine onto the passenger seat.

I moved through the sleeping parking lot and entered my building's small lobby. Wearily, I climbed the stairs, unlocked the front door, and moved to my bedroom.

The sunlight refracted through my shutters and careened into the opposite wall. The radiator had been off for hours. It was cold.

I collapsed on my bed fully clothed. The bed felt small, and the springs sank in the middle under my weight. I rolled to my wall, trying to avoid as much of the light as I could, the layers of my clothing twisting around my legs and chest. My eyelids felt cemented together; my feet were ice. I was tired. Utterly exhausted. But it would be a while before I would be able to fall sleep.

Then I remembered something. Something important. I dug my left hand into my twisted and taut jeans pocket. Eyes still closed, I pulled forth a mix of small change and Euro bills and tossed them to the floor beside the bed. I dug again, pushing deeper through the strained fabric. My middle and index fingers grasped the small square of paper folded once in on itself. I extracted it slowly, careful not to lose my fragile grip.

I opened the fold and brought the paper to my face. I lifted my eyelids. They fought to remain sealed. My vision blurred and speckled as uninviting light poured inwards while I searched to confirm the paper's authenticity. I was unable to make out the individual digits but the sight of the numerical sequence was all I needed.

I let my eyes fall shut again and rolled to my opposite shoulder. I slid the paper onto my nightstand and felt for my cell phone. I placed it on top of the paper and then fell flat to the mattress. There it would be safe. There it wouldn't go anywhere. And whenever it was that I would wake up, it was going to fix this mess.

DICIANNOVE

When I was studying in Siena two and a half years ago I met someone, Lindsay Bergen, in the final two weeks of the program. We had known of each other for the entire four months but had our first one-on-one encounter in Florence with only thirteen days remaining before our flights home.

Our connection was extraordinary, something I had never achieved before or since. We found ourselves skipping out of the good-bye parties early to spend time alone in the narrow, dimly lit streets of the medieval city. We spoke openly and mutually about never having found a bond like the one we were experiencing. Conversation was effortless and meaningful. We made out a few times. I appeared in one of her dreams.

The return to California immediately split us apart. She was from Los Angeles but studying in northern California. I was from northern California but studying in Los Angeles. We tried to catch each other over holidays, but the other person had always gone home too, or stayed at school too, or gotten sick and couldn't meet up. Communication fizzled. Distance always seemed to prove stronger than I liked to admit.

A year and a half later, with Lindsay well faded from my day-to-day life, I had opted not to travel to Miami with my family over my spring break to look at Phil's college-to-be. I had considered spending the week in San Diego with some friends but ultimately ended up in northern California, house-sitting for my parents, trying to figure out how I could have avoided making my final academic vacation one of my most uneventful breaks ever.

An old friend of mine, Greg Boschetti, showed up at the house my second night there, and we decided to eat dinner out. As with all things *back at home*, we could not decide on where to go. We drove aimlessly around Walnut Creek, indifferent to our dining options. Finally, at what must have been our thirtieth red light in ten minutes, I simply threw the car into a parking spot in front of Black's Restaurant and Pub. I locked the car door and started toward the entrance. Lindsay Bergen stood at the curb in front of me. Greg watched, puzzled, as Lindsay and I locked into a speechless, frozen stare.

What was she doing there? She told me had graduated from UC Davis and had decided to move to San Francisco instead of back to Los Angeles. Why had she come all the way out from San Francisco to dreary Walnut Creek? She said one of her friends had just broken up with her boyfriend, and they were getting her out of the city. Why Black's Restaurant? She said she didn't know.

Her purse had just been stolen, so she had no cell phone, but she gave me her work number. I met her in the city two nights later.

Our chemistry was even more potent than before. We showered each other with compliments, then insisted on rephrasing the wording to be even more personal and memorable. She told me she had been seeing someone and was considering getting married, but our inexplicable reunion was giving her second thoughts. She thought it was fate.

I never saw Lindsay again after that night. I tried visiting her office downtown on Montgomery Street after graduation—just three days before I left for Rome—but she had vanished. No one there even recognized her name.

I tend not to believe in the idea of fate and especially not in the even stricter predestiny. If fate did exist, what was it doing with Lindsay and me? Why would it toy with us so, placing us in the same medieval Italian city for four months only to have us discover our connection with less than two weeks remaining on the program? Why cause us to miss each other so many times in California after that? Why force an end to our communication? Was it to make running into each other at Black's more dramatic? Why give us one more ideal night in San Francisco and then block us from each other yet again? What would whoever was guiding this torturous game be trying to tell us? What was the point? If fate existed, by definition, there should have been a purpose.

Had fate seen me get into the car with Greg and directed us to Black's? Or had it been responsible for Lindsey's friend breaking up with her boyfriend, which sent them out to Walnut Creek in the first place? Had some unseen guiding force placed Phil onto the University of Miami acceptance list, creating the need for a house-sitter while my family visited the cross-country campus? Just how far could you take things? How far back could you trace the thread from a single act of fate before each and every step of your life became predetermined? Where did free will end and complete predestiny begin?

There was no logic to my encounters with Lindsay Bergen. It had been chance. The truth is, that if you can meet someone at some converging dot on the map of your life, then there is a relatively high probability that you can end up converging again at a future dot. If you can be somewhere in the world, no matter how hidden or exotic, so can anyone else who has shared a same point previously.

Charlotte. We had broken up the summer before starting college. It was a nasty breakup, right after we returned from our high school graduation trip through Italy. She was leaving for a state school in San Diego, which started a month before UCLA, so communication had been cut off in a bickering stalemate when she had left. That last month of summer was torturous; I could barely find the motivation to pull myself from my bed each day. September dragged, my hometown was empty, and the days were getting shorter as fall approached. Finally, my own dorm move-in day arrived down at UCLA.

My parents and I had planned on packing the car completely the night before, but ended up taking an hour that morning to top off the Explorer. We therefore hit the road an hour late. I had not eaten breakfast, so three hours into the drive we reached a consensus to stop and eat at the Split Pea, off Interstate 5. The waitress there messed up our check and we had to wait an extra fifteen minutes for the right bill. Slightly anxious after the bill incident, we decided not to fill up on gas across the street, but rather to push on southbound for another hour with the quarter tank we had left.

Interstate 5 is a six-hour stretch of absolutely nothing. Well, yes, the *something* nothing—fields of fruit, fields of wheat, fields of cows. The exits are sparse and usually lead to a solitary intersection of competing gas stations—Exxon, Shell, Mobile, Texaco. When you deem the time appropriate, you simply choose an exit at random. If you are young, you quickly reference the cheapest price per gallon and pull up to the pump. If you are older, you go with your name-brand instinct. Dad chose Shell.

He went to the bathroom while the gas pumped. I stood on the back bumper of the car, stretching my legs. The gas finished, Dad returned, but now Mom wanted to use the bathroom. So then Mom wandered off and Dad decided to use the extra time to buy some candy bars from the mini-mart.

From my perch on the back bumper, my head high above the double ski racks mounted on the roof, I watched a black Honda Civic pull up to the pump across from me. The driver emerged and stretched his arms to the sky. He looked my age—college student age. Three girls filled the rest of the car's seats.

The back right door, facing me, opened. A leg stepped to the pavement. Her pants looked exactly like the ones I had bought for Charlotte that last Christmas—baby blue warm-ups with a white stripe down the seam. It was precisely the opposite of what I wanted on my mind standing there, alone, in the middle of nowhere, five hours from *old* home, on my way to a life of question marks in a city unknown. We made eye contact as she pulled her body from the vehicle. It was Charlotte.

Imagine having loved someone every day for twelve months, the relationship climaxing in a three-week excursion through Italy, then not hearing a word from that person for weeks after a violent exchange of accusations—and suddenly having him or her materialize five feet in front of you at a gas station smack-dab in the middle of California's central valley.

We unfroze, said a few formalities, and then started screaming at each other.

What on earth was she doing there? Her friend from SDSU was giving her a ride to northern California for the weekend. What was I doing here? I was moving down to my dorm at UCLA. Why was she only an hour and a half outside of Los Angeles this late in the day? They got off to a late start packing, then the car would not start, then they finally got a jump but were unable to find one of the other girls.

This one stuck with me for years. If there were any sort of predetermined organization in the universe, this had to be it, neatly packaged in stars-and-moons wrapping paper, topped with a navy blue ribbon, and placed on my doorstep. Think about it. Had I packed everything the night before like I had planned, there would have been no encounter. Had I eaten breakfast and we had not stopped at the Split Pea, no encounter. Had the waitress not messed up our check, no encounter. Had Dad decided to fill up right after we ate, no encounter. Had Mom not decided she wanted to use the bathroom too, no encounter. And this was just from my end of things.

Had Charlotte not gotten off to a late start, no encounter. Had their car started the first try, no encounter. Had one of the girls not disappeared, no encounter. Had either of our drivers chosen one of the countless other exits at random, no encounter. Had either driver pulled into any of the other three gas stations at this exit, no encounter! It was unbelievable.

Had Dad's foot been an ounce heavier or lighter for a relatively short period of the drive we would have gained or lost a few minutes over the five-hour journey thus far. We had been fluctuating between seventy-five and eighty-five miles per hour for the entire day. And there, at that Shell station, surrounded by fields of various crops, on pumps five and eight, there was a seven-minute window of possibility for this to happen. It would have been impossible to replicate, had we tried—there were too many factors. Even trying to calculate travel speed to meet within that window, coming five hours south from San Francisco and three hours north from San Diego, would have been next to impossible.

For months—even years—after that encounter we both could not help but think fate was trying to tell us something. Were we meant to be together as a couple or meant to stay communicating as friends?

After the dramatic event took place, we continued to run into each other fairly often during holiday vacations at home. Each succeeding "normal" run-in—at a friend's house, at someone's birthday party—slightly deflated the superstitious beliefs of our fateful I-5 encounter those years before.

Today, I am not friends with Charlotte. I do not even talk to her. That encounter off Interstate 5 ultimately led to nothing. But looking back on all of the factors, at the amazing improbability, one cannot help but search for some kind of meaning. It seems to be human nature to do so.

But therein lies the problem. Whenever people talk about events being played out by fate, it is in retrospect—in hindsight. Of course, it seemed impossible that they themselves could have planned it and that only a higher force could have executed such a meticulous design. But it wasn't planned; it happened by chance. There was a minute probability which made it seem against all odds when you looked at it from the finish line, but it did have a probability nonetheless. I, no doubt, had a similar probability—close to zero but *not* zero—of running into any one of my old classmates still in California that afternoon. But when Charlotte got in that car that morning, the probability of our paths colliding rose slightly, and then happened to play out.

I am not trying to say that actions have no meaning and that everything is a chance factor. Let me get abstract for a moment. Take two parallel-universe Mikes. In one, let's say I end up getting fired from my job in San Francisco and I end up moving to, say, Chicago, to start over. In the other, I also get fired but I remain steadfast on living in San Francisco and find another position there. My Chicago self ends up meeting a woman at a bakery and falling in love with her. My San Francisco self ends up meeting a woman at a company party and ends up falling in love with her. Now, my Chicago self says to the bakery girl the day of the wedding, "It was fate that I got fired and moved here to Chicago so I could meet you." My San Francisco self says to the company-party girl on the day of the wedding, "Fate led me to this second job in

San Francisco so that I could meet you." Both are bull. It is because my Chicago self *chose* to move that he met a woman in Chicago. It is because my San Francisco self *chose* to stay that he met a woman in San Francisco. People are proactive regarding their life events. They make or break their own relations.

Back in this universe, I was walking down the side streets of Testaccio on my way to the Internet café. I had my mobile out and was scrolling back and forth over Skye's number.
>*Sarah*
>*Scott*
>*Skye*
>*Sophie*
There it was. Right in there.
>*Sophie*
>*Skye*
>*Scott*
>*Sarah*

I had sat on her number for three days since Calum had slid it across the counter at Metro Saturday night. The remainder of the weekend had passed, and I was aiming for a time when her boyfriend would be away at work. It was two thirty in the afternoon. I had to call before midweek if I wanted to set up a casual, non-weekend meeting. It was already Tuesday. I had told myself I would call after I was off the bus to Testaccio. I was off the bus to Testaccio. I was a fan of the walk-and-dial; how could you ever sound desperate if you were en route to somewhere else? I was on my way to the Internet café.

The streets of Testaccio were calm. The straight, narrow, one-way avenues were shaded at all hours of the day by the elevated buildings painted in soft yellows and reds. I passed a few people carrying grocery bags; others stood between parked cars, conversing. I glanced left as I crossed a small intersection, letting my arm with the phone go limp.

I looked forward again. I could see the intersection at Via Giovanni Branca, the street which housed the Internet point, two blocks ahead.

In one continuous motion I drew the phone from my waist and hit *Call* on Skye's number. I liked trying to act spontaneous like that, as if it would somehow nullify my obvious overpreparation.

I put the phone to my head. Immediately my brain began sending a distress signal to my hand to hang up. The adrenaline rush running through my arms helped me ignore that message. But while I was arguing with my primal alert system, I forgot what I had rehearsed saying to her.

The phone rang twice and then there was a series of four flat, chromatic beeps. Confused, I pulled the phone from my ear and looked at the screen.

>*Forwarded.*

What in the world did that mean?

I looked ahead, still walking. Only one block to go. I dialed again.

BEEP BEEP BEEP BEEP

>*Forwarded.*

I stopped. I had never seen this message before. Did it mean her phone was off? Did it mean the number was invalid? Was my phone from the States having a network error on the Italian system? Had she already left for Iceland? Had I acted too late?

I thought of Lindsay Bergen at Black's. I thought of Charlotte at the gas station. Would fate actually work through wireless phone networks and hi-tech electronics? What would it be trying to tell me? Why allow me to find her number in the first place? Come to think of it, why would anything or anyone set us off on such a start and then cause her to disappear completely?

I wanted to see fate when it was on my side. I wanted to believe we had been destined to take that walk together from Seven Eleven. To think of little baby Skye being born in a small-town hospital in the middle of Iceland twenty-two years ago. Little baby Michael was not even one, sleeping in a crib five floors up at the corner of Lombard and Leavenworth in San Francisco. We had virtually unlimited life trajectories. And it was in Rome that we had landed those twenty-two years later, first finding ourselves sharing opinions over cocktails, and then an early morning walk through the back streets of the Eternal City. It was such a romantic design.

But there was no organization to the events which followed that night. I was looking in hindsight, from the finish line, from the moment she stepped out of that train at the Cavour subway stop. Chance had put us there, a probability had played out, and now it was up to me to let her disappear or try to find her.

I switched off my phone, waited thirty seconds, switched it back on and dialed Skye.

BEEP BEEP BEEP BEEP

>*Forwarded.*

I looked up from the screen, grounded on the runway. I was at the edge of Piazza Santa Maria Liberatrice, a small two-block by two-block park, with a bricked commons leading to a gated sandbox and jungle gym. A dozen schoolchildren ran, climbed, dug, and slid about the playground, their parents occupied in animated conversation at the surrounding benches.

I spotted one girl, giggling wildly as she ran from one of the boys. The boy had a red plastic shovel in his right hand, filled with sand. The playground was a small ring and there really was not anywhere to go, but the girl moved like a bumblebee, somehow managing to elude the boy among the swing set and seesaws with her erratic motion and abrupt directional changes. The boy fell a few times, laughing still, then clumsily rose to his feet, reoriented in his direction of attack, and continued the pursuit, plastic shovel held level at all times. I followed them with my eyes.

Just you wait, you two. Wait until you are a little bit older. Wait and see how confusing it gets—when you separate from children into males and females. Wait until someone leaves you, someone you still love. Wait until you have to leave someone who still loves you. Wait until you start thinking about marriage—until you have to decide who you should spend the rest of your life with, and if that person even exists. Wait until you are older and alone, and you realize that no matter how much you may want someone and no matter how well you would treat them, those facts alone can never make them truly want you back. Just wait and see if you are still laughing then. I'll come back to this sandbox in fifteen years and you tell me how it's going.

At the university I checked my e-mail and downloaded the weather forecast—the usual Internet stuff. I glanced at my bank statement. The *one* at the beginning of my balance still sent me into a slight panic, despite knowing beforehand that it would be there.

An hour and a half later I paced back through the park. Most of the children were gone.

I caught the 716 line on Via Marmorata to my apartment. I climbed the stairs, unlocked the front door, and tossed my coat onto the kitchen table as I moved to my room. I leaned out of my window. I stared at my phone. I stood static, eyes glazed. The sun was beginning to set. I exhaled and dialed Skye.

BEEP BEEP BEEP BEEP
>*Forwarded.*

Enough. I left the phone on the windowsill and moved back to the kitchen to pour a bowl of cereal. No one was home. I had forgotten to turn the kitchen light on. The sun outside withered. The crunch of each spoonful of Special K sounded like an earthquake. Then I heard my phone ring.

I sprinted to my window, small spots of milk trailing along the floor after me as they fell from the spoon still in my hand. I grabbed the phone. The entire planet knew who I wanted it to be.

>*+393355865814 Unknown Contact*

Maybe it was someone at Metro wanting me to come into work. That would be good. I mean, it would be money. I needed that. If I wanted to stay longer and all.

I let the phone ring twice more, then chose to answer.

"Pronto?"

"Sì, ciao. Sono Skye. Qualcuno mi ha chiamato da questo numero ed io—"

"Skye! Sono Mike dal Metro! Come stai?"

"Mike! Bene! Senti, non c'è credito sul mio telefonino e sto chiamando da un altro. Puoi richiamarmi?"

"Sure, sure. I have plenty of credit on my phone. You want me to call this number or your number?"

"Call my number."

"Okay."

"Thanks!"

I hung up and anxiously scrolled to Skye's number.

>*Sam*
>*Sarah*
>*Scott*
>*Skye*

Call.

One ring. Two rings.

"Ciao, Mike! How are you doing?"

Fate!

VENTI

Skye had agreed to meet in Piazza Navona after her theater class on Thursday. We were to be at Bernini's Fountain of Four Rivers at half past seven. It was a rendezvous I had idealistically fantasized about during sleepless nights in Los Angeles, an arrangement I had secretly acknowledged must only happen in books and movies. Yet there I stood, watching the crystal streams of water cascade over the aged marble as I anxiously awaited Skye's arrival.

Every few seconds, one side of the fountain became starkly illuminated by the flash from someone's camera. Young couples, married couples, Japanese friends, German tour groups—they all took turns handing their cameras to a stranger, or leaning in head-to-head while one of them held the camera at the end of an extended arm or set a timer and scurried back to position before playing statues for the longest eight seconds of their day.

I glanced at my phone: 7:34 PM.

I tried not to read into it.

Skye entered the Piazza behind me, but I spotted her first, her hair gleaming. She was with another girl, a friend from theater class, and they began a slow clockwise stroll around the circular fountain.

I pulled my work bag from the cobblestone and circled the fountain myself to meet them both head on.

"Skye!"

"Ciao, Mike!"

We double-kissed hello.

"It is so good to see you!" I told her. It was.

"Ecco la mia amica, Irene."

I shook Irene's hand.

"Piacere, sono Mike."

She pronounced her name in an Italian accent, E-reh-ney. She was of average height, with long dark hair matching her deep brown eyes and olive complexion. She appeared slightly older, twenty-four or twenty-five.

I looked back at Skye. Already she was up to her charismatic antics, finishing a previous thought in Italian with Irene, wide blue eyes rolling, small white nose scrunching, her head bobbing left and right in overexaggeration.

Irene turned to me. "I sorry. It has been many times since I spoke English."

Was she coming out with us?

"No, that's fine," I responded, "I mean, we are in Italy; we should be speaking Italian. Mine just isn't that good."

"Irene is just learning Italian too," Skye said to me.

I stood confused for a moment.

"What is your first language?" I asked.

"It is French, of course. I am from France."

The dark hair, the dark eyes, the olive completion—she had fooled me right in front of Skye.

"You fit in very well here. You look very Italian to me," I defended myself.

I tried to get things moving with a single, resolute handclap.

"So! Where would you like to go? I know a place called Friend's over on Via delle Coppelle and there is Fluid on Governo Vecchio."

In preparation for our outing, I had spent the afternoon thoroughly studying a free nightlife publication from the newsstand across from my apartment. But neither of the girls looked impressed by my suggestions.

"Or we can just wander and find a café, or whatever," I backtracked.

"Irene has to meet someone at eight thirty in front of the church down that way." Skye pointed out the southern end of the piazza.

I wanted to time warp to eight thirty.

"So, maybe let's just walk in that direction," Skye proposed.

We began walking, Irene next to Skye next to me. I tried to read the dynamics of the situation I had found myself in. Skye had brought a friend, but that friend had to leave in less than an hour. I needed more information.

Skye handed me her children's notebook, which had just been given to her as a gift by a woman, apparently schizophrenic, in her theater class. Irene did an impression of the woman, head rearing like a dinosaur, hands streaming wildly through her hair. They were both acting extremely goofy, so assured of themselves. I had just shaken Irene's hand ninety seconds ago and already she was showing me her best Tyrannosaurus Rex.

"She tried to give me a bottle of really expensive perfume last week," Skye explained of the notebook. "And I told her I could not accept it, so today she gave me this notebook and said to me, 'I hope you will not refuse this gift. It was only one Euro, thirty cents.'"

We all laughed.

"What did you do to make this lady like you so much?" I asked.

"I don't know. I have never done a scene with her or anything."

Skye halted. She placed one hand on my forearm for balance and fingered the inside heel of her shoe.

"I have only worn these shoes maybe two times and they are hurting my feet, so we have to go slow."

Her foot dropped back to the ground, and we continued out of the piazza.

"How about we go to there?" Irene pointed to a corner building on the opposite side of the street. It was a café/pub named Bulldog.

The interior was dim and exclusively mahogany, the atmosphere warm and inviting. On each table sat a thin red candle centered in a plain drinking glass.

Irene and Skye slid into a booth at one of the tables toward the rear of the room. I dropped my bag to the floor and seated myself at the chair across from Skye. She piled our coats in the space next to her and we all directed our attention to the menus.

I already knew what I wanted, a latte macchiato, but I pretended to have difficulty selecting an item as my mind raced for topics of conversation which could include Irene. Everything I had prepared—tell me about your town in Iceland, tell me what it is like being dyslexic, tell me the top-ten things you don't like about your boyfriend—was too exclusive for a three-way conversation.

Theater class. There was something they had in common. I milked it for all I could.

How many students were in the class? Twelve. How many foreigners? Three. What script were they working on? Romeo—pronounced *Ro-MAY-o*—and Giulietta. When was the production? June.

"I'm hoping to still be here in June," I told them. "I'm trying to make my money stretch through spring until the summer rush begins and Metro can hire me full-time."

"You like to work at Metro?" Irene asked me.

"It's not perfect. It was better when Skye was still there, of course," I smiled at her and she chuckled. "But it is good. I like nightlife. I like going out at night. And one of the bartenders, Mariano, has been teaching me some bartending basics."

Both Skye and Irene had appeared startled when I had said that I liked nightlife.

"If you need money," Irene started, "and you like to work in the night, you could be a ... a ... a stripper."

I smiled large, but waited for someone else to initiate the laughter. No one did.

Irene continued, "You make much more money, and it is a thing of night."

"I'll keep that in mind if Metro fires me," I said.

She had to be joking. At least a little bit.

"You could be a stripper too!" Skye said to Irene. And then they both laughed. As if for her the idea was completely preposterous.

"I only do striptease for one-man audience! One man!"

So Irene had a boyfriend. The clue was not helping me crack the case. My investigation was put on pause while I gave the waitress my order. Skye's phone rang. She picked it up and happily greeted someone. I turned to Irene.

"What do you do here in Rome?"

"I am student at the university."

Skye was giving directions in Italian to whoever was on the other line.

"What subject do you study?" *And wasn't it almost time for her to leave?*

"I study the philosophy."

The waitress placed our drinks on the table, as Skye returned to the conversation.

"You don't have to work tonight, do you?" Skye asked me as she placed her phone next to her glass of red wine.

"Actually yeah, at ten."

I had mentioned the events of Saturday night to Skye on the phone—how Mariano had stuffed my bag full of liquor from Metro—and she insisted I recount the event in detail over the table.

The girls sipped their wine as I described the night. I finished my miniature café macchiato in about thirty seconds; a drink I had ordered by accident when I said *café* before macchiato, which meant *espresso*, instead of *latte*, which meant *milk*. Then Skye's phone beeped and rattled on the table. She read the screen while I continued my narration. I focused the story toward Irene who seemed politely interested even though she really had no reason to be, given she knew none of the names I was mentioning. Skye typed away on her keypad.

"So, anyway, it was one really crazy night," I concluded. Stellar recap.

Irene looked at her watch. "Well, I must go. I am happy to meet you."

We shook hands, Skye passed her coat across the table, and Irene left. Finally.

I gathered myself as Skye worked to remove her sweater. The ring of its neck caught on her nose. She tugged harder and the cotton gave, revealing her face in an instant, frazzled blonde bangs matching the dazed look on her face. We both laughed.

Her head turned down and left as she placed her sweater atop our two coats on the seat next to her, exposing for the first time a long earring hanging from her right ear. A small brown feather fanned at her shoulder, strung on an extended silver line which fastened at her earlobe. I had seen nothing like it. She turned back to me. Her other ear remained naked.

"Skye. That earring is spectacular."

"Thank you. It belonged to my grandmother," she said, accepting my compliment and delicately fingering the feather ending with her hand.

I brushed the burning candle between us away to the left of the table and leaned in toward her.

"Can I ask you a question about your dyslexia? Or is it something you don't enjoy talking about?"

I was so sensitive.

"No, sure. Go ahead."

"I know you told me that you never read the schedule in the kitchen at Metro, and you wanted me to help you read the menu that night at Seven Eleven,"—*that was a magical night, wasn't it*—"but you just sent a text message, right?"

"Yes, I mean, I'm not like *way* dyslexic. There is a degree of dyslexia you can have." She created fists with her hands and placed them on the wooden table. She bounced her right hand. "If you are really dyslexic you cannot read anything at all." She bounced her left hand. "If you are only a little dyslexic you just read slowly and maybe have some troubles spelling."

She slid her left, not-so-dyslexic fist two inches inward.

"I am about here," she said. It was far less dramatic than I had assumed. But she was dyslexic nonetheless.

"So I could type you text messages, and that would be fine?" For some reason it sounded weird on the way out.

"Yeah, that is no problem."

Good.

"So. Iceland. I want to kno—"

"Heidi!" Skye cut me off. I looked left to the girl at my shoulder.

"Heidi, this is my friend, Mike." Skye turned to me. "Heidi used to work at Metro too."

I introduced myself, and Heidi filled Irene's spot at the table. She told me she was from Sweden, but she seemed extremely comfortable speaking in Italian.

"You worked at Metro?" I asked her.

She turned to Skye. "Lui parla l'Italiano?"

"I speak a little bit, but English is better for me," I answered before Skye could say anything.

"I was worked—works?" Heidi started, "… working at Metro, but I breaked too many things so they told me a night to not to come back tomorrow."

The girls shared a laugh.

"You agree that you broke too many things?" I asked her.

"Yeah. I have five, six glasses on the tray, and," Heidi mimed dropping the invisible tray. "There was no one near me. Dario asked me, 'Che cazzo stavi pensando?'" *What the fuck were you thinking?* That gave us all a laugh.

The image was pretty hilarious—Heidi delicately placing five empty beer glasses onto her tray, one by one, turning slowly to the empty room, and then proceeding to drop every last one to the floor.

"So, how much of Italian do you speak?" Heidi asked me.

"I studied in Siena for four months, so I understand the grammar. It is the vocabulary that's the problem." I took a long breath and shifted positions in my seat. "Here is the thing. In California I went to a very, very good university. Almost everyone in the United States knows my university—"

"What is its name?" Skye asked me.

"UCLA."

Skye turned to Heidi.

"Have you heard that school name?" Skye asked through her teeth, as if to soften the blow if Heidi were to say she had not.

I needed Heidi to pull through for me here.

"Yes, yes I have known it."

Thatta girl.

"So, at that university I studied communication studies which included things like the study of language, and English composition, and media writing. So, in English, I have a very, very large vocabulary." This was taking an eternity to explain as I made sure to enunciate everything clearly and leave definitive spaces between words for Heidi. "In California, I was the friend that other friends came to when they needed help with a problem—a problem about work, or a relationship, or whatever it was. But in Italian I ... well, here is an example. Did you work with Roberto, Heidi?"

"Yes, he was very quiet."

"Compared to Mariano he is. But he takes great care of me. He gives me rides home on his motorcycle, and he insists I take his tip money most nights."

"He gives you his tips?" Skye asked, taken aback.

"Yes, sometimes he—"

"Why?"

"Because he appreciates the work I do. I don't know. Anyway—"

"Weird."

I paused to be sure we had moved on.

"He has seemed troubled recently. He and Mariano had some kind of fight and I asked him in Italian if he was stressed—I can only talk to him in Italian—and he said yes. But because of my small Italian vocabulary, I cannot even ask Roberto what is wrong. He is a great friend to me and gives me his tips and gives me rides and I am unable to even understand what is making him feel so sad."

The girls took long breaths and nodded noticeably which seemed to signal they had understood my point. But the punch had not landed as squarely as I would have liked.

"But you like work at Metro?" Heidi asked me.

"It is okay. I'm not really making any money, but I am trying to just get through to tourist season when they could hire me full-time and I could support myself off that job."

Wow. Mike and Metro, the two subjects I wanted to avoid tonight with Skye and I was revisiting both. Where was Iceland? Where was Skye's family and siblings? Her passions? Her aspirations? Mike and Metro were on their second spin this hour. How was that possible?

"How much do you pay of rent?" Skye asked.

"Five fifty a month."

Both girls wowed in astonishment.

"That is too much money!" Skye told me. "It would be so easy to find a cheaper place in Porta Portese."

I wanted to dare Skye to help me. To find me something cheaper. To find me something closer to where she lived.

"I actually would like to live more in the center—and with Italians, so I am forced to speak it more often."

"You aren't learning at Metro?" Heidi asked me.

"I learn simple things but Mariano and Isabella speak more English the—"

"Stella!" Skye cut me off. Again. I looked left to the new girl at the end of the table.

"Ciao, sono Stella," she waved to me.

Stella had dark-rimmed glasses and a backpack slung over one shoulder. She was obviously Italian.

"Hi, I'm Mike." I didn't even try. I wondered if she could tell I was agitated, my mental gears stripping from the repeated accelerations and sudden stops. I prayed these two strangers sitting in on my romantic evening escape with Skye accounted for both the phone call and text message and that no one else was set to arrive.

Stella turned to Skye as she filled the final remaining seat at our table and pointed to me.

"Lui parla l'Italiano?"

My God.

"Un po' ma parliamo in Inglese." Skye answered. "Puoi parlare l'Inglese?"

Stella turned to me.

"I speak very little of English," she said.

"That's okay."

I focused back on Skye. It was probably rude, but I was realizing that any one-on-one time had expired. I was going to have to leave for work soon, and I had gotten nothing of any substance across to her.

"Anyway," I continued the earlier conversation, "I can speak simple Italian at work, but at home I live with all international people so my conversations are all in English."

How had I landed smack-dab in the center of a self-pity party?

"Mike, where do you come from?" Stella asked me.

I turned to her. "I am from California."

I turned back to Skye.

Wrong night, Stella.

"So, if I lived with Italians I would be able to use the words I look up in my dictionary and they would stick. Now they don't stick. I look them up and know them for an hour but they don't stick."

The conversation was pathetic. In my peripheral vision I could see Stella intently trying to follow my speech. Then Heidi said something to her in Italian and they began talking to each other. I let their side of the table go. Skye continued to focus on me, possibly out of interest, more likely out of empathy.

"You would be surprised how much you know," she told me. "You just need an American to come out and you translate between an Italian at a bar and the friend and you'd see how much you know."

"I can express all the basic stuff; it's just so difficult when it comes to real conversation. I run all my errands around Rome only in Italian. I am learning more each day. I could have never done this after Siena. But I should be better by now. I should be much better."

This must have been the exact opposite of a turn-on.

"I know. I was just like you—we all were." Skye gestured to the table but could only mean Heidi and herself. "My first three months in Sardegna I never spoke a word. But then one day I just made myself start doing it, and now it is easy."

"I know! I know." I slapped my forehead. "It's just so frustrating."

"And I really wouldn't become stressed about the money problem. I mean the worst that can happen to you is you can't pay rent and you are kicked out of your apartment."

Wait—wait just one second.

That *was* the worst that could happen. And it was an absolutely horrific scenario. I would have nowhere to even sleep at night.

"You would just have to stay on someone's floor or couch until you got another work. In the summer it will be easy to find more work," Skye continued.

I had never even considered that possibility. Why?

"You know people here," she told me. "You know me; you could sleep on my floor until you got another work."

I leaned back off the table. "I guess you are right," I acknowledged.

I could make out bits of the Italian conversation between Heidi and Stella next to me. They were talking about food and seemed to have given up on the café's menu in front of them. Heidi leaned toard Skye and asked if she was hungry, but Skye had already begun reemphasizing her previous point to me.

"And you need to start speaking Italian wherever and whenever you can."

Skye turned to Heidi and answered her question in Italian, explaining that she could eat but was indifferent. Then she turned back to me and was abruptly hit by a bolt of awareness. Her eyes burst as the revelation flooded her brain.

"Here! Starting right now we—"

Frazzled hands fanned at her face. She restarted. "Da adesso parliamo solo in Italiano. Faccio io l'inizio."

Stella turned to me and spoke in English.

"Mike, do you have hung—... err ... are you hungry?"

"I'm not that hungry, but we can go with you if—" I turned back to Skye. "Are you really not hungry?"

Skye's eyes moved up and left, off into space, her chin followed. The corners of her lips curled down, her eyebrows raised, her eyelids fluttered. One hand rose to her ear and bent it ever so slightly in my direction. *I can't hear you!*

"Are you ... ahh. Hai fame?" I asked quietly, wearing a sheepish smile.

She held her pose and leaned her body toward me. Her eyes squinted toward the ceiling. *What was that?*

"Hai fame!" I screamed.

Content with my effort, her body unraveled, returning to normal as she slouched back in her seat. She was amazing.

"No, non tanto. Andiamo con loro, pero. Va bene?" *Not really, but let's go with them anyway. All right?*

"Sì. Certo. Va bene," I answered.

"C'è una pizzeria trenta metri da qua," Skye explained the location of the nearest pizzeria. "Hanno pizza al taglio." Stella and Heidi smiled eagerly. Skye looked back at me.

"Ti piace pizza al taglio?" *Do you like pizza by the slice?*

"Sì," I started. And then ran with it. "C'è una pizzeria ... umm ... vicino alla casa mia si chiama Pizza Luigi. Umm ... È pizza al taglio e mangio lì due, tre volte alla settimana. È buonissima." The phrase had gone pretty damn well. *There is a place near my house called Pizza Luigi; it's pizza by the slice and I eat there two or three times a week.*

I could feel Stella's frozen stare locked on my profile. I turned to her. She looked utterly perplexed.

"Ma lui parla l'Italiano!" she called to Skye across the table. Damn right I spoke the Italian!

Skye began handing back coats from the pile next to her on the booth. She replied to Stella while passing her jacket. "Ma certo. A Metro tutti parlavano in Italiano e lui capiva quasi tutto. Ma appena che lui ha scoperto che io parlo l'Inglese, insisteva che lo parlavo con lui." Of course I had insisted on speaking English with Skye at Metro! I had to be absolutely certain of our exchanges! She was too important to jeopardize with verb confusion and incomplete vocabulary!

Stella turned back to me.

"Ma perchè non hai parlato in Italiano quando sono arrivata io?" *Why didn't you speak in Italian when I arrived?*

"Perché è troppo frustrante!" I insisted.

"È troppo frustrante!" She repeated in a ghastly tone, *it's too frustrating*, throwing her head to the ceiling. She turned to Heidi. "Lui ha detto, è troppo *frustrante*! Una parola letteraria! Lui parla l'Italiano! Per tutto questo tempo pensavo che non parlava nemmeno una parola!" I was infused with confidence and having a ball. Of course I knew the word for *frustrating*. Explaining why I could not speak Italian in Italian was becoming my most practiced speech and I had looked up all related words in the dictionary.

Everyone around the table rose in preparation for leaving. I grabbed my bag from the floor. Everyone was smiling and laughing and shaking their heads in amusement. Skye handed me my coat. I looked her in the eye.

Take me to your Rome, Skye.

The four of us broke out the front door to Corso Vittorio Emanuele II. The sound of traffic—the buses, the scooters, the taxis—was a sharp contrast to the quiet café interior. I looked at my phone. It was 9:51 PM. It would only take only a few minutes to walk to the Campo from where we were, but the girls were heading in the opposite direction.

"Skye!" I called out.

All three stopped and turned.

"Oh. Umm, I have to get to work, actually. It was very nice meeting you both."

I stepped toward Heidi and Stella and shook their hands.

I turned to Skye. She extended a hand to shake but I pulled her in with one arm and we kissed cheeks. As she fell away I ran my hand down the length of her left arm and took her hand in mine. I looked her in the eye once more.

"Skye, listen. I'm not going to see you around your apartment. I'm not going to see you at work. I'm not going to see you in theater class. Skye, don't disappear."

She smiled an intricate and multistage Skye smile, one which involved her entire body. She laughed and nodded her head in assurance. I let her hand fall to her side and took two long, slow steps backwards away from her. Stella and Heidi turned to resume their walk; Skye's eyes remained fixed on mine.

Please, don't disappear.

VENTUNO

A portion of my courses at UCLA had focused on the mass media: television, magazines, film. One film class in particular had been exceptionally extensive—four hours a day, two days a week, the class itself split in half: two hours of lecture in our fully functional movie theater followed by a two-hour film screening. We covered the birth of Hollywood, the founding of the major studios, even some of the clubs the early stars frequented. But the most prominent moment that semester had been when our professor told us that almost every traditional Hollywood film followed the same basic storyline; it was simply the setting and characters which changed.

I did not know a lot about movies, but I did know a lot about music. And I knew that if you looked at the major mainstream hits over the past few decades, you would find almost every one spoke of the same subject—a connection with another person. Whether that connection was being born, broken, or mended, it was this theme that ran through nearly all great and widely admired music.

From there, I thought about the more typical Hollywood movies I had seen in my lifetime. Yes, they had been predictable; they had been overly dramatic, but despite these facts, I and most everyone else who saw them enjoyed them. And those hit films, like the hit music, had been about connections between people—usually a romantic connection between a man and a woman, but not always.

So, why was it that we continued to watch and listen to these same movies and same songs? Why was it that a new obstacle which tested a clichéd bond between two people, or an altered chord arrangement which backed a banal emotional expression, made that old fundamental concept feel refreshingly novel and so incredibly satisfying?

I had thought about this for weeks and it was not until my psychology midterm the next month that my hypothesis was conceived. Humans are social creatures. To not seek out human interaction is to be antisocial, or antihuman to a certain extent. This is why people who are overly solitary are labeled by society as quirky or weird or abnormal—because it is not normal to *not* seek out human-to-human connection. And it is this trait of being human—this trait so deeply engrained within our circuitry—that is triggered every time a movie or song makes us feel. It does not matter if our rational brains can see straight through the contrived plotline or acknowledge the improbability of the impossibly heroic situation—the pleasure emanates from a part of the body deeper than the cognitive.

From this I had built my understanding of why I had such trouble believing in fate, yet still felt so often that a larger system must be at work. In movies, in books, and on television, recurring characters are never brought into a scene without reason. Never. They always have an impact on the storyline. They always end up providing a crucial piece of information or advice, or take part in a critical event which affects the main character.

Each of us lives in our own movie, where we play the leading role, and when a new character begins recurring in our script, those deeper inner workings become engaged. What is this character here for? How will he or she affect the plotline?

It would have made sense to have this outlook when it was first wired into our internal systems thousands of centuries ago—thousands of centuries before you could commute an hour by car or train to work, thousands of centuries before airplanes and buses could move you halfway around the world overnight, thousands of centuries before one human could live among three million others in a single, sprawling metropolis. Before all of this, every recurring character in your film most likely did affect your plotline. They did prove pivotal at one point or another in your small, stationary village, or tribe, or community.

I stood against the wall at Metro, waiting for the speed washer at my side to finish its cycle, watching Mariano pour a cosmopolitan. Mariano had become a main character in my script.

I looked right, to Roberto, who was placing three slices of strawberry onto the edge of a finished frozen daiquiri. I then looked down to Isabella waiting patiently at the counter with her tray, ready to deliver the drink to the appropriate table. Both Roberto and Isabella had become main characters as well. And they were all affecting my plotline.

Who else was a main character in my film? My roommates: Nina, Ayden, Aleksia. They were all main characters, though they seemed to be popping up in fewer and fewer scenes. But the gauge for which I labeled cast members had less to do with the frequency of their appearances and more to do with the influence of their respective scene.

Skye was not Private Harris, who had just entered the script one page before our descent to the surface of the Martian planet—where there was sure to be a laser firefight in which she would be killed only four short minutes after her introduction. In the film of my life, I was the star, and Skye was a definitive main character in my script. And because of this I felt—I *knew* something significant had to happen with her. That was just how every movie goes.

"So, Michael. When am I going to see you outside of this bar?"

That was Morgan. She was six beers deep and talking to me across the counter as I polished stemware at the backbar.

Morgan was a cute girl, twenty-one years old, hazel eyes, and had become increasingly dedicated to flirting with me come the end of each passing night at Metro. But she was American, from Chicago, and a student at the American University of Rome. Those were the two worlds I had left behind in California. Morgan was a minor character in my script, a humorous subplot.

"I'm not sure what to tell you, Morgan."

I crouched to the speed washer and pulled a warm basket of glasses from inside.

"How about some feedback here, Michael."

"Feedback on what? You?"

"I think I've made it abundantly clear that I find you attractive; I would like some feedback from you."

"I think you are a very cute girl."

Morgan's face winced as my words hit her ears. Her upper body twisted to the table of girlfriends at her back.

"He thinks I'm *cute*. Oh God!"

I fought to recover.

"Yeah, I do. So what?"

But I knew what. I had just landed a direct *I'm-not-interested* left hook to Morgan's temple. But she was not the type to simply give up. She turned back to me.

"Do you have a girlfriend, Michael?"

I broke eye contact; squinting instead past her to the illuminated wall on the opposite side of the room. My body rocked back and forth while I sucked air in through my teeth. I did this for about five seconds before Morgan finally said something.

"Ahh, I see."

I understood what she was seeing. She was seeing, *There is a girl that I am hooking up with regularly but our status as exclusive has yet to be mutually determined.* And I was fine with that. It was a hell of a lot better than, *There is a dyslexic Icelandic girl who used to work here that I am holding out for despite the fact that she has a boyfriend and I rarely see her.*

"Listen, Morgan. I'm going to be straight up with you. You are cute. But you are at a bit of a disadvantage here."

"I'm at a disadvantage?"

"Yes. I moved to Rome to experience something … non-American."

She stared silently.

"Do you know what I'm saying?" I asked.

"So, is your girlfriend Italian?"

I groaned and looked toward the ceiling.

The house lights ignited. It was two o'clock and time to close down and clean up.

I left Morgan with her beer, stepping back to the sinks and starting to extract the pieces of fruit from the empty cocktail glasses before placing them into the small, white, circular baskets to be washed.

"Michael," a new voice in front of me started, "You come with us to dance drum and bass tonight?"

That was Vittoria. She was dropping off a tray full of cocktail glasses stuffed with used blue napkins and black straws. She was Skye's replacement and for this I had tried to resent her, but I simply was not able to. For one, I was too clearheaded a person to place any sort of blame for what had happened to Skye on Vittoria. And secondly, she, like Isabella, went above and beyond to make sure I always felt included and welcome. Even in those first nights that we had worked together, she would always find time during the night to speak with me in poor English about my weekend or my old apartment in California. She was such a sweetheart.

"Sure. I would love to go. I've never been to a drum and bass club."

Drum and bass: Electronic music on speed. This would prove interesting.

"Great! It will be a very fun!"

Vittoria sank back into the ocean of anonymous figures. I topped off the first bin of glasses and loaded them into the speed washer. I sprang back to the sinks and focused on keeping the multiplying glasses under control.

"Michael, I got you something."

I looked up. It was Morgan, holding a lime. One she apparently had just taken from the fruit tower to my left.

"Wow. Thank you so much." I took the lime from her hand and gently placed it back alongside the others on the top tier of the tower. "I am going to put it right here so I can look at it while I work."

My vision returned to the sinks.

"So, is your Italian girlfriend a better kisser than your American girlfriends have been?"

I stopped.

"Morgan. Listen. I never said I had an Italian girlfriend."

"All right, all right. You have amazing eyes. Can't you feel our connection, Michael?"

I would not say Morgan's persistence did not have a certain charm to it, but I worked to keep things platonic.

"I do indeed enjoy your company."

I caught a glance of Morgan's wrist as she pulled from her beer. *Destiny* was tattooed across the underskin.

"Interesting tattoo. Is that a belief or a life philosophy or what?"

I pulled a basket of glasses from the washing machine, replaced it with a basket of dirty ones, and then returned to the clean basket to unload things to their respective locations.

"Both—a belief of structure in the universe."

There we had it. She believed in structure in the universe and I did not. It was clear things would never work out.

"Do you have any other tattoos?"

Morgan's right boot hit the countertop. She unzipped the black leather, exposing a fiery ring of interlacing hearts circling her ankle.

"I like it," I told her.

"Thanks."

She zipped up again and dropped her foot back to the floor. By now most everyone except for the staff had cleared out. Morgan's friends were still at their table, watching us and laughing hysterically.

"You have some great teeth, Michael. I bet you didn't need braces as a kid."

"You need to get a book and start writing down all these lines of yours."

"I just call them as I see them. So, Michael, where is the after-party tonight?"

"I'm actually heading out to a club with some co-workers."

Dario came walking out from the back room and began kindly ushering everyone to the door.

"Okay, girls. Sorry, but it's time to go now." He was sweeping the air upwards with his hands and arms.

Morgan downed the remainder of her beer and joined her friends slowly making their way toward the glass front doors as they adjusted exposed bra straps, fixed chic winter coats, and slung designer purses over their shoulders.

"I'll see you later tonight, Michael. In my dreams."

I laughed and watched her blow me a kiss as she exited. I shook my head and returned to the sinks. I could feel Mariano staring at me. I turned to him.

"Yes?" I asked.

"Why did you not fuck her!"

"What?"

"Why did you not fuck her? She is a cute girl!"

"Mariano, it's not that simple. I fe—"

"Why did you not fuck her!"

He had already turned back to his station to resume covering the leftover fruit with plastic wrap. I simply shook my head and continued attending to the remaining glasses in front of me.

I had seen it coming—the Mariano incomprehension of not wanting to copulate with any two-legged human female that expressed a physical interest. What I also should have seen coming, but had not, was the advance made by Morgan.

She and her friends had been to Metro nearly every Thursday, Friday, and Saturday night that I could recall. I remembered one of the first nights I had seen her—the night Mariano, Isabella, and Carmen had almost quit. She had been sitting with that group on the couches in the back of the club, talking with Dario as we cleaned. She had been the one who asked Dario my name as I passed them on the way to the kitchen.

My goodness. Was I a main character in Morgan's script?

Could it be possible that the way Morgan viewed me was the way I viewed Skye? And that the way I viewed Morgan—with complete and absolute romantic neutrality—was the way Skye viewed me? Were Morgan and I two main characters in two separate scripts chasing fictional plotlines which ultimately led nowhere? The ink ran off the edge of the page into an abyss of meaninglessness.

I stood with Vittoria, Isabella, and Mariano, who exchanged Italian as we huddled in a circle in front of Metro's doors. A small blue Italian-Honda-Civic equivalent appeared from around the corner of the Campo. Davide hopped out from the driver's door.

"Ciao, bello!" Mariano exclaimed, extending his arms.

They embraced.

I looked toward Davide's car. His door had been left open and there was another figure in the passenger's seat—a woman.

My eyes shot to Isabella. She fumbled with a cigarette and gazed distantly across the dim and gradually emptying piazza, avoiding Davide and Mariano's enthusiastic exchange.

"Ciao, Mister Jones!" Davide smiled at me.

"Ciao, Davide, come stai?"

We kissed hello.

"Sto bene! Vieni?"

"Sì, sì."

Everyone began crowding around Davide's car. Mariano turned to me.

"Davide takes us to my car. We go from there."

The car was a two-door and I circled around to the passenger's side. The anonymous woman had moved to the back seat. Mariano and Isabella climbed in after her and pulled the seat backwards, locking it into place. I looked at Vittoria, standing next to me.

"It is okay if I sit on the …" she started. "… on your …"

"On my lap?"

"Yes!" she laughed.

"Sure. That's fine."

"It is a quick travel," she assured me.

I climbed into the front seat, stuffing my black bag between my legs. Vittoria climbed in on top of me. Everyone in the car was giggling.

The interior was cramped, and Vittoria's upper body contorted awkwardly along the ceiling of the interior as Davide pulled out of the Campo and toward the Tiber.

Italian was flying all over the place. I brushed Vittoria's hair from my face.

"Oh, excuse me!"

"It's no problem, really."

"I am too much weight? Do your legs hurt from me?"

"No, no! C'mon." She was such a sweetheart.

A voice came from the back seat. "Michael, why did you not fuck her!" Mariano chuckled at his own outburst, and then began explaining the situation to Davide in Italian.

We made it to Mariano's car which had been parked at the mouth of an alley off Viale Trastevere. We spilled from the automobile as if it were a clown car, body after body emerging from the single open door.

Vittoria, Isabella, Mariano and I stepped toward Mariano's micromachine. The woman with Davide climbed up into the front seat. Mariano circled with me to the passenger side of his own car and tossed Vittoria the keys. They were jabbering in Italian.

Considering Mariano was sure to light a joint within the next ten minutes, the key toss had been a smart move. Give the keys to the one with her head on straight, so loopy here would not drive us into an ancient ruin on the way to the dance club.

Vittoria unlocked our doors and we climbed inside.

"Mariano, what the hell happened to your windshield?"

A spider web of fractures ripped through the front glass. It looked as though he had smashed into something.

"Nothing much, man. Just a little accident."

"It doesn't look little," I insisted.

"It was nothing, man."

It was quiet for a moment. I waited for Vittoria to start the ignition, but instead she gazed down at Mariano's lap.

The Italian started up again. I was in the back seat next to Isabella and directly behind Mariano. My vision was blocked by the faux fur-lined hood of his enormous winter jacket. He was surely rolling a joint. Possibly multiple joints.

Their Italian was too fast and contained too many pronouns for me to understand. I stared out the window down the vacant Viale Trastevere in the direction of the Tiber as I let the strings of unintelligible words hit my eardrums. I still loved how that language sounded—rhythmic and musical.

Mariano's seat pressed back into my knees. I found a break in the conversation.

"Mariano, can you move your seat up?"

"What?"

"Muoviti avanti, per favore."

"Hold on bitch, I am just almost finished."

I stared back out the window. The Italian resumed. We must have sat there in that lifeless automobile for ten minutes.

What was taking so long? This had to be the greatest set of joints ever rolled. And I was not intending to smoke a single one of them. Though I was sure to inhale plenty from my position in the backseat of the vehicle.

Mariano turned and said something to Isabella. Isabella fished out her night's salary, stripped a ten-Euro bill from the bunch, rolled it into a cylinder, and handed it to Vittoria.

That was exactly the problem I had with this, right there, naked and in plain view, painted in a stark black and white. The money you earned at a job was handed to you from your employer, and then twenty minutes later you handed that exact same money to someone for weed. For a drug. For a few hours of detachment from reality. Was I the only one who enjoyed his reality? Who found ways to use what he earned to try and enhance rather than distance himself from actuality?

There was another break in the conversation. This time Mariano spoke. "Why did you not fuck her!"

"Mariano, drop it. And move your seat up already!"

Vittoria turned to me from the driver's seat. She was holding the rolled ten Euro between her fingers like a cigarette.

"No, Mike. I understand what you say. Do not to listen to him."

Thank you. At last, someone who understood. And how nice it was for her to side with the American she barely knew against her own Roman friend—even if the subject was petty and he was a bastard.

I liked Vittoria. I was glad she was becoming a regular cast member.

Mariano proclaimed completion and then inched his seat forward, finally releasing the pressure on my knees. He continued to shuffle objects in his lap, placing unseen items onto the dash. Vittoria watched him and smiled. The ten Euro was still between her fingers. She brought it to her nose like a tube of sinus decongestant.

She was so sweet. She was the kind of girl you could clearly envision in thirty years. You could see how her facial characteristics would develop—how her small but distinctly arched nose would become her most prominent profile feature. You could imagine how she would be considerate but firm with her children, how she would teach them to be strong and confident at an early age.

Mariano carefully raised a postcard from his lap to Vittoria's chin and she expertly took one of three lines of cocaine, sniffing the short white trail through the rolled Euro and into her right nostril.

Huh.

So.

That was cocaine.

Vittoria passed the bill to Isabella who took the second line.
"Professionista!" Mariano applauded her performance.
Isabella then passed the bill to Mariano, who looked at me.
"Would you like some?"
I paused.
"No, no thank you."
He took the third line himself, then kicked open his door and swapped seats with Vittoria. I guess he was driving after all.

I thought about Mariano's question. *Did I want some?* The truth was that I did want some. Throw out any cliché you'd like—*you only live once, don't knock it till you try it,* whatever. When it came down to it I was simply curious. I had done my share of downers—alcohol, marijuana—and I hated their sedative nature. But cocaine was something new, something on the opposite end of the spectrum. And the fact that the media so often sensationalized the drug had not done much to curb the curiosity either.

I had never actively pursued obtaining it myself, of course. And I would never have ingested anything I had stumbled upon alone. What the hell did I know about cocaine or cocaine culture? I had never done Ecstasy for the same reason; too many idiot kids who thought they knew what they were buying were in actuality swallowing a whole mixture of laced chemicals in the form of those so-easily-obtainable pills. But I trusted Davide. That guy was a purebred cokehead. He knew what to get and where to get it.

I guess I just did not want to do it there, in that cold, cramped car, on the way to a location unknown. The trip could be a paranoid disaster. Where was the right place to get strung out? Was there such a place?

Mariano kicked the car into gear and barreled onto Lungotevere. I was unable to tell if he was simply excited about the night's plans or if the coke was already hitting him, but he was driving even more sporadically than normal.

He darted between the other scattered vehicles sharing the road as if they were construction cones fixed to the pavement.

We raced along the Tiber. A traffic light ahead in the distance turned yellow. Mariano opened the gas and downshifted. We had to be going seventy.

The light turned red. We were still thirty meters or so from the intersection which formed a T, requiring a turn either right into Trastevere or a left across the Ponte Sublicio. A van and three scooters slowly pulled from their waiting positions at either side of the dark intersection and began crossing trajectories ahead of us.

Mariano let off the gas, preparing for a left turn, with zero intention of stopping. Our car swallowed the repeating left arrows painted on the street below. We were ten meters from the red light.

The van and scooters were visible, but out of our direct path. The intersection appeared clear.

We shot through the red light, beginning a multi-lane arc, wheels fighting for grip under the centrifugal force caused by our velocity.

That was the first time any of us saw it.

A monstrous two-car tram was rumbling down the tracks lining the Ponte Sublico. It was coming from the left, the same direction we were turning. It was right on top of us.

I could see the helpless expression of the conductor through the webbed glass of Mariano's windshield. How had none of us seen it? The tram was massive. We must have simply not registered it; the trams were supposed to stop at midnight. I could read the LED display above the conductor's head.

Deposito. *Out of Service.*

Isabella and Vittoria screamed. My head cleared; my body relaxed. There was nothing I could do at this point.

Mariano reversed the wheel, aborting the turn, rapidly shifting the weight of the car from right to left and aiming us straight for the stunted marble wall lining the bridge. The ground shook and the car rattled as the tram rolled behind us, inches from our rear bumper. I could not believe it had not hit us.

My eyes shot forward. We had about five meters before we hit the side of the bridge. Mariano spun the wheel left again. The weight of the car shifted left to right.

The front right tire collided with the curb and climbed to the narrow sidewalk, then the rear right tire. The car straightened, my door inches from the stone wall.

Mariano accelerated off the sidewalk back to the cobblestone of the overpass.

Isabella smacked Mariano across the head. Vittoria, smiling, cursed at him. I took a deep breath and shook my head as I watched the lights reflect off the Tiber out my window. Mariano laughed to himself.

We sped down Via Marmorata toward Piramide. It was the same way Mariano drove me home most nights. Maybe I was better off asking Mariano to drop me off at my apartment. Maybe I had better save the drum and bass thing for a different night.

We barreled past the pyramid, its white marble stained black at the edges, its apex thrusting toward the moon. The sight of it had grown comforting over the months. It meant I was almost home, only a few blocks from my front door, a fact that elicited a flooding of relief during long walks back from Trastevere, or rainy-day returns from the center, or cocaine-fueled chauffeur rides down Via Ostiense.

We were two blocks from my turnoff.

I should say something.

One block.

I should tell them to just leave me at my apartment.

We careened past my street.

I reached for my seatbelt. If I was going to see this through, I had better take the few precautions at my disposal.

I pulled the strap over my chest and felt around the seat to my left for the buckle. Nothing. I wedged my hand between the back and bottom cushions. The seat obviously folded down and my buckle was dangling in the trunk space. Nothing. I felt and searched and looked again and again but could not find the buckle for the life of me. Then Mariano yelled while jerking the car into a U-turn.

"Cazzo! Sto andando da Mike!" He *was* going to my place. He realized he had missed the turn. Thank God.

I must have misunderstood something earlier. I thought I had agreed to go with them but Mariano *was* driving to my place. I must have nodded in agreement to something I had not understood but which had signified a changing of my plan. I had thought it was strange we were continuing down Via Ostiense, past Testaccio, toward nothing but apartment towers and sleeping storefronts.

Mariano doubled back. We were three blocks from my right turnoff.

This had been a lucky break.

Two blocks.

Chance was putting me out of possible danger tonight.

One block.

I had to start opening my mouth more often.

We rocketed past my turn and the pyramid appeared a second time. It gazed down triumphantly upon us as we circled the piazza below before shooting off on a new direction. It then faded out the rear view and the Coliseum approached in the foreground.

My mind raced over what Mariano had said. Literally he had said *I am going to Mike's place.* But I had read the context wrong. I had read the context how I had wanted it to be. He had said he was going to my place, but by mistake, on an erroneously programmed autopilot.

We curved around the rear of the Coliseum. I watched its illuminated features pass by Isabella's window, a stark yellow glow lining the curved marble of each archway against the black of the night sky behind.

I remembered the first time I saw the Coliseum. It was in summer, four and a half years ago, with Charlotte. I remembered approaching it from the forum, reaching its base and staring upwards. I remembered the first thing I had thought.

It's not *that* big.

And it was not big by modern standards. But as we had slowly circled the amphitheater that hot afternoon in June, I fixed my eyes on the slabs of marble composing the uppermost portions of the mostly intact northern wall. I picked one slab and focused on it, on its weight, on its dimensions. It was enormous. And there it was, one hundred and sixty feet up, situated into position by men with ropes and levers and pulleys before the invention of forklifts and mechanical cranes. The risk of loss of life in completing such a project must have been monumental.

That day had been the first time I had ever really envisioned Rome as it was when it had ruled the world. I placed my mind back those one thousand nine hundred and twenty years. I imagined myself, still age seventeen, there at the foot of the arena, but in the Rome of the past. I would have been an adult in that world. I might have grown up on a villa outside the capital. The tallest building I would have ever seen would have been our single-story farmhouse. I would have moved to the urban center for work, for excitement, to see the big city.

I would have stumbled my way through the flurry of the forum, the overrun marketplace engulfing, the frenzied main boulevard overwhelming—all the marble, all the human creation, all while the rest of the world lived in frail huts and aimed merely to survive. And then I would have caught sight of the Coliseum.

It would have been the largest, most magnificent and confounding structure I had ever set eyes on. And to think it had been built solely for the purpose of spectacle. I would have never thought such things could exist in the world. I would have never imagined humans could dedicate such time and resources to a single elaborate creation. It would have taken my breath away. Rome would have taken my breath away.

It had been that day, standing there with Charlotte, lost between the world of the past and the world of the present that only the Coliseum could blend together so vividly, that Rome did take my breath away.

I had declared to Charlotte that at one point in my life I would live in the Eternal City. And it was two and a half years later that I had stood at that same spot with Leighton, starry-eyed, happily lost among the stripped pillars and scattered chunks of marble, and told her my plans and told her I was not kidding and told her it was going to happen one day.

The structures of Rome humbled me. The number of people who had lived and died on that very ground throughout the city's illustrious past humbled me. And the Coliseum represented both.

The Coliseum had seen Rome at its peak and had watched Rome fall. It had watched entire generations be born and entire generations die. It had seen innocent men murdered in front of crowds of cheering onlookers. It had seen Christianity spread throughout the Western World. It had seen the invention of the automobile and the airplane. It had watched the nations of the world fight one another—twice. And now it watched me, watching it from the window of Mariano's cramped white Fiat, our lunatic driver weaving through the streets while strung out on cocaine.

Who was I to the Coliseum? No one. And if I was no one to the Coliseum, then who was I to history? To the world? To anything? If Mariano lost control of the car right then and we careened into the brown stone wall on the opposite side of the street, killing all of us instantly, how was I any different than the beggar who had died of starvation at the foot of the arena two thousand years ago? I was not any different. The Coliseum would not care. History and the world would not bat an eyelash.

I rummaged again for my buckle. Still nothing. Mariano cut into a side alley and I quickly lost orientation. He then threw the car behind a trash dumpster, cut the engine, and everyone climbed out from the vehicle.

I shut my door and shot Mariano a confused look. The three of them began walking toward a set of double doors across the small alleyway. I trailed them and Mariano dropped back and placed his hand on my shoulder as we walked.

"This is not my favorite pub of Rome, but we need to stay here for few minutes."

The bar appeared closed, the street devoid of sound and motion. In the distance, through the narrow gap at the end of the tight alleyway, I could see one side of the Coliseum arching into view before bending back out of sight.

Vittoria knocked on the wooden double doors. A young Japanese man, late twenties, long black hair tucked behind his ears, Benjamin Franklin spectacles barely clinging to his nose, opened them. He was skinny and adorned with various jewelry in his ears, on this wrists, and around his neck. He was someone you would expect to see in a Japanese rock music video.

"Thiao Vithoria!" He had a terrible lisp.

"Ciao, amico!"

They kissed hello. I followed in line behind Isabella and Mariano, each of us stepping up and into the small and eccentric lounge. Numerous golden Buddhas watched us from shelves fixed high into the burgundy walls. Twenty or so candles provided all available light, fighting a losing battle against the overpowering blackness. The décor was cluttered—colorful beads strewn randomly about.

We moved to the back of the main room and sat on a triplet of sofas framing the square table at our knees. A circular tin of coals at the center of the table bled orange warmth onto our faces.

"Michael, do you have a telephone card?" Mariano asked.

"I have a credit card."

"That is not too thin enough."

He pulled a small bundle of white paper from his jacket pocket. It looked like one of those firecrackers that popped when you threw it at the ground. He twirled the paper at its top, untwisting it, and shook the cocaine onto the table.

The clumped white powder absorbed yellow and auburn as pulses of flickering candlelight came streaming in from every angle.

It felt strange to be staring at the small pile of cocaine. It felt strange that I knew these people. Isabella handed Mariano a phone card and he began chopping the clusters into a fine grain. It was just as I had seen in the movies. But this was real.

It felt like the first time you witness a car crash on the freeway—when you realize lanes are really just streaks of white and yellow paint. They are not physical boundaries. They do not inhibit anyone from driving anywhere. And when you see those cars collide, it just looks so peculiar—as if your windshield is a movie screen. Cars are not supposed to collide like that. The lanes are supposed to keep them apart.

I was not supposed to be two feet from a pile of cocaine. I was not supposed to know this person so expertly cutting and dividing the pile into three even white lines. But there it was, there he was, and there I was. It was simply a physical substance some people bought, he was simply a person I had grown to know through work, and I had simply shared a ride to this abandoned bar where everyone was sitting around a table doing coke. Literally it made sense, but it just looked so peculiar—as if we were all playing dress-up, acting out a movie in which young adults in Rome do cocaine.

"Would you like some, Michael?" Mariano asked me.

'No. No, thank you."

This definitely was not the place.

Davide and the woman from his car appeared at the front door. They greeted Japanese Rocker and made their way through the faint candlelight to our table.

I turned to watch Japanese Rocker through the darkness. He remained at the front of the bar, apparently talking to someone. I looked harder. I could make out two shadowy figures a few feet across from him. I had thought we were the only ones inside.

Davide and the woman squeezed onto the comfortable, but now crowded, couches. Davide pulled his own firecracker from his jacket pocket and carefully emptied more cocaine onto the opposite corner of the table. Directly across from me, the anonymous woman removed her jacket and smiled.

"Ciao."

"Ciao," I repeated.

She looked familiar. I felt as if we had met somewhere before, briefly.

I turned left toward Isabella. She had a rolled Euro bill in her nose and was leaning down to the first of the three lines Mariano had prepared. She was a matter of inches from the table when she exhaled too strongly, scattering the fine white grain across the glossy brown wood. Her body shot upright, her hand covered her mouth, her eyes pouted, and she looked at Mariano.

Mariano shook his head, laughed, and used the phone card to gather the dispersed substance in front of her.

Silly Isabella had blown the cocaine everywhere.

I glanced forward to the anonymous woman again. Now another lady was sitting on the couch next to her. The new woman was dark skinned, older, slightly overweight, and was rocking back and forth.

Anonymous Woman turned to her; they were practically shoulder to shoulder.

"Ciao, come va?" she asked.

The older woman's eyes bulged, the pace of her rocking quickened, she opened her mouth and pointed her finger inside, as she expelled a deep groan. It was upsetting. It was the kind of thing you pictured homeless people on the street doing. And not the homeless beggars or musicians who held out cups for donations. This was the type of distressing homeless person who you crossed the street to avoid, someone who appeared hopeless of recovery to any sort of normal existence, someone so disconnected from reality that she was capable of doing anything at anytime without any rationale.

Anonymous Woman replied, "Lo so, lo so." *What* did she know? She knew what this crazy woman was experiencing? Could a seemingly normal person become this for a night with the wrong combination of drugs? With too much cocaine? Had Anonymous Woman been there? Been that far gone? She looked too young and healthy and normal to know anything about that. She was a friend of Davide's and Mariano's. What did she know?

I looked left. Isabella and Davide took synchronized lines, their nasal inhalations continuing as they pulled their heads from the table and placed a thumb on the appropriate nostril to assure nothing was wasted.

Japanese Rocker appeared on my right and placed a glass of red wine on the table between Mariano and myself. We thanked him. Isabella handed Mariano the Euro bill. He looked at me.

"You sure you do not to want some?"

"No, I'm fine, really. I'll have some wine, though, if that is all right."

"Sure, yes, drink man!"

I took the glass in my hand and slouched back into the sofa seat. I needed a break from the world of the table, even if that break was simply leaning back, tilting my head, and closing my eyes. I pulled at the wine and wandered in my blackness.

Numerical figures shot into my mind—numbers of shifts at Metro, salaries, wages per hour. I had begun experiencing this nightly as I lay down to sleep: various budget projections based on fictional schedules over the next four months, searching for a minimum income that would allow me to extend my stay through June, and then searching for a necessary monthly, weekly, and daily income to reach that minimum.

    A vision of Roberto replaced the equations. His face read great sadness. We were in an alley standing next to his motorcycle. He was saying something to me but I could not understand him. I could never understand him.

    My thoughts hastened to the present. In my mind I watched Isabella, Mariano, and Vittoria take lines. I saw Anonymous Woman talking to the stranger at our table. I wondered if she was still there but dared not open my eyes.

    It was there in that vacant bar, at that cocaine-dusted table, that I understood something. If part of surviving in Italy was acceptance, then I had better get to accepting that I was never going to be able to express myself in Italian to the degree I wanted. I was never going to communicate sympathetically and elaborately with Roberto. I was not always going to understand where Mariano was driving us. I was never going to receive full financial security, even for a minimum base income, from Metro.

    I breathed in deeply, eyes still closed, and pulled again off the wine. I sealed my eyes tighter. I drown out the conversation at the table.

Skye.

...

Skye.

Mike, ciao! There was the craziest old man at the market to—

Skye, stop.

What is it, Mike?

Skye. We need to stop this.

Stop what?

Stop meeting here.

But I thought we were—

You aren't real.

Mike, we worked together at Metro. We—

The real Skye is out there, out in the physical, and you are hurting her. We are hurting the real Skye by meeting here.

But, what about how you read me restaurant menus? About what an inspiration we are to other couples and to parents and—

Skye. None of that has happened. None of it. The real Skye knows nothing of these things.

But—

You need to go.

But Mike I—
Go.
...
Skye.
...
Skye!
...
Good.

I opened my eyes. Everyone was standing, zipping overcoats, and collecting purses. I finished the last of the wine and stood with them, fixing my jacket and stepping toward the entrance behind Vittoria. We each shook Japanese Rocker's hand, I thanked him for the wine, and we emerged to the dimly lit alleyway.

We climbed into Mariano's car. Davide and the woman with him climbed into his vehicle, which was parked behind us.

We accelerated down the alleyway in tandem and exploded onto the main Via Labicana. The Coliseum engulfed the horizon.

We stopped abruptly at a flashing yellow traffic signal at the foot of the Piazza del Colosseo. It was a large four-way intersection, and the few scattered cars were taking turns crossing in a counterclockwise sequence.

Surprisingly, Mariano waited his turn, then shifted the car into gear and moved into the intersection. Davide followed, riding our bumper, his headlights illuminating our car's interior. The Coliseum looked monstrous from my vantage point at road level in Mariano's miniature vehicle.

Suddenly Mariano hit the brakes and spun the wheel. The headlights from Davide's car whitewashed our seats as our bumpers grazed. Both cars began circling the sparse intersection. Isabella and Vittoria began laughing wildly.

Two other vehicles which had begun across the intersection slammed on their brakes, their headlights bowing to us as we made not one, but two circles within the wide junction before spiraling off onto one of the avenues.

Isabella, still laughing, slapped Mariano across the back of the head. Vittoria, smiling, cursed at him. I took a deep breath and shook my head as I watched the lights of the Coliseum flicker between the trees lining the roadway. Then I laughed too.

"I'm sorry, Michael, but we do dancing another night," Mariano said to me.

I looked at my phone: 4:55 AM.

"That's fine," I replied.

We sped past the pyramid, down Via Ostiense, and past my turnoff. And that was fine too. What would I have done in my apartment anyway? Sleep?

We pulled up to Mariano's complex and entered the building with Davide and his friend. The six of us crammed into the tiny elevator and rode it to Mariano's floor, where we entered his apartment.

This time he turned on all the lights. The room was much brighter than I had remembered and everyone was overflowing with whispering conversation.

I sat down on Mariano's bed between Isabella and Vittoria and rubbed their backs.

"How are you feeling, girls?"

"Very, very well!" Vittoria responded.

Isabella turned to me. "Mikey, I just—I just think you're the best!"

Mariano stepped past me to the stereo. He removed a CD from its case and placed it into the deck. The label had looked familiar. He pressed play.

"Ladies and gentleman," he stated, "this is the music of Mike!"

I had brought a handful of CDs with me in my guitar case. The tracks were a collection of rough ideas I had recorded over the previous years. After I had played the song on Mariano's acoustic guitar the first night I met Davide, Mariano had asked me if I had anything else he could hear, so I had brought one of the demos in to work for him.

"You really have some talents." Mariano looked across the room to me.

He then made his way back to the circular wicker table where Davide was dividing more lines of cocaine on a kitchen plate.

Davide's friend appeared from the bathroom and sat herself down Indian style on the floor in front of us. Her head bobbed to the music. Isabella, to my immediate left, began speaking with her in Italian. Vittoria, to my immediate right, turned to face me.

"Mike, this music is very good. Really, I ... uhh ... complimenti! I don't know how to say in English, but complimenti!"

"I understand. Thank you."

Mariano appeared in front of me. He handed me the plate. It was porcelain, hand painted; a thick yellow ring dotted with orange flowers lined the circumference. Five lines of cocaine radiated from its center.

"It is a present from Davide," Mariano said, handing me a rolled twenty-Euro bill.

I looked toward Davide, still sitting across the room at the table. He leaned back in his chair, smiled and waved to me with one hand.

"I don't really know how to ..." I started.

"Here, I can help you!" Vittoria interjected.

She took the plate and held it at my neck. I used my now-free hand to plug my right nostril while placing the rolled twenty in my left. Davide's friend pumped her arms to the ceiling and chanted.

"Mike! Mike! Mike!"

How did she know my name? She knew everything.

I leaned toward the plate, making sure to exhale before I got too close. I paused at the tip of one of the lines. I glanced up, my eyes locked with Vittoria's.

"Go, Mike!" she smiled.

She was such a sweetheart.

I inhaled steadily through my nose, dragging the bill slowly across the plate's glossy finish, a single white line vanishing magically behind me. I pulled my head skyward, continued to inhale, and placed a thumb to my left nostril.

"Grande!" Davide applauded from his chair.

The girls clapped and bounced lightly on the bed. I handed Vittoria the twenty and fell back on the mattress.

Everyone was moving to the rhythm of the music as they conversed. Soon Isabella and Vittoria fell back onto the mattress with me. We were all giggling.

"Mikey, I just—I just think you're the best!"

"*You* girls are the best! I have no idea why you are so nice to me, but thank you."

The plate came around again and we sat up briefly to take another line. I flopped to the mattress again, my feet uncontrollably bouncing to the music—my music—emanating from Mariano's stereo. I ran my tongue around the inside of my mouth repeatedly.

It was true. You really could feel it in your teeth.

Welcome to **Wells Fargo** Online Banking …

Your statement as of **March 01, 2005** is

Cash Accounts

Account	Account Number	Available Balance
CHECKING	XXX-XXX0385	$ 797.51
SAVINGS	XXX-XXX6608	$ 100.02
		Total $897.53

VENTIDUE

One of my favorite words in the entire English language is *nightlife*. Maybe you think that is a bland choice. Maybe you would have expected something more dramatic, like *illustrious* or more tortured, like *insatiable*. Those are good words too, but *nightlife*, if you take a moment to really look it over, is a term loaded with implications of modernity and human achievement.

It was relatively recently that *life*, as far as human beings were concerned, ended at sundown. *Life* was restricted to the daylight hours. The time for living followed the sun. It told you to rise in the morning and retreat come dusk.

In many parts of the world life is still constrained in this way. But in the parts of the world that I had had the good fortune of living in—the cities of San Francisco, Los Angeles, and, most recently, Rome—the setting of the sun meant less the ending of the day, and more the birth of an entirely separate world.

In major metropolises across the globe, people have achieved control over what was once considered unmanageable on a scale larger than a campfire or row of torches—people have achieved control over light. Today we have windowless casinos where time seems to never move, and we have cities that never sleep. We have harnessed electrical energy and spread it through infinite webs of wiring to lift our four-star hotel elevators and light our expansive and exhaustive networks of roadside streetlamps. We can power masses of audio speakers, which reproduce digitally recorded music played on electric turntables in chic lounges, where people drink and dance and socialize, most oblivious to it all—to the progressive development that went into creating a whole other life for civilized man.

It is a life of neon lights and guest lists, velvet ropes, and colorful cocktails in exquisitely shaped glasses, men and women dressed in the height of fashion who have spent hours preparing themselves to exit from the life of the norm—of the daylight—and enter a second, new life, of the night. It is a life that is an extremely modern phenomenon and one which celebrates human invention and creation. It is the defeat of the darkness, victory over the black. The recapturing of time stolen—time previously rendered useless and reserved for creatures nocturnal. It is an entire world that exists beyond the constraints of the sun. A world that should not be. A second life apart from that which was conceived naturally. A *night life*.

I liked the word *nightlife*. I liked the concept. Time repossessed. Defiance of the natural order. But the night is far more than a mere extension of the day. The night is another world. And the energy of this other world—of this night life—is something in itself a bit darker, a bit shadier, a bit more suspicious and mysterious. Even if you do not frequent the see-and-be-seens, even if you do not happen to live in one of the world's major urban capitals, even if your normal bedtime is quarter past nine after a rented DVD you watched with your two cats, you too have felt the effects, the power, the influence of the night.

Why is it that so many first kisses happen after dark? Is it simple probability? Simply a statistical fact that you go out to Chinese dinner or to the latest Hugh Grant import flick—for her sake, of course—around dusk, and it just so happens to be dark by the time you are back at the front steps of her parents' house, or are on your third round of liquid courage at the local Irish pub, or are sitting parked in your nineteen-eighties Toyota Camry, the engine off, light jazz trickling from the three functional speakers, the two of you staring anxiously into each other's eyes instead of the beautiful view of the stars above or ocean below or city ahead in the distance? Is it simply that people have to work during the day and therefore only get to the tantalizing and passionate and tempting at a later hour? Or is it something more?

I remember the period of life when sleepovers at your friends' houses were a weekly event. It must have been around middle school—sixth to eighth grade, or so. Before that time, there was the stage in elementary school when you were too young to conceptualize such an idea and playtime was cut off well before nine o'clock. There was also the period of high school afterwards, when you outgrew sleepovers at your same-sex friend's houses—that concept now considered strange and emasculating—and you instead snuck around your neighborhood trying to have scandalous and secretive late-night encounters at a girlfriend's house, which were achieved by elaborate window escapes and bed stuffing—stunts which were, in retrospect, so obvious and contrived that you must thank your parents for playing along so well with your missions impossible.

But that period there in the middle, sixth to eighth grade or so, where you would call home after delivered pizza and ask if you could spend the night at Charlie Marshall's and Mom would ask to talk to Mr. Marshall and he would confirm it was a welcome idea and you would set up a pair of sleeping bags in the living room and switch off the overhead lights and just lie there with your best friend—those are some of the most revealing and intimate memories I have from childhood.

Opinions, judgments, beliefs, embarrassments—regarding everything from siblings to girls at school to puberty to sex to the very relationship with the person with whom you were conversing—they just came flowing freely from our consciousness to our tongues as we laid there in the faint illumination of the room's modest nightlight. Why was none of this ever discussed during the day? Why was it so easy to get these ideas to snowball lying there on the floor in the darkness? Why in the world would we get up the next morning and never discuss some of the issues—really relevant stuff—until the next sleepover or sometimes never discuss it ever again?

Now we are older, more self-conscious, and do more self-editing. But the night still pulls at our subconscious, our subliminal, our secrets dying to get out. Why do candlelit dinners bring people closer together—make them feel as if they are the only ones in existence at that particular place and time? There is something that happens to us when we refuse to exit consciousness and instead push onwards, alive, awake, led by the artificial and man-made long after the sky has extinguished, the horizon faded to black, and the world shrunken to that of the diameter of light thrown from the nearest lamppost, or wax candle, or living-room nightlight.

"My coup likes your coup."

I was sitting in the Bulldog Pub, the sight of my romantic evening train wreck with Skye. Carmen sat across the table from me, a hopeful expression lingering on her face.

"Actually you would want to say *my cup* is like *your cup*," I corrected.

"My coup is like your coup," Carmen repeated.

"It is kind of confusing. In English we use *like* to both mean things are similar and to say we are pleased by things or people. It's not the same as Italian or Spanish where the object does the pleasing."

Carmen stared at me blankly. I had put far too many words into my explanation. I decided to clarify through examples.

"My spoon *is like* your spoon. *I like* coffee. My cup *is like* your cup. *You like* apples."

She exuded an *ahh* of comprehension, smiled and nodded, and began skimming through her textbook again.

Carmen had been frequenting an English language course but had not been able to afford the reenrollment fee for the new semester, so she had bashfully asked me if I would meet with her once a week so she could keep in practice and maybe have me explain a few things. I had kindly agreed, and already we were nearing the end of our second such meeting.

We had met in the center at quarter to five, giving us an hour's time for lessons before Carmen had to start her shift at Metro. Our previous lesson had gone well. I had even printed off the lyrics from a couple famous Beatles songs and pulled from them to highlight some useful expressions. But this particular evening I felt distracted and detached from the table.

Carmen looked up from her book and slowly formulated a question.

"When do you get up at morning?"

"What?"

"At morning, when do you get up?"

"Oh, *in the* morning. When do I get up *in the* morning."

"Wha—?" Carmen looked down at her book again.

"*In the* morning. *In the* afternoon. *At* night," I clarified.

Carmen looked back up at me, frustrated.

"Ma come mai è diverso? *In the, in the, at?*"

"I don't know why *night* is different."

Carmen returned to her book. My vision drifted off over her shoulder and out the set of windows at the front of the pub. How was it already dark outside? I looked at my phone lying next to my empty cappuccino cup.

It was 5:47 PM. I had woken up just four hours ago, a mere hour and a half had passed since I had left my apartment for the first time that day, and the sky was already pitch black. And today was nothing out of the ordinary. It seemed three hours of sunlight was becoming normal for my daily routine now that my body clock was set on my weekend work hours and winter was squeezing the days dry of illumination before they even seemed to begin.

"Carmen, we have to get you to work."

"Cosa?"

"Lavoro. Devi andare a lavoro." I pointed to the time on my phone.

"Ahh, giusto."

We pooled a small group of Euro coins to pay for our cappuccinos, gathered our things, and exited Bulldog to the main Corso Vittorio Emanuele. Carmen's phone rang and she brought it to her ear. She began talking in Italian to whoever was on the other end of the line, as we crossed the street and entered a small alley which lead into Campo de' Fiori's northern end.

As Carmen continued her Italian conversation on the phone next to me, I returned to my own thoughts—thoughts which seemed to have faded from their optimistic state along with the cocaine high of Saturday night.

In my head I fought for a correct and undistorted perspective of myself. I fought to take a definitive stance in evaluating my recent actions. Yes, I was learning a second language. Yes, I was tutoring a Peruvian girl for her English classes. And yes, I was interacting with people from all over the world. But what could be said about what I had been doing in Rome if framed differently? I was living in a European county, working in a bar, and experimenting with drugs. The unoriginality of the skewed, but undeniably valid, statement pierced my soul; it shook my foundation. Rome had to be about more than killing time and drug experimentation under the all-too-common pretense of self-discovery. I was better than that. I was smarter than that.

I thought back to the brightest day I could remember. It was June. Los Angeles. Graduation. It felt like that day had occurred a lifetime ago—in another life, in another *world*.

A vision of King Arthur abruptly materialized in my head—not the story with all its moral undertones and selflessness, but rather the image of that preadolescent Arthur in the first moments after he tore Excalibur from its stone sheath.

The sword had been built for a grown man, someone who had endured a great amount of training and was fit enough to yield such a weapon. The blade's weight would have been massive, immense, colossal when matched up against the still immature child, his muscles undeveloped, his training nonexistent—yet whose small fists gripped the lethal instrument's thick metal handle. He would have wavered for a moment under its weight, searching for equilibrium.

I pictured that graduation hall at UCLA. It had been filled to the brim with little adolescent Arthurs. The story might have been different, but the image was the same.

We had begged for our freedom—our liberty from the academic system and its credit requirements and fixed scheduling. Every ten weeks our futures, blocked off in half-hour increments and conveniently color coordinated, had come spitting forth from the mouths of our ink-jet printers. "Enough, already!" we had said. "Tell us what further units you require we complete and let us go! We are ready! We are adults!"

We had heard the lecture a million times from a million different people. Wielding a weapon as powerful as our own life paths required discipline, it required strategy. Our parents had warned, our professors instructed, our counselors guided. But we had said we knew, we were prepared, so set us free already. We screamed as we tugged with all our might at that sword encased in that stone sheath. And on the day of our graduation, when the blade finally loosened from the rock and came ringing free, we had gripped its handle with all the confidence in the world, and acted as if we had suspected its overbearing mass, and hid our slight stumbles as we found initial equilibrium.

And then we had taken a first determined swing—a swing so confident that we had fooled even ourselves into thinking we were indeed as prepared as we had thought. Some struck at a career, others at graduate school. Still others struck at places, at cities, at countries. Leighton struck at New York, I struck at Rome. But our muscles were underdeveloped, our training incomplete. And soon we found ourselves midway into a swing we could not stop. The momentum was too great. Wielding our Excalibur had proved less controllable than we had so assuredly presumed.

It had become unclear whether we were the ones swinging that sword or if it was the sword which was swinging us. The immediate reaction was to bite our lips, to play it cool, to wait for things to slow to the controllable again. But our minds screamed to take immediate cautionary action. Could someone be hurt? Could we hurt ourselves?

Carmen and I entered the Campo as she finished her conversation and dropped her mobile into her purse.

"Mi aspetti mentre cambio?" she asked me. I had nowhere to be. Sure I could hang out a few minutes.

"Sì, certo. Ti aspetto al bar."

We pushed through the double glass doors of Metro, and I made my way to the bar while she continued to the back stairwell.

There was someone working behind the counter whom I did not recognize, someone who worked the day shifts and would be off in ten minutes when the night shift began. I politely waved and smiled and we exchanged *ciao*s.

I leaned onto the glass bank and stared at the back of my hands. They reflected green from the illuminated glass. My eyes panned upwards and across the backbar ahead—the five glowing shelves of whiskies and rums and gins and vodkas and cognacs and liquors. I then glanced to the sinks—to three upside-down martini glasses, one margarita glass, and a pair of shot glasses.

I lifted myself from the counter and turned to face the double glass doors I had just stepped through. Outside, the various streetlamps rooted in the floor of the Campo spread yellow radiance to the cobblestone below. The sliver of sky I could make out was jet black.

It occurred to me as I stood there waiting for Carmen to emerge and thank me for my brief English lesson, that my favorite word had become my commonplace. And I questioned whether it could have been healthy to live exclusively in a world that should not be—in an energy that was so abnormal.

I tuned back to the main room and spotted Carmen climbing the final stair to the main floor of the back room. But instead of continuing forward toward me, she doubled back and disappeared into the kitchen.

I did not feel like staying there any longer. Metro, the night—it all felt suddenly so contrived. I pushed off the bar and headed toward the flapping kitchen doors myself. I had to get out of there. I had to distance myself and start to think—to formulate a plan.

I pushed into the kitchen and stopped. Roberto was sitting on top of a white floor refrigerator in the far corner. He saw me and said nothing. Instead, he rubbed his forehead with one hand and tapped the ash off the tip of his lit cigarette with the other.

Carmen appeared at my side. "I am sad," she whispered.

"What's wrong?"

I looked toward Roberto again. His eyes met mine from the opposite end of the kitchen. He took a drag off his cigarette and then looked back toward the floor as he exhaled.

"Roberto is ... is going away."

How I hated that kitchen.

VENTITRE

I stepped to the textured metal grating at the entrance to the GS supermarket. The automatic glass doors split down their center and glided outwards as I moved between them and onto the white reflective flooring inside. The hum of refrigerators and fluorescent lighting added to the overall climate of complete neutralization.

I grabbed a red plastic hand basket from the stack next to the shopping carts and made my way down the first aisle. I stopped about halfway in; it was a fitting perspective for taking in the numerous shelves of refrigerated pastas and cheeses.

I quickly scanned the price tags to narrow my options. The GS brand tortellini appeared to be on sale, judging that below them sat a colorful red and yellow sales tag as opposed to the other white and blue ones. I stepped toward it and read the price description.

Promozione ~~E 1,84~~ ... E 1,15.

I manhandled four packages into my basket. Content with my decision, I continued toward the end of aisle number one, about to really dive into the evening's shopping.

But before I did, I double checked my jeans for my GS Spessa Amica discount card—a card I considered invaluable for the three-Euro-and-seventy-eight-cent average savings it provided me on my bi-weekly grocery purchases.

I found the card so symbolic to my steadfast disciplined spending, that on a few rare occasions—definitely more than once—I had stranded my half-filled shopping basket in the middle of the fruit section while I literally sprinted the short three blocks back to the apartment to grab the card from its position between the salt and pepper shakers above the sink.

I fingered the plastic card in my back pocket. It looked as if I would not be breaking a sweat this evening.

Next in the supermarket's progression of refrigerated merchandise came the milk. I did not care much whether I purchased whole milk or two-percent, as long as the expiration date was as distant as possible. I actually did not even really know if they had two-percent milk in Italy, but I had been told the green containers were low-fat and the blue were whole.

I peered across the first row of sealed cardboard pinnacles.

Da consumarsi entro: 10/03/05. I pulled my cell phone from my pocket to check the day's date. *07/03/05*. In Europe's dating method, the day is written first, followed by the month, then the year. I had switched my phone to the same format in an attempt to instill the new system into my daily habits, but I continued to find myself embarrassingly confused when trying to sort out the ludicrously short string of numbers.

It was the seventh of March, two thousand and five. *07/03/05*. The green-boxed milks expired in three days, on the tenth of March, two thousand and five. Three days. That was a terrible *da consumarsi*.

I moved up a shelf to the blue milks. I tilted the first one forward on its edge and read the date printed on the back. *13/03/05*. Better. Six days to consume that carton. And that was only the first milk I had checked on that row.

I dug four containers deep and delicately extracted a single blue carton. I flipped it gently in the palm of my left hand, my right still occupied with my red plastic basket, and it landed on its belly, *da consumarsi* date facing upright. *18/03/05*. Now that was a winner. For the next eleven days I could feel free to consume the milk I had purchased with zero sense of urgency. Eleven days.

I dropped the prized carton into my basket and swung into the next aisle. Eleven days. That was over a week and a half. I could not remember the last time I had found a carton of milk that would last as long. Given the sea of confusion I had found myself swimming in lately, it amused me that a carton of milk could provide such fulfillment.

I scanned the glass containers of pasta sauces. I placed four *sugo a basilico* at ninety-nine cents apiece atop the packaged tortellini. I then moved past the spices and to the end of the aisle.

18/03/05. That milk would last past the middle of March. How many days were there in March, anyway? Ah, yes, March, the dreaded thirty-one-day month with zero U.S. national holidays to help out. How I had despised March during my academic career.

I handled a few loaves of bread. I would never understand why bread in Italy was always so much harder than the bread you could buy in the States.

18/03/05. My goodness, that milk would last past the middle of March. Two weeks after that milk expired I would have to pay rent. That meant I would have to draw money from my bank account. I did not even have one thousand dollars left. Next month would be the last month I could survive on that money.

I took a satisfactory loaf from the shelf and moved forward to the cereals.

18/03/05. My flight back to California, as it stood, was three weeks after that. Could I still change it if I wanted to?

I pulled a family-size Special K box from the top shelf. I had never seen the family-size boxes of cereal before at this supermarket.

18/03/05. Skye. When was the last time I had seen her? February, I think. It must have been the middle of February when we had met in Piazza Navona and gone to Bulldog. Had it really been almost a month since I had seen her?

I changed aisles a final time, the dry pasta aisle proving the last useful one to someone on a budget such as mine. I pulled three boxes of Barilla penne from the center shelf, found three respective spaces in my basket to prop the boxes in, and turned back toward the registers at the front of the store.

18/03/05.

I reached the single open register and placed my bin at the mouth of the rubber conveyer belt. I began unloading my items, watching them being carried away one by one toward the cashier as she finished scanning the items of a young Italian woman with a stroller in front of me.

By March 18 I would have been in Italy for five months. Had I been eating exclusively pasta for five months? Was that bad for my health? It could not be that bad for my health. Could it? Was five months a long time to eat only pasta? The tortellini had meat inside. At least, the ones that were not four cheeses did.

The woman in front of me accepted her change from the cashier and placed her final item, a six-pack of Peroni beer, into the black netting on the back of her stroller. She fished one hand through the four plastic loops created by the two loaded grocery bags and moved off toward the front exit.

"Sera."

My eyes darted back to the cashier, who was already scanning my humble selections.

"Ciao," I responded while moving forward to face her.

"Tessera?"

I pulled my Spessa Amica card from my pocket and handed it to her. She passed it over the scanner and the computer expelled a monotone beep before she handed it back to me. I rounded the counter and began bagging my items as they came sliding toward me, one beep at a time, from the cashier's left hand.

I was still using my Spessa Amica card to save money every time I bought food to eat. This would be another three-Euro-and-seventy-eight-cents saved. And that money had to be adding up. I was still playing this smart.

I could make it through April. I could make it through spring to summer, to more work, to sunshine. I would just have to make some things happen—tell Dad I wanted to move my flight another few months and start thinking, really thinking, about how else I could make some immediate Euro, no matter how small. I could do this. I could make it happen. All four seasons, back to back to back to back.

"Scusi."

Jesus, how could it already be the middle of March? It was not the middle of March yet, but how could it be so close to the middle of March? How had that happened so quickly? I had a flight for the second week of April. April came after March, and it was basically the middle of March already!

"Scusi, signore."

I looked up to the cashier. She stared at me through her thick, brown-rimmed glasses. She was holding the blue milk carton in her hand. What did she want?

"Sì?"

"Fuoriesce questo cartone." What the hell was she trying to tell me about my milk? I glanced down to my cluttered and illogical bagging job, then back at the milk. The carton was the only item left to be scanned. I looked at the cashier and rumpled my eyebrows in perplexity. "È ... rotto," she said in a highly enunciated fashion. She ran a finger across the carton's bottom and then extended the digit toward my nose. A thin layer of hazy white liquid masked the skin of her fingertip. She then pointed back at the conveyer belt. Short smudges of milk streaked the dark grey rubber. My milk carton was wounded.

"Lei vuole prendere un'altro?" *Do you want to go get another one?*

I stared at the carton for a second. A single white drop formed at the container's back left corner, freefell through the stale air-conditioning, and collided with the stainless steel counter.

"No, grazie. Non lo voglio," I replied. *No, thank you. I don't want it. And no, I don't think I'll take another one.*

I quietly paid for the rest of the items, crumpling the receipt and various change in my palm. I lifted my three shopping bags from the metal counter and turned toward the front exit.

And you know what else? That milk carton can go fuck itself.

VENTIQUATTRO

"It's five Euros!" I screamed over the music, as I slid a pint of beer across the illuminated counter and to a man standing at the bar opposite me.

He passed me a ten-Euro bill and I turned back to Dario at the register. He was talking with Roberto in Italian—well, he was screaming at Roberto in Italian to be heard over the music.

From the little I had overheard and had been able to understand, I gathered that Dario was trying to convince Roberto not to leave Metro and was apparently willing to use even the busiest of times to reemphasize his argument.

I held the ten-Euro bill out to Dario. Spotting me out of the corner of his eye, he took the bill and held it in his hand as he continued his discussion with Roberto. I waited patiently for the change. After about sixty seconds I glanced back to the tall, dark-haired man still waiting for his change at the counter. I twisted back to Dario. He noticed my restless stance and broke conversation with Roberto for a moment.

"How much is this guy paying?"

"Five."

Dario immediately returned to his Italian debate. He drew five one-Euro coins from the register and held them toward me in an enclosed fist. I cupped my hand beneath his and he let the coins fall without ever breaking eye contact with Roberto. I turned back to the bar and slid the coins over the counter.

"Sorry for the wait."

The man nodded his head, took the coins off the glass counter, and stepped away. Almost immediately two young women squeezed into his place.

"Due gin e tonica!" I glanced back to Roberto and Dario. Roberto had his back to me. They remained in heated discussion. *Two gin and tonics*. I could make that.

I stepped from the sinks and moved to Roberto's station, where I filled two glasses with ice from the container at my waist. I fingered through the numerous bottles of alcohol and lifted a bottle of Gordon's Dry Gin from the third row in. I poured it carefully into each of the glasses, one at a time, counting off two ounces as I had practiced with Mariano. I placed the bottle back on the counter and grabbed the soda gun. My thumb fingered the capital T, and I filled the remainder of each glass with tonic water. I placed the soda pistol back in place and took the two gin tonics in my hands.

"Fourteen Euro!" I yelled and placed the drinks in front of the girls.

"Cosa?" one of them replied in Italian. Ah, yes, Italian.

"Umm … quattordici Euro," I reiterated.

The girls handed me a twenty and I tuned to Dario and Roberto again. I held the bill in their direction but this time received no acknowledgement. Both Roberto and Dario's hands were lost in gesture; their mouths fired off the Italian rapidly. I glanced to the girls.

"Un momento!" I assured. But now Dario had his arm over Roberto's shoulder and was talking more privately into his right ear. I spotted the register just to the left of them, the drawer half open. The spot where Hassan usually sat was vacant. He must have gone to the bathroom or outside for a cigarette.

I slid past Roberto and placed the twenty in with the stack of ten or so others. I fingered a single Euro coin from its respective slot and pulled a five-Euro bill from another. I stepped back to the girls and handed them their change.

"Grazie!" They smiled in unison.

That left only one person still standing in front of Roberto's station. I did not even have to look to know Roberto and Dario were still occupied, as I could hear their discussion beginning to battle the level of the music again. So I stepped up to the short, spiky-haired, black-poofy-jacket-clad Italian myself.

"Un rum e coca e due gin lemon!" he barked. *A rum coke and two gin lemons.* It was a bit more complicated but still a manageable enough order. I went to making the drinks, shoveling ice into three cocktail glasses and placing them on the black rubber bar mat in front of me. I poured the rum first, then the gin, then carefully fingered the soda pistol and completed the second half of the two-part mixtures.

"Venti uno!" I screamed across the counter.

"Quanto?" he screamed back.

"Ven-ti un-o!" I yelled, this time enunciating each syllable.

"Ventuno?"

Ah, jeez. Twenty-one was *ventuno* not *venti uno*.

"Sì, sì," I blushed as I took the fifty-Euro bill from his hand.

I turned to the register. Dario and Roberto were gone.

I stepped back to the sinks and stared down the length of the narrow walkway, the fifty-Euro bill still clutched between the fingers of my right hand. Mariano was at his station halfway down the bar. He was already packing up with great haste, spinning colorful tops onto his juice bottles and throwing random items of fruit into the small refrigerator at his knees. I spotted Hassan seated at the last glass table at the back of the room, fingering an unlit cigarette. Dario and Roberto were nowhere in sight.

I stepped back to the register. It was wide open, waiting to be used, a rainbow of Euro bills bursting from the black metal partitions. I slid the fifty underneath the pile of four others and slowly gathered the change.

I stepped up to the young Italian waiting patiently at the bar, dispensed the two bills and four coins onto the glass counter, pronounced my best *grazie*, and then skipped back to the register.

I extended my right hand and my fingers delicately met the extended metal drawer, applying light pressure as the drawer began to slide closed. But the further in it slid, the greater the springs inside pushed back in resistance.

I stared down at the overflowing Euro still visible. There must have been over two thousand Euro cash in that small black drawer. And no one had seemed to be keeping any track of what was going in or out of it. Prices were exchanged verbally and change handed on the fly without any receipts being printed or computer notes added, in order to keep the flow of client alcohol consumption moving smoothly and seamlessly.

I looked back towards the sinks and the small fraction of the bar visible from the register. There was still no sign of Dario or Roberto. My hand held equilibrium with the springs inside the register, balancing the drawer half open as my glance returned once again to the abundance of unrecorded currency.

Would they have known if I slid a single blue twenty-Euro bill from the center divider and into my right pant pocket? Would they have had any idea at the end of the night? How could they? They would have never had the slightest idea a bill had gone missing because no one knew how many there were supposed to be in the first place.

One swipe—one quick, fluid swipe and I could double my salary for the night. Instead of walking out Metro's double doors with twenty Euro in my pocket, I could be walking out with forty. That would be huge for me. And how much would twenty Euro harm them anyway? The register was stocked to the brim.

Two swipes. I could pull two quick swipes and it would not even take five seconds. Two quick swipes and I would have all the money I needed to pay for groceries for the next two weeks—a budget freebie on my graph-paper accounting record. With just two quick swipes in less than five seconds I could leave tonight with the amount that I normally made in an entire weekend. That would really be huge for me—that would make a real impact on how much longer I could squeeze expenses out of my disappearing funds.

I stepped away from the register. It drifted open behind me as I moved to peer down the bar again toward Mariano.

"Mariano," I screamed, "where are Dario and Roberto?"

He replied without looking up from his rushed fruit packing and bottle tossing and counter tidying. "They have been to the kitchen! Begin to clean the station of Roberto! I want to leave fast tonight!"

I dropped back to the register a final time. Now completely open, the deepest partition of the drawer was left uncovered, exposing another short stack of fifty-Euro bills to the dim green light of the back bar.

Three swipes, not only quick, but strategic, and I could leave with enough Euro to cover the difference between my bank account and what I needed to pay rent for April, for next month, for the month in which my money was projected to finish, for the month that otherwise would hold my flight back to California. April signaled the beginning of spring, and could be the final month I would have to push through before the tourist season would take flight and I would be able to find full-time work. Three quick, strategic swipes and I would be able to see all four seasons of Rome—back to back to back to back.

The white house lights ignited. Everything in the room lit up stark and vivid. Shaken, I slammed the register closed and jolted to the sinks.

I felt cowardly and weak. I felt like I had been under the control of some twisted puppet master. That could not have been me. Those thoughts could not have been mine. I was a college graduate from a respected university. I was a good person. I was an honest person. I frantically rinsed the glasses at the counter in front of me and dropped them to the basket at my waist.

The topic of money had been raised often during my years in university. When talking about job opportunities and career decisions, the debate of working for a higher level of money or working for a higher level of personal satisfaction had become a repeated and trite debate. Everyone—and I mean *everyone*—had condemned any idea of sacrificing personal respect or values—or even personal time—for a fatter bank account. We had all joined together in defiance of the alluring power of the buck. We had thought its dark side exposed, conquered, tamed, and under control by our ability to live self-aware and think well-informed.

But for us, the desire for additional money in a career had been synonymous with the desire for absurdly impractical sports cars and oceanside mansions. Money had never, ever represented things as simplistic as groceries and rent—food on the table at dinner time and a roof over our heads. The way we had all grown up, these things were a given. Meals and apartments were just ... there. They were simply issued with life. Money, in the form of a better salary or a bonus or a tax refund, would mean it was time to treat yourself to something extra—a new cell phone, a pair of sneakers, a couple new CDs, or a better car stereo. The thought of struggling to scrape together enough cash to pay for a small single room in a shared flat and purchase discounted supermarket-brand pasta at the grocery store had never once crossed our minds. How could that possibly have ever been a problem?

As I stood there at the sinks of Metro, my hands trembling while I fumbled to wash the last of the dirty glasses, these thoughts poured through my mind. And it dawned on me just how many people in this world would have been revolted, absolutely disgusted, to hear the debates of myself and my fellow university students—students composing a demographic declared so cultured and so well-experienced that we were positioned to lead the generations of the future, but were instead so sheltered and implausibly naïve that we could never have understood the perspective of the majority of the world's population, no matter how much we claimed to have been taught to objectively empathize. It was dawning on me that to many—most likely to Mariano and Roberto, to all bartenders and waitresses in Rome, to countless others in Italy, to millions back in the United States, and now, suddenly, soberingly, to me as well—those small, convenient, rectangular paper notes actually represented food and shelter. They represented the basis of life. They represented survival.

I cleaned the entirety of Roberto's workstation and changed downstairs. Hassan handed me a single blue twenty-Euro bill as I emerged from the stairwell, and I found Mariano typing a message on his phone just outside the front glass doors.

"Did Roberto leave already? I never saw him again after he disappeared with Dario."

Mariano looked up briefly from the phone's small screen, just enough to acknowledge my presence before returning to his typing, and we both began to walk out of the Campo and onto the narrow Via Giubbonari.

"No, he still talks with Dario. I think this will be the last weekend that he works with us."

"Why is he leaving? What is Dario saying?"

"I don't know, man. He just has another work. Probably more money."

There was silence for a few moments. Mariano's thumb skipped across the buttons of his mobile phone.

"Where are the girls?" I asked. "I don't want to go out tonight—are you guys going out, because I can take a night bus or something," I told him.

Mariano remained focused on his phone as we curved onto the main Via Arenula. "No, man. They are going to their home. Do not to worry. I take you home."

He then sent the message he had been working on and we stopped quietly at the corner of Lungotevere, obeying the traffic signal despite the fact that we had not seen a single car pass us for the entirety of our short trip thus far.

The light changed, and we moved onto the Ponte Garibaldi. I could make out the dome of Saint Peter's Cathedral upriver. The lights lining Lungotevere reflected bleeding streaks of gold onto the calm, dark water of the Tiber. The streets were vacant, apart from the two of us, our breath misting upon hitting the frigid night air as we walked.

Mariano's phone let out a short chime and he drew it to his face.

"Merda ..." He turned to me. "Yo, man, would you like to have twenty Euro tonight?"

I glanced at my own phone for a second. It was two forty in the morning.

"For doing what?" I asked.

"I must to ask you for a favor. It is nothing too difficult."

"What do you want me to do for you?" I asked again.

"It's nothing, man. Do you want twenty Euro or not?"

I thought about Mariano's cryptic offer. I was sure the favor he was requesting was bound to be juvenile, most likely irresponsible, and quite possibly illegal. I wanted to go home—just go home and go to bed. But my financial situation was real and the presented scenario tempting. On my fifteen-minute ride back to my apartment with Mariano I could match the money I had made cleaning glasses and emptying trash cans for four hours.

"I guess I can do it. But I really just want to get home. And I wish you would just tell me what it is."

"Great. Don't worry about it, man, it will be something too easy."

We reached the narrow alley where his car was parked and climbed inside. The streetlamp directly above ignited the splintering fractures still spread across the front windshield. Mariano started the car and we sped onto Lungotevere.

There was silence.

I ran my forearm up the passenger side window and my fingers fiddled with the rubber seal at the top of the door.

Twenty Euro was a good deal for me. No matter what it was, it would be in my best interest. And at the same time, it was something Mariano wanted me to do for him—maybe even needed me to do for him. Everyone would be benefiting.

I wondered if I would be able to make the favor a recurring duty—something I could do two or three times a week. If I could help Mariano with this three times a week I would be doubling my total weekly income. Maybe this could be my in. Maybe this could allow me to push through April—to the end of this freezing winter.

Mariano switched on the radio and the baritone vocals of the Crash Test Dummies crept from the speakers at our knees and into the cold dark interior of the car.

"Who is this group?" Mariano asked after a moment's thought.

"The Crash Test Dummies."

"Ahh, yes, yes." Mariano laughed for a second to himself. "When I was little, I wanted to be a crash test dummy." He mimicked the sound of cars colliding and threw himself against the steering wheel.

"I hope you've grown out of that phase."

"No, not really." He laughed. "Does the way that I drive scare you?"

He pressed on the gas and began hugging the right side of the road dangerously close to the triplets of garbage dumpsters which lined the Lungotevere opposite the river. He looked over at me as I remained calm and mute.

"You never say that you are scared," he spoke, "but I think you are scared."

He pressed the gas further and hugged the side of the road closer. The dumpsters whooshed three at a time as they sped by mere inches from my door.

My untouched seatbelt waved lightly back and forth at my head, the cold metal buckle brushing against my ear as if to remind me of its suspended position.

The acceleration continued. Mariano spoke again.

"Say something."

He began to concentrate closely on the containers, focusing more on them than the road itself. His right hand grasped the steering wheel and quickly calibrated for the reduction or augmentation of space needed to create the minimum possible and not collide with the large metal bins.

"Say something! React!"

We sped faster and the whooshes melted into single, pulsating rushes of air for every set of dumpsters we passed. It was impossible to tell at this point whether the front end of Mariano's car would clear the next set or glance off them, sending the car into an immediate spin and inevitable roll which would throw both of us—neither with our seatbelts fastened—through the already fractured windshield and onto the pavement outside.

"You—" I started, then stopped in silence again.

"I what? Tell me! Finish!"

At that moment there was a sharp explosion of sound as the passenger side mirror struck the first of four garbage dumpsters, sending a shower of plastic and glass across the window and door at my side.

"Mariano, quit it!" I burst out.

He nodded his head in acknowledgment, released the gas pedal, and let the car drift toward the center of the quiet main road again.

"Why do you remain so quiet? Why does it take so much for you to speak?"

"Listen," I raised a finger to his face. "You live your way, and I'll live my way, all right?"

"All right, man. But I think it would be better for you if you ... if ..." He shook his head. "Never mind, man. I'm sorry."

The reckless driving exhibition had brought us quickly to Via Marmorata, the final straightaway which led to the pyramid. I could make out the very tip of the marble-coated apex above the tree line ahead. I would have been almost home.

Mariano cut the wheel right, and suddenly we were flying through Testaccio. We navigated a half dozen right-angled turns before popping back out to Lungotevere, continuing southward along the Tiber.

"Where are we going? I assume this has to do with the favor you need me to do?"

"What?" he asked.

"Never mind."

I struggled to understand Mariano. The things he told me, the things he believed—which of them were valuable and to be considered, and which were the ludicrous talk of a madman?

"Are you scared to die?" he asked quietly.

I stared at him for a moment. He continued to watch the road, perhaps more engaged in contemplation than in guiding our vehicle.

"No. Eventually, no. But I would rather it not be any time soon—like tonight in this car. And I do not think it is bad to take simple precautions to be sure that doesn't happen."

The metal of the seatbelt buckle kissed my right ear.

"Do you want to know when you are going to die?" he continued.

"No, no, I don't. I mean ... if I did, I guess I would be able to ... I don't know."

For a moment there was only the thin, solitary sound of the radio.

"Do you want to be awake when you die?"

"Jesus, Mariano, I don't know, do you? Do you want to be awake when you die?"

"Yes."

"Why yes?"

The wind outside began to whistle as it rushed along the seams of the car's boxy chassis.

"I think everything in the life is an experience. I know you cannot to remember, but to be born is an experience, to grow old is an experience, to have sex is an experience. And to die also is an experience. And I want to be awake for that experience, to try to understand that experience."

The buildings once lining the left side of Lungotevere had disappeared and been replaced with patches of dirt and weeds. A chain-link fence ran parallel to the road, twenty meters from its edge. The shoulder looked deserted; a few random cars left carelessly abandoned here and there, some missing tires.

In the distant darkness ahead grew the broad face of a towering stone wall which formed the foundation of a major-looking bridge crossing the Tiber. The wall seemed to block the road completely, creating an ominous dead end. Mariano slowed the car and pulled off into the dirt. He cut the engine and switched off the headlights.

"We have arrived."

He reached for his small bag and pulled a wad of Euro cash from inside. He counted off four blue twenty-Euro bills and handed them to me.

"Here you go, man. Keep one for you." He then pointed toward the bridge ahead of us. "Just walk to the bridge and tell them you want three. That is it."

"Tell them I want three what?"

"Say to them in Italian. *Tre*. That is all."

"Three what?"

"Do not to worry."

It was too vague.

"Why can't you do this yourself?" I accused.

"I just cannot, man. It takes two minutes. Go, and then we go home."

I shook my head and opened the passenger door. Scattered fragments of the shattered mirror sprinkled to the dirt below. I stood at the open door and slid one of the four twenty-Euro bills into my jacket pocket. I stared toward the wall of stone ahead in the distance. I could make out faint arches of metal gating at its base. I ducked my head back into the car.

"Where do I go? How do I know where I'm going?"

"Just follow to the lights."

"The lights?"

"Yeah, man. Follow to the lights."

I pulled my head out and squinted toward the bridge. I was unable see anything but blackness at its base. I ducked my head again into Mariano's car.

"There are no lights. It's all black down there."

"When you get close you will see the lights. Follow to them."

"Mariano, why can't you tell me what I'm doing? Why can't you do this yourself?"

"Listen, you are just buying for me a thing. It is nothing too big."

Weed. That was what this was about.

"I'm getting you weed? Is that it? Why can't you walk over there and get it for yourself? I don't understand."

"I cannot go."

"Why?"

"I just cannot, man!"

"Tell me why you can't go!"

He exhaled and stared out the front windshield. That was when I noticed again the fractured web of cracks which ran through it. Mariano turned back to me and saw the expression of comprehension run down my face.

"I had some problems the last time I came to here. I cannot go to there again."

I stared at him for a moment and said nothing. Then I pulled my head out from the car, slammed the door shut, and began a fast, determined stride toward the base of the bridge.

This was fucking ridiculous. This was absolutely fucking ridiculous.

I could see nothing but blackness ahead of me, and I would be at the foot of the wall in less than a minute. I rubbed the three twenties between my numbing fingers. It was fucking freezing out here.

To my right, the dark water of the Tiber crept slowly and silently southward. I was twenty meters from the base of the massive overpass. Two large metal gates arched forty meters upwards. I could make out the road continuing onward beyond them. They must have been passageways for government or military vehicles only.

Then a sudden, small pulse of white neon light flashed from inside one of the two towering metal gates. I stopped and listened to the faint hum of traffic passing along the bridge above. I glanced back toward Mariano's car, now a substantial distance behind me. There was no one else in sight.

I turned back to face the wall. A double pulse of white neon light burst soundlessly from the left gate once more.

Follow to the lights.

I stepped in the direction from which the light had come, moving slower now as I struggled to gain some sort of visual orientation as to who or how many people were waiting just beyond the heavy bars of metal. As I stepped closer still, my eyes adjusted, and almost instantly I was able to make out a half dozen silhouettes, quietly roaming against the massive dim arch of light created by the open gate of the opposite side. As I reached the thick metal poles, one of the figures stepped to meet me and said nothing.

"Tre." I extended the three twenty-Euro bills through the dark rods. They were pulled from my hand. Just behind the faceless person directly in front of me, the other silhouettes continued to shift and pace back and forth. I could hear the faint resonance of metal—possibly a knife or a small handgun.

What if they recognized Mariano's car from here? They had seen us pull up. Jesus, they probably heard us arguing and screaming at the car's door. Apart from the faint hum of traffic above it was dead silent under the bridge. What if Mariano owed them something? God, what if it he had hit one of them with his car? What if that was how his windshield had been broken? What would they do to me? What if none of them understood English? Could I explain myself? Would they even care?

I felt plastic pressed against my left palm and instinctively grasped it. I turned away and shoved the small bags into my jacket pocket. I hurried back toward Mariano's car.

This wasn't worth twenty Euros. This would not be happening again. Mariano would have to figure out his own weed problems for himself.

I reached the car and climbed inside.

"Let's get out of here."

"Do you have the three bogs?" he asked.

I drew them from my jacket and tossed them to his lap.

"Thank you, man," he said.

"I'm not doing this again."

"All right. As you want."

He started the car and circled back in the direction from which we had come. I pulled out my wallet and slid the twenty-Euro bill Mariano had given me next to the solitary other from Hassan.

I had thought I was in control of money. But in its growing absence it was clear that it, in fact, was in control of me. Having money meant control—control over the devious temptations at Metro and control to refuse favors for people who could not solve their own problems. Without it, however, the thoughts that were beginning to run though my head were those of a scavenger and pusher. These thoughts were crazy—thoughts which six months ago I would have considered absolutely insane. And this time it was not the kind of crazy that was the envy of the timid and regrettably apathetic. This time it was the bad crazy.

VENTICINQUE

Traditionally, spring is about life, rebirth, the beginning of something—a brighter time and season. If you look at nature during the months comprising the spring season, you will see this is true. The trees adorn themselves in a fresh layer of green, flowers emerge and open to the amassing daylight. But to me, spring had always felt like an end.

Maybe academia had engrained this mindset into my head. In that world—the world I had been living in practically every year of my conscious life thus far—spring meant the academic year was coming to a close, that friends were moving home for the summer, that acquaintances were flying to Washington DC for internships. Spring meant the unraveling of fixed class schedules and weekly lunch meetings. Spring meant leases were up, and regular social institutions were due for review. Spring was unstable and unnerving and nostalgic.

Last spring had marked not only the end of an academic year, but the end of academia, of my time in Los Angeles, of my time in California indefinitely. It was the end of an entire world. And although the final week of March in Rome provided a stunning preview of the physically beautiful spring to come, mentally it felt no different than the springs of the past.

It was Saturday. For the past week the sky had been flawless. The sun threw warmth delicately onto our arms and faces. I had even managed to sport a T-shirt and jeans as I ran errands around the center.

The city was beautiful and unfaltering. And I had constructed a cheery papier-mâché exterior for myself to match the encouraging weather, while inside I felt uninviting and unsure and was frantically trying to sort out some kind of plan.

I crossed the wide Via Giovanni Giolitti, dodging taxis as they departed their stand at the foot of Termini station. I had taken the short metro ride north from Piramide and was headed away from the station and toward the narrow Via di Manin, which stretched three blocks south before colliding with the northern wall of the Santa Maria Maggiore church.

Dressed in black boots, grey slacks, and a dark, pin-striped dress shirt casually untucked, I hopped to the sidewalk, my black bag bouncing lightly at my side, my feet striding in the direction of Piazza Santa Maria Maggiore.

The narrow streets teemed with life. Maybe it was the weather, maybe it was the time of day, maybe it was due to the weekend, but I could not remember the last time I had seen the city so alive.

I paused at the light of Via Amendola. It quickly turned green, and I stepped with the others from the curb to the cobblestone. My legs moved involuntarily, my mind consumed elsewhere.

My return flight to San Francisco was in just over two weeks—nineteen days. Had I accomplished everything I had wanted to accomplish? What had I come to Rome to accomplish? I had no answers.

I split a group of young Italians eating gelato as they strolled northbound. I rolled my shirt sleeves to my forearms. The temperature was perfect.

I thought back to October, to the moment I had first exited Termini station to these very streets. What had been my goals then? Find an apartment, find an Italian social network, find a job. They had been so basic. I had accomplished all three, but had that really been it? Why had I not thought beyond such fundamental objectives?

I hesitated as a swarm of scooters buzzed across the intersection at Via Farini in front of me. Then I crossed, glancing right to a pair of businessmen passing a runaway soccer ball back to a group of elementary school children.

I stepped up the opposite curb and began the final block of Via di Manin. With each step forward I watched the final buildings on either side of the narrow alley open like theater curtains, steadily revealing the broad, towering wall of the Santa Maria Maggiore church.

I broke from the narrow streets and entered the expansive Piazza Santa Maria Maggiore. It was ten minutes to four. My phone emitted a short chime and I opened the new message.

<Sono davanti alla chiesa, dove si entra> *I'm in front of the church, where you enter.*

I circled Santa Maria's western corner and began along its southern wall.

If I were to stay in Rome it was going to be a battle. My three nights a week at Metro had helped stretch my money to this point. But I did not even have enough left in my bank account to cover rent and food for another thirty days.

Remaining in Italy would mean finding another position somewhere in the city immediately.

The past week I had set off around the center, hopefully casting out résumés in an attempt to gain additional income and, therefore, additional control. I had passed through a couple of pubs near the Pantheon and one restaurant on Via Nazionale, but their responses had not been promising.

The owners at the two pubs had told me they were not seeking extra staff. And the restaurant manager had told me to return with the proper visa documentation—documentation I did not have and could not legally obtain. It felt unsettling similar to my search in November, as if I were experiencing my second month in Rome all over again, only with four thousand dollars less in the bank.

I reached the front of the Chiesa Santa Maria Maggiore. Steps cascaded from the two double-door entrances, radiating outward as they spilled into the cobblestone lake of the piazza. Groups of teenagers free from school for the weekend lay scattered about the tiered stone, basking in the welcome afternoon sun. A trickle of tourists weaved their way between them as they cautiously moved into and out of the cathedral. I began circling the sprawling entrance, my eyes scanning the figures as I walked.

Was this life in Rome worth fighting for? Would these relationships I had such trouble grasping prove sturdy enough to carry me onwards? Could they give me the strength I would need to in turn fight for them?

I spotted a small figure centered on the steps. She sat mute among the flurry, head buried in a thick paperback, blonde hair—almost white—woven into a long braid which ran down the back of her maroon long-sleeved shirt. She slouched forward over the book in her lap, her nose mere inches from the text, her finger carefully guiding the position on the page—a curious twelve-year-old examining a chart on insects.

I was searching for solid ground, for a reason to stay, for motivation, for purpose.

"Skye."

Her finger held its position on the page and she squinted up at me. I shifted my head to the left, my shadow hopping from the stone steps to her face.

"Mike! Ciao! Come stai?"

I had to know. Whether I was to return to California in two weeks or in two years and never see Skye again for the rest of my life, I had to be sure. I had to leave no doubt that I had, in fact, been wrong, that she was not meant to be a main character in my script. So, after I had spoken with the manager at the Flann O'Brien on Via Nazionale where Skye now worked, and he had told me that I did not have enough experience to be a waiter nor a valid permit to work, I had marched straight to the front of the restaurant, caught Skye on her way from the kitchen to a table, and told her I had to see her.

She had agreed enthusiastically, of course, and said she would call me the next day, which she did, of course. She was lively and complimentary on the phone, of course, and there she was, where and when she had promised. And more importantly, here *we* were, one on one, finally alone among the city's 2.7 million residents.

"Did you get my message?" she asked.

"The one just now?"

"I realized this piazza is actually pretty big!"

"I did. That was thoughtful of you."

I turned away from the church entrance as she gathered herself and rose to her feet. Her voice interrupted my spin. "Wait. Can we go in, really quick? I realized when I got here that I have lived in this area for seven months and have never been inside this church once."

I laughed. "Sure! Let's go."

We weaved through the scattered Italian students and quietly entered the cathedral, trailing a Japanese couple with matching JanSport backpacks. Inside the cavernous lobby sat more young Italians, hair spiked, jeans torn, designer sunglasses resting on the bridges of their noses, whispering to each other as they cooled off among the glossy marble and seamless shade.

I paced slowly with Skye across the colorfully tiled flooring toward the front of the vast structure. Every inch of the ceiling and walls was bathed in artwork—every angle lined in gold.

"Do you believe?" she whispered.

"No. At least, not in the sense of this organized form."

I happened to be in accordance with the obelisks, in this case.

Her head bounced lightly in acknowledgement. Our meandering crawl reduced to a full stop as Skye gazed toward a circular mosaic centered at the front of the basilica. My eyes turned from her cheek and followed her stare.

Distinctive colored bits of stone formed Mary being crowned by Jesus. Thick golden halos encompassed both of their heads.

"Do you?" I asked.

Skye shook her head and then began moving back toward the entrance.

"I have been to so many churches here that they have become so ... they are too much."

We broke back to the afternoon daylight and started away from the piazza.

"So, this is your part of town. Is there a café or something you like around here?"

"Well, can we get some gelato?"

"Of course we can get gelato."

"Good, because there is a great place down this street."

We started down one of the side streets jetting off Piazza Santa Maria Maggiore.

"How did the talk go with Signor Sanna at our restaurant?" she asked.

"Not very well. He asked me about my Permesso di Soggiorno which expired back in January. I just told him I didn't know when it expired and I would be back with the information but there really isn't any information to take him."

"Your permesso is already expired? How can that be?"

"Because we aren't part of the European Union, so we only are allowed three months in Italy."

"Three *months*?" Skye exclaimed. She scrunched her nose as she looked over at me.

"How long is *your* permesso good for?"

"Until two thousand and nine."

My mind heard the year but had trouble registering it. It was another four years away. Skye could live and work in Italy with no problems for another four years. For some reason I had assumed she had a permit valid for a year, or at most two years. But *four years*.

"Wow." It was all I could muster. Maybe it should not have, but the fact that my permit had expired after three months made me feel foolish. I must have sounded so foolish to Skye and her four-year permit.

"What are you going to do?" she asked.

"I don't know. I mean, if I have to fly home, I would be going back to California, which is a great place. I've had an extraordinary six months here, and I have a great life waiting for me back at home."

That was not totally true. It was not false either, but there was no way I knew that for certain. Just because I would be a legal citizen in California, and I had a nice degree from a nice university, did not imply that I would find a rewarding job or gain a steady social network or have anything better or worse than I had in Rome. It simply meant I would be able to walk into a Coffee Bean and not have to lie during the application process.

"Eccoci qua!" Skye announced as we turned off the sidewalk and into a small gelateria. She rubbed her hands together and leaned in to inspect the flavors. A young woman in a red apron appeared in front of her.

"Prego."

"Prendo una coppetta da due Euro con nocciola e …" Skye trailed off as she leaned to the left, continuing to inspect the numerous flavors.

"E pistacchio!" she exclaimed, her finger darting toward the tub behind the glass covering.

The woman behind the counter began shoveling the gelato into the small paper cup, laughing to herself at Skye's overly enthusiastic delivery. Skye exchanged a two-Euro coin for the gelato and the apron-laden woman, still giggling, turned to me.

"E per Lei?"

"Prendo la stessa cosa, grazie," I told her.

She began making a replica of Skye's order.

"Your accent sounds better," Skye started, speaking with a mouth full of nocciola. "You must have improved a lot by now, huh?"

I slid two one-Euro coins across the counter and took my cup. Skye and I stepped back to the street.

"Improved since when?" I asked her.

"Since I first talked to you at Metro on New Year's."

"Maybe I have. They still speak a lot of English to me at Metro, and it is all English at my apartment. I try to study on my own, though, and I did speak a lot of Italian with Roberto. But he left recently."

Skye threw a spoonful of pistacchio into her mouth.

"Roberto quit now too? Everyone is leaving Metro. Federico was the first. Did you know him?"

She must have been talking about the Federico that Mariano had introduced me to at Seven Eleven.

"I met him once, but never really knew him."

"No one wants to stay at Metro!" she laughed.

Skye made a sudden halt at a shop window. The clothing inside appeared to be secondhand, vintage, really funky stuff. She lifted one hand to the glass to shield the reflecting sun as she peered inside.

"This place looks really cool. I will have to come back here," she said.

Her head darted left and right as she examined the cluttered racks of garments. Her hand squeaked along the glass and she pulled away for a second, observing the green streak of ice cream she had left behind.

She pulled her shirt sleeve over her fist and attempted to wipe the streak clean, but it seemed only to grow larger, smearing and spreading with each pass of her hand.

She looked back at me with raised eyebrows and shrugged. I spooned a dollop of gelato into my mouth, smirked, and shook my head at her.

"If you want to go inside we can just—"

"Oh, no!" Skye interrupted. "The lady inside is giving me a really scary look!"

I peered through the window myself to see a thickset woman shuffling toward us from inside the shop. Her right hand karate chopped the air as excited Italian streamed from her lips. On her third or fourth monstrous waddle, she knocked a stack of vintage hats off their rack and to the floor, adding even more fuel to her red-hot burning temper.

Skye stiffened her body, smiled ear to ear, and proceeded to rapidly wave her right hand toward the infuriated woman who was nearly on top of us. Then, seeing that her attempt at resolving the situation with a friendly gesture had failed, Skye looked to me, and with two stark blue eyes expressed a vigorous, *let's get the heck out of here*!

Our cups fell to the stone sidewalk and we took off running. Side by side down the center of the narrow roadway we ran. Our feet pounded the cobblestone, two Skye strides for every one of mine. She hugged her purse to her chest, I swung my bag to my back. There was no need to run but we ran anyway. And it was the most fun I could remember having in months. We rounded the next corner and paused to catch our breath. We were both laughing.

"She was really pissed about that window!" I blurted out between gasps.

"Seriously! I couldn't believe how mad she looked! I wasn't staying around to see what she would do!"

Skye tilted her head up the street to our left.

"Let's go up this way."

We climbed the short street, our breathing slowly returning to normal. At the summit of the roadway we hit what appeared to be a giant medieval stone wall. It must have run twenty meters high. Various forms of greenery overtook the metal fencing at its top. Skye looked at me.

"Have you been to this park?"

"There is a park up there?"

"Yeah!" She pointed to a stairway of stone ascending into the wall a few meters ahead. "You want to see it?"

"I want you to show me." *Show me more of your Rome.*

We scaled the rocky stairs, their cracks filled with weeds and moss. I followed her higher. The clamber of traffic softened to a smooth hum as we reached the top. I strode after her from the last step onto a thick stone pathway.

The park was small; I could see to each end from where we had entered. A dozen grass islands floated in the small sea of mixed grey gravel. A pair of wooden benches accompanied each island, split by small metal trash bins. Various trees lined the park's perimeter. It was peaceful and calm.

"Do you know where we are?" Skye asked.

"Not exactly, no."

She continued forward, feet crunching on the small stones with each of her swift steps. I followed her and then recognized the Vittorio Emanuele II Monument at eye level in the distance between the trees lining the park's opposite end.

"I didn't realize we were so close to Piazza Venezia."

"Yeah, cool, huh?"

We reached a metal railing at the park's edge. She carefully leaned outward.

"And down there is Via Nazionale."

I leaned over the railing as well. Thirty meters below buses and scooters and taxis rumbled down the main boulevard.

"Want to sit down over there?"

I followed Skye's finger, expecting to find one of the park's twenty-some unoccupied wooden benches, but instead discovered a ring of rock surrounding one of the grass islands.

"That looks perfect."

Just perfect. Thirty meters above all the mess and confusion. Above the bank accounts and work permits. Separated from the disorder of the Rome below, this Rome would be ours. We sat shoulder to shoulder, our faces aglow in the evening sun. This time there would be no interruptions, no distractions.

"You have to tell me what on earth your town in Iceland is like, Skye. I can't even imagine."

She inhaled excitedly as she turned to face me.

"You know, you should come to Iceland with me! I bet you would love it! I'm going in June for a week."

It felt good to hear her say that. Not because I had any realistic intention of actually traveling to Iceland with her, but because it assured me that all my tangent daydreams and runaway fantasies had not been unfounded. She had played a role in it all. That was not to say what she was doing was wrong or even intentional. But hearing such a request—as blunt and naked in form as this one had been—it was clear how even a single phrase could plant a seed which instantly sprouted into countless stems of prospects and possibilities. Who would not have fallen in love with such ideas?

Our conversation pushed forward as the sun paced itself toward the distant horizon. Iceland: small population, dark nearly all day in winter, the hottest summer day only as warm as that particular spring day in Rome. Siblings: one brother, older by a year, also into theater, her parents having conceived him in their early thirties—an extremely late age to have children relative to other Icelanders. Her passions: stage theater, both as a teacher later and an actress now, but never behind a camera and never to get famous. Aspirations: to complete her current acting course, which would allow her to apply to the most prestigious theater school in Italy, located in Rome, and, if she were accepted, to begin the two-year program next fall. Gelato: always the creamy flavors over the fruity flavors. Always.

It was all there—everything I had wanted to cover. For two hours we sat side by side, perched high above Via Nazionale, matching blue eyes alternating between a fix on each other and a gaze beyond the treetops to the white marble of the Vittorio Emanuele Monument II coated orange by the afternoon sun. For two continuous hours there was always something which had us laughing or contemplating or rambling off when we hit a question we had yet to solve for ourselves. And for two hours there was nothing. There was no real underlying exhilaration. There was no attempt at visually subtle but perceptibly forced physical contact. And, barring the preposterous trip to Iceland, there was no list of future plans growing to an improbable length the more we spoke.

Maybe calling it *nothing* was being too harsh. There was respect, there was gratification, there was empathy. But as seven o'clock approached and we rose from our stone seating to begin our decent to the chaotic Via Nazionale below—back to the engaged Rome—the picture was unmistakably clear.

I had thought the fact that Skye and I we were both foreigners had bonded us, and maybe that fact did account for a majority of the connection we had. But Skye had a plan for next fall. Skye had a *plan*. I did not. I was directionless.

Her world, even as an immigrant, was played out in Italian. Her friends and colleagues spoke the local language. And I did not. I spoke English.

Skye had a permit to stay for the next four years. She had the ability to build a true life in Rome. And I did not. My permit was long expired and I should have been back in the United States months ago.

I walked beside her, back across the gravel and down the cracked steps to the alley below. I felt quiet. I had asked everything I had wanted to and had received all I had needed to know.

We continued to the end of the block and turned onto Via Nazionale, beginning a slow stroll up the busy sidewalk. Endless traffic—buses and taxis and scooters—clambered down the main roadway to our left. Teenagers and businessmen streamed passed us on both sides, often brushing one of my shoulders as I listened to Skye recite a story about work the night before.

We reached the outdoor seating of the Flann O'Brien, Skye's new workplace and the restaurant where I had been turned down for a bus boy position due to lack of a valid work visa.

That Permesso di Soggiorno had been worthless. What could anyone accomplish in three months?

We faced each other in the middle of the frenzied sidewalk.

"Am I only going to see you once a month from now on, Skye?"

She laughed. "I guess so, huh!"

I guessed so, too.

"I would really like to see you more than that. It's difficult, though? You have your circle going through work here, and your apartment, and I have my circle going at Metro and at my apartment. And for any overlap ... it just ..."

"I know," she nodded.

I took a deep breath and slid my hands to my pockets. My eyes fell to my shoes.

She understood. For any overlap to occur it would take divergent energy. And for what, at this point? For pleasant conversation? For an agreeable friendship? People did not fight for such things. There was not supposed to be the need.

I pulled my eyes from the ground and instructed my cheeks to smile.

"But it was really nice to see you. Thank you for meeting me."

"Really, it was really nice to talk with you too. I had a really good time."

I believed her. She did enjoy seeing me. But I was a minor character in her script—an amiable subplot.

We kissed cheeks.

"You can come in if you want. I mean I have to start working, but you can."

Skye, if you aren't happy with your boyfriend, you should say something. I don't know if you know me yet. Maybe if you got to know me better you would see me differently. Even if I have to leave Rome a lifetime before you ever do or he ever does, if he does not make you light up the way I know you can then why are you with him? For the now, for today, why?

"I actually should get going," I told her. "But say hi to Heidi for me."

"Okay, I will! See you soon! Buon lavoro e ci vediamo a presto!"

I aspired to say something novel in Italian back to her. I fought for something so articulate that it would shake the foundation of what she thought I could verbalize. I searched to say something that proved I could fit right into her Italian-speaking world. I had been studying at my apartment and speaking with Roberto at work. I wanted so badly to show her how infinite my potential could be if only surrounded by the right people.

"Ciao. Ci vediamo," was all that came.

Goddamn my worthless Italian.

Skye turned, took three quick steps down the alley of patio seating, and pushed through the right front door. The door swung shut behind her.

I stared at my reflection in the glass. *Guinness* was painted across my chest. Rivers of pedestrians streamed passed me. They appeared in the framed glass rapidly, each for only a second.

I watched my expressionless face flicker behind a man in a suit on a cell phone, a woman in sunglasses and too much makeup, a pair of teenage boys. They flashed in front of me and behind me, and some headed north and some south, but all of them moved with such purpose.

I turned southward myself, and began what would be a long walk down Via Nazionale to Piazza Venezia, and then to the Campo. I had three hours to walk what would take twenty minutes.

The sun fought for position in the sky. The days had become noticeably longer lately. The temperature was perfect. The sky to my back: lavender; above: azure; ahead: auburn. The gradient was stunning. Leave it to a girl to make such an evening feel *blah*.

I did not mean to say it was Skye's fault that I felt melancholy walking down Via Nazionale under such a brilliant stained-glass ceiling. I also did not mean to say that women were evil or trouble or any other stereotypical comment regarding relationships with the opposite sex. What I meant was: leave it to human nature; leave it to that overpowering connection our emotions make on their own accord, which in one swift blow shatters all sensible reasoning regarding a situation. That was what I meant.

Leave it to a girl to make an entire country feel expired.

Welcome to **Wells Fargo** Online Banking ...

Your statement as of **April 01, 2005** is

Cash Accounts

Account	Account Number	Available Balance
CHECKING	XXX-XXX0385	$87.65
SAVINGS	XXX-XXX6608	$100.02
		Total $187.67

VENTISEI

Language is a funny thing. You don't notice most of its intricacies when everyone around you speaks your mother tongue. But when you hear people casually conversing in a language you know nothing about, it is hard to believe your own language has the ability to sound just as seamless and cryptic to them as theirs does do you.

I remember my first day of Italian lessons in Siena. Our sweet, plump, grandmother-esque Italian *professoressa*, Sandra, jumped straight into all the ordinary orientation formalities—her name, where she was from, an introduction to the city, and the course, an overview of the syllabus—but she did so exclusively in Italian.

Her voice hit my eardrums and registered in my brain just as every voice had before hers, yet I could not for the life of me understand a single thing she was saying. Of course, I was able to pick out the articles—*un, una, il, la*; yes, I ruffled assertively through my stack of handouts and successfully retrieved whichever photocopy she had briefly held up to the class amidst her lecturing, sure my face read great concentration and attentiveness. But I was not following a thing.

It had gotten me thinking. If I would have walked outside and found a young Italian man, around my same age—maybe even of the same disposition, musical preference, dress, etc.—and I had sat down with him over a drink and spoken to him in the exact same way I had spoken to every single person in my entire life up to that point, he would have been unable to understand a single word I was saying to him, much less the concept. And when he would have spoken back to me, my ears would have listened just as they had listened to every single person in my entire life up to that point, yet I would not have been able to understand a single word he was saying to me.

So what is a *word* then? I had taken an introductory phonics course my final semester at UCLA where we learned that words were composed of sounds created with exhalations of air which may or may not vibrate the vocal chords. This is teamed with positions of the tongue within the mouth and various lip contortions.

My ears would have physically *heard* the young Italian's words, but that would not have been enough. I would have derived no meaning from any of his lung-scrunching, tongue-twisting, lip-rounding exposition.

Words appear to be full-bodied objects, spirited and bursting—bursting with imagery and memories and color. Words can cut and heal, soothe and burn. They can be weapons for vengeance or tools for rebuilding. But when one examines them more closely, one can see that words are actually hollow and lifeless, mere placeholders for larger ideas and abstract concepts which exist only in the intangible. Their meanings are volatile and imprecise, and simply a best attempt to articulate into the physical world infinitely more complex thought processes which take place exclusively in our minds.

Take the word *bull*, for example. Say the word out loud once, and tell me what concepts and imagery come to mind.

Bull.

Horns. Rodeos. Cowboys.

Say it again.

Bull.

Spain. Running. Danger.

Now say it out loud twenty-five times in a row.

Bull bull bull bull bull bull bull bull bull bull bull bull bull bull bull bull bull bull bull bull bull bull bull bull bull.

Now what comes to mind? The way the tongue presses against the pallet of the mouth. The strange gargled *lul* sound composing the second half of the word. It does not even sound like a real word anymore. How is it possible that such a vocalization—a string of four symbols on a page—could have trapped such concepts as *danger* or such imagery as *Spain*? There had been nothing at the word's core—nothing inside of it once it had been broken down. The word had simply been a placeholder for whatever we had elected to fill it with based on our experiences.

I had thought the word *Rome* was fixed. I had thought it was unwavering and perpetual. I had seen it written a thousand times before I had landed at Fiumicino International Airport in October of two thousand and four.

Rome.

Vespas. Cobblestone. Pizza.
Rome.
Italian. Foreign.
Rome
Halfway around the world.
But now *Rome* had changed. It had been gutted and restocked.
Rome.
Metro. Seven Eleven. The pyramid.
Rome.
The 23 bus line. The carnival. Cocaine.
Rome rome rome rome rome rome rome rome rome rome rome rome rome rome rome rome rome rome rome rome rome rome rome rome.
Nina, Ayden, Aleksia, Mariano, Roberto, Isabella, Carmen, Vittoria, Morgan.
Rome rome rome rome rome.
Hassan, Dario, New Year's Eve.
Rome.
Skye.
Rome.
Bliss.
Rome.
Rejection.
Rome.
Confusion.
Rome.
Alive.
My mobile phone rang.
>*Caller ID Unavailable.*
I pulled the phone from the windowsill, cleared my throat, and answered.
"Pronto."
"Mike."
I was unable recognize the voice.
"Pronto?" I repeated.
"Mike, it's Leighton."
"Oh—Leighton, you didn't sound like you."
"Well, it's me!"
"What time is it over there? It's like lunch time, isn't it?"

"Yeah and I'm taking the rest of the day off. My friend Randi and I are going to have a picnic in Central Park. And then we are going to check out this open-air art exhibition in the Village."

"That sound's great."

"It should be. How are things in Rome? It seemed like you stopped replying to my e-mails."

I paused. "Things are all right."

Leighton hesitated a moment. "Mike, what's going on? You sound, like, deflated."

"No, it's just that I've just been lying on my bed and thinking about stuff or—whatever." I pulled myself upright on my mattress. "So, things are going well in New York, then?"

"They're really good and really bad. And then really good again. It's still cramped and loud and dirty, but I'm starting to feel more comfortable with feeling uncomfortable—if that makes any sense—and that's become an exhilarating feeling."

"Sure it makes sense."

"I feel like this is where I want to be right now. And where I should be."

"And work?"

"Oh, work is work. You know, *work*."

"I'm glad you're feeling better. I'm happy for you."

"Yeah, I'm happy for me too. Listen, this is probably costing me a fortune without a phone card, but I just wanted to call and say hi. It seemed like I hadn't heard a word from you in so long."

"Thanks for calling, really. I'll e-mail you soon, I promise."

"Okay, bye Mike!"

I placed the phone back onto the end table. Good for Leighton. I was happy she was working things out for herself.

My phone began to ring again. I looked at the display.

>*Caller ID Unavailable.*

I pressed the small black button corresponding with *accept call*, switched hands, and placed the mobile to my opposite ear.

"Leighton?"

There was a pause.

"Excuse me?" a foreign voice replied.

"Err ... sorry, who is this?"

"Is this Mister Gyulai?"

Strange.

"Yes."

"Hi, this is Amanda calling from STA Travel to confirm your flight from Rome's Fiumicino airport to San Francisco International next Friday, April fifteenth."

Amanda had caught me off-guard. I felt I needed more time to respond to her request for confirmation. Actually, that was not true; I felt like I *should* have needed more time to respond to Amanda's request for confirmation. But I guess I did not. What was there to factor? I was in a country illegally and was out of money. It was that simple.

"Mister Gyulai, are you there?"

It just felt so rushed there in real time, ten seconds into an international phone call.

"Mister Gyulai, I—"

"Yes, yes I'm here. I'm sorry. Yes, you can confirm my ticket."

"Great. Have a safe flight back to California."

"Thank you."

I placed the phone on my small bedside table and slid down to the wrinkled white sheets. I would have to inform the landlord, Giulia. But that could wait until tomorrow. And I was sure no critical arrangements would need to be made at Metro due to my absence. I rested my hands quietly atop my abdomen and breathed deeply through my nose.

California.

Beaches. Palm Trees. Los Angeles. San Francisco.

California.

Dad ... Mom.

California.

Halfway around the world.

VENTISETTE

The night sky of Rome is something one rarely notices, with all the earthly visual distractions which compose the city constantly stealing one's attention. I was seated, staring skyward, examining the blackness above to see if I had been missing anything after all these months. The star count was decent, better than Los Angeles, but nowhere near the speckled black canvas stretched tight over places like the Hawaiian Islands.

My vision fell forward. My eyes met Neptune's.

Thunderous water cascaded over the jagged marble at his feet and spilled into the shallow illuminated pool of the Trevi Fountain.

The small piazza was vacant as the hour closed in on three in the morning. The next forty-eight hours would be my last in the city. I was sure I would be back to visit, to walk through my old neighborhood of Piramide, to swing by the Campo. But in regards to living, integrating into the city, watching from the other side of the glass, this would be it.

A light drizzle cast a hazy mist into the air; it polished the smooth marble surrounding the fountain. I sat silently on the wide stairway descending to the Trevi's base, dead center across from Neptune, my hands pushed deep into my coat pockets, my closed umbrella resting at my side. The streetlamps emitted a faint yellow hue which mixed with the stale blue of the night to paint a dull two-tone, coloring all immediate surroundings.

You lied to me.

The light sprinkling dampened my face.

Michael, I did no such thing.

My eyes held locked with the god of the sea.

You owed me love.

I owed you no such thing.

I refused to blink. Moisture collected on my eyebrows and lashes.

One coin to return to Rome. Two coins to fall in love. You owed me love.
I did owe you to fall in love. That much is true.
Love, to fall in love—what is the difference? And I achieved neither.
That is not true, Michael.
It is true. Try to explain to me how that is not true.
You did fall in love, did you not?
Of course I did not. To fall in love requires two people and it requires emotional reciprocation.
For one person to fall in love does require two people. But emotional reciprocation is unnecessary.

My fists tightened in my coat pockets.

Your argument holds no logic.
Were you in love with Charlotte?
Of course I was. And that was years ago.
And was she in love with you?
Yes she was in love with me. We fell in love with each other. The emotions were reciprocal. That is what romantic love is.
And tell me: at the end of your relationship, were you still in love with her?
Of course I was still in love with her.
And, at that point, was she still in love with you?
…
Were the emotions reciprocal then?
I looked away … I shook my head. Then I turned back.
That was different. That was the closure of a relationship. We had already fallen in love together.
Answer my question. In those final months of your relationship with Charlotte, were you in love with her?
Yes.
And was she in love with you?
…

I looked away again.

Now tell me, does falling in love imply reciprocity?
…
So tell me, Michael, did you indeed fall in love here in Rome?

I faced Neptune a final time. I leaned forward and pulled my upper body towards him.

You are deceiving.
Michael, I gave you what I promised.

VENTOTTO

"So you just fucking moved here to bartend without knowing anyone?" Tomaso was sitting on three stacked boxes of Jack Daniel's whiskey at the back of Metro's underground stockroom. A glowing cigarette was dangling from his lips, streaming a thin line of smoke into the air.

"Not to be a bartender, really. I just wanted to live in Rome."

"And you just fucking moved over here by yourself?"

"Yeah, pretty much."

"That's fucking insane, man."

Tomaso had begun working at Metro the previous weekend as Roberto's replacement. He had been to both the States and London many times and his English was nearly perfect.

It was Thursday, around two thirty in the morning, and I was helping Tomaso collect bottles to restock the refrigerators and backbar upstairs before we left. My flight to California was in six hours and I had spoken with Dario earlier in the week to tell him that this would be my final night working at the bar.

"How much do they pay you here?" Tomaso asked.

"Twenty a night."

"Twenty fucking Euros a night!"

"I come in at ten, though."

"That's fucked-up man! I can't believe they only pay you twenty fucking Euros."

Tomaso took a drag off his cigarette. He exhaled slowly, as his head dropped back to the notepad in his hand.

"Two bottles of Havana Seven and one Baileys," he read.

I turned to the wall of liquor at my shoulder and pulled the requested bottles from the shelves. I placed them into the large cardboard box we had filled with the other various beers and liquors which had run out during the night.

"Is that everything?" I asked.

"Yeah, that's everything."

Tomaso rose to his feet and flicked his cigarette to the tiled floor. He looked at me as I hoisted the clunky box of bottles to my waist.

"Do you know how much fucking money you can make bartending in the States?"

"Way more than you can make here."

"Hell, yeah, you can. Jesus."

We both climbed the stairs to the main floor and I passed the box over the bar to Mariano. Dario, standing at the front doors, motioned for me to join him. I stepped away from Tomaso and Mariano, leaving them to organize the bottles.

Dario extended his hand to me as I approached. "Here is your twenty for tonight."

The single blue twenty-Euro bill, folded once in on itself, passed from Dario's fingers to mine.

"Thank you."

He nodded his head in acknowledgment. I went to step away but he continued. "Have you enjoyed your time in Rome?"

"Yeah." I stopped. "I have. It was a pleasure to work with everyone here."

"Good." He paused briefly and looked off toward the wall. He put his hands into the pockets of his slacks and continued.

"I talked with Hassan, and we both think you are a good worker—a hard worker. If you'd like—if it's still a possibility—we can take a look at the schedule and try to add you as one of the waiters on the floor working full-time."

Huh.

That had been unexpected.

"I know money was an issue with you staying and we like the work you do and we could see if we could work something out."

"I'm very grateful to you both but ... my flight is tomorrow, and I've already packed up all my things at my apartment and—"

"You're flying out tomorrow?"

"Yeah, well, today if you count today as Friday."

"I hadn't realized it was that soon."

We both stood in silence for a moment.

"Well, I figured I would offer."

"Thank you, really."

Isabella, Carmen, and Vittoria pushed through the glass doors at our side and out into the piazza. Excited Italian streamed from their lips. I heard Tomaso and Mariano following closely behind, and I turned back to them. Mariano had my tote bag in his left hand and shoved it into my chest as he passed me.

"Let's go, motherfucker!"

I turned back to Dario and shook his hand. He gave a final farewell.

"Have a safe flight, then."

"Thanks."

I pulled my coat from my bag and took off after the five Romans walking feverishly out of the Campo.

"Where are you guys going?" I called as I caught up to them from behind.

"We are going to have a drink for your last night with us," Mariano answered.

"You guys don't have to—"

"Shhh-shh-shh!" Isabella cut me off.

"I'm taking the girls with me," Tomaso said. "We'll meet you there." They then turned down a nondescript side street.

Mariano and I continued our normal route to his car.

"Where are we going?" I asked him.

"To Seven Eleven, if it is all right."

"Sure, of course that's all right."

"We wished to take you to someplace of nice, but I think it is the best place open still at this hour."

"No, no. That sounds great. But you guys don't all have to come for me. I—"

"You are our friend, man. We want to go out with you."

The walk was silent as we turned down Via Arenula toward the Ponte Garibaldi. We paused at the stoplight along Lungotevere. It turned green, and we stepped off the curb to begin our walk across the bridge.

"Are you sad to leave Rome?"

"I'm not really sure. I'm sad to be leaving you guys." I was in a way. But exactly how sad—melancholy, upset, devastated—I was unable to gauge.

Mariano smiled. I continued. "Rome is just—it's weird for me right now. I'm not sure ..." I trailed off.

"We all like you very much also."

We reached Mariano's car and silently climbed inside. He apologized for the stack of textbooks on the passenger seat and tossed them into the back of the small vehicle. Then he started the car and pulled out onto Lungotevere.

The radio was off and the wind whooshed over the front windshield and along the rubber seals of the car doors. The engine hummed and pitched up or down with each gear shift.

"I am going to miss to work with you. Really," Mariano said, breaking the silence for a moment.

I laughed.

"No, truly. It is hard to find workers like you in the Italy. It is always a pleasure to work with you."

"Well, thank you, Mariano."

There was silence in the car again. I debated reciprocating the praise, but it would have sounded too scripted and insincere if I were to play a tit-for-tat game of complements. The engine hummed. The wind whooshed.

"But I think it may be right for you to go back in California."

"Why do you think that?" Why would he say that? Did he not want me here with him? With Isabella and Carmen and Vittoria? Why would he think something like that? I thought he had said we were all friends.

He took in a long breath and looked over at me. I could see his mind was buffering the English required for his response. I locked eyes with him for a second and then turned my vision back to the road.

"Red light, Mariano! Red light! Rosso!"

His vision shot forward as he slammed on the brakes, but we had already passed into the intersection. The streets were vacant of traffic and he crouched over the steering wheel and peered up through the fractured windshield just in time to verify that the traffic light we were speeding under was indeed *rosso*.

We both could not help but laugh.

"Some things never change, Mariano."

I was shaking my head and grinning as he began speaking again. "Roberto, for example. I like Roberto very much, and I think he is a good person, but the brain of Roberto is made for the work as a bartender."

"Okay."

"But I think that your brain ... I think you have ..."

I watched Mariano's profile as he now watched the road. His mouth was open, waiting for the right words to emerge. His left hand guided the steering wheel; the fingers of his right formed a claw which slowly rotated as he tried to manifest the concept in English. Then he looked over to me, just long enough to make his statement. "I think you have a beautiful mind."

I was unsure whether it was the fact that in Italian the word *bello*—directly translated in English as *beautiful*—meant everything ranging from *nice* to *pleasant* to *attractive* to *exquisite*, or whether perhaps Universal Picture's 2001 internationally recognized blockbuster *A Beautiful Mind* had influenced that particular choice of wording, but Mariano's comment had been undeniably flattering.

"Truly," he told me, "have you thought about doing something similar to psychology?"

"I actually have thought about it, yeah. Many of the classes I took at UCLA were psychology classes."

"You have qualities that a lot of persons don't have. For example, you know when to listen and when to talk. I do not have that. I just always want to talk."

"I thought you said I didn't speak up enough."

"Ehh," he thought for a moment. "Sometimes for yourself you do not say enough, but you know how to say things to others. Like what you told me of the coat and the weed. The way you said was very ..." he looked to me, "sensato?"

"Sensible?" I guessed.

"Maybe, I don't know. But I enjoy very much to talk to you about many things."

"So you think I should be a psychologist?"

Mariano smiled and turned to me for a moment. "Yes, you have the face of a doctor."

I laughed. "What does that mean?"

"A face to trust."

We both chuckled and looked forward again, watching the city's sleeping buildings pass by through his cracked front windshield.

"Why did you not go out with Morgan?"

"Mariano, please."

"No, not to fuck her. Just to go out."

I thought for a moment. It seemed obvious.

"She is a student and is American. I'm not here for that."

"But you are an American. And you studied in Italy before. It means you both like Italy and both like to travel outside of the America. I think you are very similar to each other."

I reviewed his points. They were valid.

"I guess it doesn't matter now," he said.

"Exactly, it doesn't," I replied thankfully.

There was a moment's pause.

"I have to tell you somefing," Mariano then began. "I told Isabella and Vittoria about what I made you to do the other night."

He glanced at me. I was unsure where he was going with this.

"For the twenty Euro," he continued.

"Mariano, listen I—"

"And they got very angry with me and—"

"Mariano I wouldn't have—"

"And they were right!" He raised his voice for just a second. Then, reading my accepting silence, he continued in the calm tone of the previous statements.

"I should not have made you to do that. It was wrong."

"Mariano, you didn't make me do anything. If I really didn't want to do it I would not have."

He looked unsatisfied.

"I feel," he thought for a moment as he guided the vehicle. "I feel like you are one of the only persons who I can trust." He glanced at me again, then back to the road. "But I should not use your trust in this way. I will not to do it again. I mean, I know you are leaving, but if there was a—"

"No, I understand," I cut him off. "But don't worry about what I choose to do. I am a big boy, Mariano."

He nodded.

We turned onto the Ponte Vittorio Emanuele II. I stared out my window as the large marble statues lining the bridge passed to my right. Manicured stone swirled around the angels' feet and wings, exaggerating further their animated stances.

I looked left to Saint Peter's Cathedral, illuminated in all its historical and architectural greatness as it moved into, and then quickly out of, Mariano's driver's-side window.

"I feel bad. You will go back in California as an attic."

"A what?" I asked.

"A drug attic."

"Oh, an addic*t*." I bore my teeth and emphasized the final *t*.

"Attic*t*," Mariano repeated.

"What are you even talking about? First, we have only taken drugs a couple times. And second, I had already smoked weed before I came here."

His eyes connected with mine. "And the white stuff?"

I rolled my eyes to the roof. He faced the road again.

"I'm not addicted to anything, Mariano."

"You should not to do that stuff. I know I did it too, but I have seen in my books what it does to your brain. It is bad for your 'ealth."

"I know it's bad for your *h*ealth, but I did it *one* time."

"Okay, okay. One time every six or eight months for somefing special is okay, but it is very bad if you take it more. I was attict to it in the past."

"You were addicted to it?"

"Yes, I took it too much. But now only once or two times a year. And never, never take some pills. Have you sawn what the pills do to your brain?"

"No."

"I have studied the pictures of the brain in my books for the university. You have the brain that works three hundred percent to that normal. It is not safe."

"Okay."

"Promise to me you will never to take them."

I laughed.

Mariano turned the car sharply into the narrow alley which housed Seven Eleven and pulled alongside the curb between a set of motorinos. He cut the engine and looked at me with genuine concern.

"The pills can to hurt your art—your creation. They can to hurt your beautiful mind. Promise to me."

My smile faded as my face matched his sincerity. "I promise."

"Okay." He held his stare. "Now get out of my car, motherfucker."

We climbed from the vehicle's small white doors and walked across the alley to the entrance of Seven Eleven. The female bartender stood just inside the entryway smoking a cigarette. She exchanged ciaos with Mariano as he entered and smiled at me as I passed.

We descended into the bar's cavernous main room and found Isabella, Carmen, Vittoria, and Tomaso at a mahogany table towards the back. The crowd was sparse—two couples nursing cocktails at separate tables and a pair of strangers occupying two of the seven barstools.

We crossed the room and I went to slip into the booth seating next to Vittoria. As soon as I hit the seat to slide up next to her, she began to pout. "Oh, Mikey, I will miss you a lot."

My eyes met Carmen's. She was smiling at me, a phrase on the tip of her tongue. "You will lack me very, very much."

I laughed. "Mi mancherai anche tu," I told her. I looked across the table. "Tutti voi mi mancherete." *I'll miss you, too. I'll miss all of you.*

Tomaso spoke from across the table. "Why don't you take that job Dario talked to you about?"

"You heard that?"

Vittoria spoke before Tomaso could reply. "Come to work with us at the tables!"

I had started shaking my head at the first word of Vittoria's request. "Guys, my flight is tomorrow—it's *today*. And I will have no apartment. I already told the lady I am leaving. I told her last week and she has someone new for my room."

Isabella jumped in. "Roberto is looking for a new apartment. You ... you could live together."

"You think Roberto would want to live with me?"

Isabella's eyes grew large as if the answer were an obvious one. "I fink that ... that ... that ... *uh* everyone wants to live with you because you are so clean and so ... so ... *uh* ... nice and ... and ... and *tranquillo*."

Huh.

It was an impossible idea at this point. Fortunately, the waitress appeared at the head of our table, distracting the group by asking for our orders. We recited a variety of simple mixed cocktails—two rum and cokes, a vodka tonic, two gin lemons, a vodka orange—and the waitress, who was apparently also the bartender, returned to her position across the room and behind the counter to fix our drinks.

Tomaso started again. "It is too bad, man, because you would be a fucking good bartender."

"How can you even know that? We worked two nights together!" I refuted.

"I can see it. You are a good worker. You are comfortable with the bottles. You are precise."

"I don't know," I resisted.

"You know I teach a bartending course? I could get you a discount probably. I might even be able to teach your class."

Bartending school in Rome ... no, it would have been impossible. There was no way. I shook my head and fell back to my previous argument.

"We weren't even that busy tonight, Tomaso. You work with me two times and you think I am something special."

Mariano spoke at my shoulder. "Mike, everyone that they work with you says the same. Everyone."

Huh.

I kept shaking my head. My face still displayed skepticism, but as my eyes panned the faces of my Italian coworkers sitting there at the table beside me, my doubt was contested by head nods endorsing Mariano's remark.

The waitress-slash-bartender-slash-doorperson appeared with our drinks. We all reached for our wallets, but as I pulled my single folded twenty-Euro bill from my pocket both Isabella and Vittoria let out a frantic chain of *no*s and pushed my hand back under the table. I thanked them as they paid, and we all took our glasses from the wooden tabletop and raised them to the air. We held them there for a moment, arms extended toward the rafters, our glasses forming an arching array of colored liquids. Vittoria called out skyward, "To our dear friend, Michael!"

"To Mikey!" Isabella announced.

"To Mike!" Mariano and Tomaso overlapped.

We drew the glasses down to our lips and pulled from their rims. We placed them back on the table. Vittoria threw her arms around my neck. "I will miss you!"

Mariano waved his hand through the hair of the back of my head.

"We will all miss you."

Maybe I had not been paying enough attention. Maybe I had gotten distracted. Maybe after all the self-loathing, after I had so assuredly brushed the tortured self-portrait of the foreigner who no one cared about—that no one would invest in—maybe I had been wrong.

Maybe it was true that after six months of living in Italy I was not yet on anyone's fictional wedding invitation list. Maybe I was not having philosophical conversations in Italian at cafés at the foot of the Pantheon come the weekend. But maybe, when everything was said and done, and everything taken into account, maybe these relationships were real. Maybe these interactions did carry a mutual value. Maybe, just maybe, these people actually did give a shit.

Huh.

VENTINOVE

At 6:35 AM my alarm went off. I opened my eyes, my head lay motionless. I could hear Ayden rummaging around the kitchen. The dark room came slowly into focus, my life once again packed into three suitcases and a guitar case grouped in the center of the blank bedroom.

I had made it back from Seven Eleven around four. I must have slept no more than two hours.

Ayden knocked lightly on my door, and I sat up on my mattress while rubbing my eyes and calling for him to enter. He opened the door halfway and spoke in a loud whisper from the doorway.

"Good morning, Michael. Would you like a cup of tea before we go?"

He had offered to help carry my luggage the short trip to the Stazione Ostiense at the end of the street.

"Oh, no. Thank you, though." My voice was deep and raspy. "I actually have to go over to Giulia's right now to get my deposit back. I told her I would be there at six thirty."

"Why don't I meet you at her building with your bags in ten minutes?"

I reached through the darkness for my shoes and slid them over my feet, still wearing the socks from the night before.

"Are you sure you can carry all four bags over there?" I asked him.

"I think I can make it across the street. It is you that has to travel with them all the way to California!"

He laughed, and I smiled and nodded. Ayden then returned to the kitchen, leaving my door half-open.

I gathered myself and stood. I had slept in the same jeans and long-sleeved shirt I had worn out the night before, an outfit I also planned to wear to the airport to avoid any need to open a suitcase zipper the morning of departure.

In the darkness, I stretched my arms to the ceiling, rose on my toes, then relaxed my body and moved across the room.

I pulled my wallet and phone from the empty desk, picked my long black coat from its unpacked position atop my luggage, slid my arms into its sleeves, and hoisted it to my shoulders. Just outside my doorway the apartment's single active light threw Ayden's shadow starkly from the kitchen across the entryway floor. I stepped through it and out the front door.

Outside, the cool morning air rushed over my cheeks, ears, and nose. The crispness tingled in my throat and sinuses. Scattered gravel thrown from various potholes crunched below my sneakers as I moved through the apartment parking space toward Giulia's building. A motorino was kick-started somewhere nearby; the proceeding revving of the engine echoing off the walls of the complexes.

A young businesswoman holding a briefcase and motorcycle helmet exited Giulia's building, allowing me to catch the door, and I climbed the stairs to the first level. As I approached her door I could hear the clanging of silverware and sputtering of a frying pan. I knocked lightly, and quick footsteps heralded her welcome. "Michael! Hello! Come in, come in."

I entered the apartment and moved with her to the kitchen.

"I'm just making some breakfast. I have to run to Trastevere at seven."

I searched for a light topic of conversation but my short-lived concentration led me to nothing. I reached into my jeans pocket.

"I have the keys to the apartment here." I placed them on the kitchen table in front of me.

"Great. I have your deposit in my room. Just one second." She cut the burner and moved a pan of three over-easy eggs to the opposite side of the stovetop. She then disappeared down the hallway.

I took a look around the kitchen: pots, ladles, a spatula, a calendar of London, three pastel coffee mugs flipped upside down and drying next to the sink.

I rubbed my eyes. Maybe it would have been wiser to have slept more. I had hoped I would be able to sleep on the plane. Giulia skipped back into the kitchen with a white envelope. She handed it to me.

"It should all be in there, but count it to be sure."

I opened the unsealed flap and spread the numerous fifty-Euro bills across the amber tabletop at my waist. I then picked them up one at a time, adding their denominations.

Fifty. One hundred. One fifty. Two hundred. Two fifty. Three hundred.

I took the six accumulated bills between my hands and tapped them into alignment on the table.

Three fifty. Four hundred. Four fifty. Five hundred. Five fifty.

"All here."

Giulia was watching me as she forked her eggs from a small plastic bowl. "So what will you do when you get back to California?" she asked.

I placed the money back into the white envelope and folded it once in on itself. "I'm not really sure, actually."

Giulia looked at me, took two more chews of the egg in her mouth, then swallowed. "If you ever are back in Rome for a vacation or anything you can always stay with us."

A vacation in Rome. The concept seemed strange, somehow abnormal. Vacationing in a city where you knew the bus routes and supermarket locations.

"Thanks. I think Ayden is downstairs with my stuff, so I better get going. But thanks for everything. I had a really nice time here."

"We enjoyed having you as well. Good luck in California!"

"Thanks."

Giulia led us out of the kitchen, bowl in hand, and opened the door for me as I left. I descended the single flight of steps, bouncing down two at a time, and met Ayden just outside the front entrance. He was waiting patiently beside my bags, blue ski jacket zipped to his chin, a light mist coming off his breath.

"All set, Michael?"

"All set."

I crouched at my green JanSport backpack for a second, unzipped the side pouch, and slid the envelope from Giulia inside. I closed the pocket, lifted it to my back, and picked up my guitar case.

Ayden took my black duffle bag over his shoulder and extended the guiding arm of my rolling suitcase. We then set out in the direction of the Stazione Ostiense.

A thin layer of grey cloud cover neutralized the sky. A 716 bus rumbled down the street in the opposite direction followed by two small cars and a motor scooter—the first commuters passing us as Rome geared up for another day.

The five-minute walk to the station was mostly silent. Ayden too asked me what my plans were for California. *To use my degree* was the best I could come up with. Maybe something back in Los Angeles. Los Angeles was nice.

We quickly reached the end of Via Matteucci, descended a single escalator, and entered the station's underground lobby. Inside, a set of television displays listed departure times and track numbers. We found our way to track thirteen and climbed the steps to the outdoor platform.

Ayden propped my suitcase upright and gently dropped my black bag to the ground. We shared the platform with two dozen others—Italians commuting to work or to the airport as well. I checked my phone for the time. The train would be arriving at any minute.

"You know, Michael, the apartment is going to be very different without you in it."

I looked up at Ayden. "I feel like I barely see any of you these days. I figured you wouldn't notice much."

He laughed. "No, no. From the very first days I knew you, you were the one most excited about this place—about this city. Me and Nina and Aleksia, we would laugh about your enthusiasm for it."

"I still really like it. I do." I thought I did. "But California is a great place as well."

"I know. It is just that we all thought you would be here longer than any of us. We were sure of it."

I had been sure of it, too.

A blaring monotone from a horn diverted our attention. We looked up the railway to see the approaching cream and turquoise Trenitalia rumbling toward us along the final curved stretch of tracks before the straightaway lining the platform. Our eyes remained fixed as we watched it overtake us, hissing and rumbling and squealing past as it decelerated. Ayden turned to me a final time.

"Well, Michael, know that you will be missed."

The doors of the now-stationary train rattled open beside us. I gathered my luggage, gave an appreciative nod to Ayden, then turned and stepped on board. Almost immediately the doors slid shut and the train began moving again.

I inched sideways down the car's narrow isle, muscling my bulky baggage past the mostly vacant seating. A few rows in I found two open pairs of seats facing each other and dropped myself and my four bags across them. I sank into the cushioned seat and stared out the window as the train accelerated over Via Ostiense. I could see various taxis speeding down the center lanes; scooters and small colorful cars dotted the outer ones. In the distance a 23 line bus was disappearing toward the pyramid.

I felt empty, neutral, detached from everything—as if all the extreme emotional highs and lows of the previous months had finally collided and exploded to dust.

I sat there, staring out the window as the train reached full speed. Within five minutes I was watching ever more sparse neighborhoods pass by through the glass. I felt no eagerness to arrive at Fiumicino International. I would have been content to simply sit there forever, comfortably slouched deep into the blue and green cushioning, watching the world pan left to right in front of me.

I had landed at the very airport I was heading toward just six months ago with so much fire and drive, ambition, and determination. I would have done anything to stay, to make local friends, to be given even the smallest seed of opportunity to work and earn Euro. Yet, I slumped in my seat, indifferently speeding away from a full-time job offer backed by a supportive group of locals. I was content just watching it all pan by, left to right.

My mobile phone rang.

>+*19255551282*. Home

I answered.

"Hello?"

"Hey Mike, it's Dad."

"You guys just getting ready for bed over there?"

"Yeah, but I wanted to check your arrival time for tomorrow."

"I'm getting in at 3:55 PM, I think. It's British Airways flight BA117."

"That's what I have down here. So we will meet you right outside the baggage claim, then. We will probably be there at quarter to four and just hang out."

"You and Mom?"

"Yeah, she is going to take a half day from work and come out with me."

"Good."

"You know ..." There was a pause on the other line. Dad held a slight hum, letting me know he was about to finish this thought but he had to check something first. I heard a door creak shut on the other line. "... I didn't mean to leave you hanging with all that stuff about Mom and me when you were leaving."

"It's fine."

"I know I sort of brought up a bunch of things and then left you in the dark there for a while and—"

"It's fine. Really, I can imagine there was a lot to work out."

"Anyway, we are okay. We are really good, in fact. We've been going into the city a lot to see the foreign films that are playing at the independent theaters. You know, the Italian Film Festival is coming up next month—you should come with us."

"That would be fun."

"There is supposed to be some four-part series by this director named Marco Giordana. Have you heard of him?"

"I haven't, no."

"The movie is something like four hours long because—"

"Can you tell me—err, sorry."

My interruption had been uncharacteristic and I dropped my question. But I had not registered the last thing Dad had said. I asked him to continue. "What film is this?"

"No, go ahead. Can I tell you what?"

I paused for a moment. "What was it? What did you do? What did Mom need from you?"

I heard Dad take an extended breath on the other line. "It was nothing she needed from me. I think ... I think she just needed what everyone seems to need when they feel lost."

"Which is?"

"Time."

I stared out my window. In the foreground a wooden fence ran along the railway, its horizontal crossbeams blurring into fluttering streaks of brown as we sped onward. Just past the fence and extending to the horizon was a field of head-high grass, a brown dirt road splitting the ocean of green every few seconds. The sky remained pale, grey, neutral.

"Anyway, we can talk about the film when you get in. I just wanted to make sure I had the right stuff written down. We love you, and we'll see you tomorrow."

"Today you mean—no, tomorrow for you is right."

Dad laughed. "See you in eighteen hours!" he said.

"There we go. Eighteen hours it is."

I pulled the phone from my ear and watched the display as the line disconnected. I slid it back into my pocket and faced the window again.

Why did Skye have to quit? Why Roberto too? Why was Nina leaving? Why were people not happy where they were? It was an ironic thought, for it was that exact freedom of movement—that ability to create prospect and chase opportunity—which I had preached as being the greatest benefit of finishing academia. I had up and left California. I had up and left the entire United States. And now it seemed I expected all the benefits of this freedom of movement for myself, yet demanded everyone else remain locked in place, static, convenient constants in the formula I was attempting to develop and live by. Personal freedom had been my most celebrated argument, and now I was trying to nail down everyone in my immediate world.

Outside the window the wooden fencing changed to metal. Soon concrete and parked cars replaced the fields of green. The train began a subtle, angled arch as the parking structures of the Fiumicino Airport came into view.

The tracks leveled again, straightening into the final stretch as the train decelerated and the passengers around me began to stand and pull luggage from the overhead compartments. I gathered my own things from the seats and slowly made my way off the train.

I followed the signs to concourse C and stepped onto one of two moving walkways leading down a short corridor. I flexed my shoulders to fight the weight of my backpack. My right hand guided my rolling suitcase, the left tightly squeezed the handle of my overweight guitar case. I had slung my black bag across my neck and the strap pulled at my collar.

At the end of the corridor I stepped off the walkway and a set of sliding doors split open in front of me. I pushed forward to the British Airways desk, wound my way through a miniature labyrinth of guiding ropes, queued behind three other travelers, and dropped my guitar case and work bag to the floor. Almost immediately two of the three passengers were called to check-in stations and I kicked my luggage forward with my feet.

I felt so melancholy lately, so critical and cautious. Could it have been an effect of the world I had been living in? And which world was that? The world of living in the darkness of night? The *nightlife*? Or the world of the Italian economy? Maybe the world of an immigrant? Could it simply have been the effect of the post-academic world—that elusive *real* world? And regardless of which world these influences were originating from, were they having a permanent effect, or was this a phase? How do you know when you are not being yourself, and how do you know when you are changing as a person?

A family joined the line behind me. One of the attendants shouted from the desk ahead. "Will the next two passengers please come forward to stations four and seven!"

I pulled my things from the floor and shuffled to station four. I dropped my guitar case and rolling suitcase onto the large metal scale. I pulled my bag off my neck and placed it behind the two others.

"Checking three bags today, sir?"

"Yes, those three there. My backpack I'll keep with me."

"All right. May I see your passport?"

I unzipped my Travel Safe pouch, extracted my passport, and handed it to the attendant. She hit a few keys at her computer and then reached to the printer under her desk. "You will be leaving from gate 22C. There will be no need to check in again at the departure gate; however if you need assistance boarding or have a special request for your in-flight meal there will be British Airways attendants available to help you."

She slid the boarding pass along with my passport across the counter. I slipped my ticket into my pant pocket and slid my passport back into my waist pouch.

"Have a safe flight home."

I moved back to the main lobby and followed the signs to the security screening. At the foot of the metal detectors and X-ray machines, I emptied a half dozen Euro coins from my pockets and placed them into a small, grey plastic bin along with my phone. I pulled my belt from my pant loops and kicked off my shoes.

I placed the bin, my backpack, shoes, and belt onto the conveyer belt and looked to the official just past the detector. He waved me through and I collected my things on the other side.

The waiting area at the gate was expansive. A couple hundred people lingered around the boarding entrance. Some stood, others sat in one of the various padded blue seats arranged in symmetrical groups and fixed into the thin grey carpeting.

I dropped my backpack to the ground and sat in one of the seats myself, two seats to the left of a mother gently rocking a baby stroller and one seat to the right of a large man reading a newspaper.

I scanned the faces of the other passengers across from me. Some were obviously American, others obviously Italian. The majority were hard to decipher.

A young couple stood together toward the front, her back pressed against his chest, his arms around her waist and locked at her stomach. Her neck stretched upwards as her lips met his.

Why did I have to meet her? Why here and why now? What would it have been like had we not met? How would I have been feeling then?

It was impossible to know. What had happened was irreversible. She was a dark-red sock thrown into a wash of bright white. She had colored everything. For better or for worse, there were tints of her everywhere.

I thought of where Skye would be at that moment. She would have most likely been quietly asleep in her small single bedroom near Piazza Santa Maria

Maggiore. I imagined her face was peaceful, her body at rest below two layers of covers pulled to her chin.

It had not been fair of me to place such weight on her. It had not been fair to her; it had not been fair to me; it had not been fair to Rome. But did acknowledgement of that fact make how I was feeling any less real? Could I deny my emotions because I could find fault in their place of origin? Could one disprove an emotion or find truth in an intuition, or did absolute truth or fallacy require tangibility? Could one use reason to derive happiness? Could one, at the very least, use reason to neutralize sorrow?

A British Airways attendant moved from the large check-in desk to the adjacent podium and retracted the black rope which blocked the jetty leading to the aircraft. He began organizing a set of papers, while another attendant, standing behind the check-in desk, reached for the intercom. She pulled it to her lips and the depression of her index finger was met with a short static crackling from the speakers above us.

I was suddenly aware of my heart beating. It echoed inside of me and sounded as if it were underwater. My breathing was regular, but I found myself conscious of each inhalation and exhalation.

If I had chosen to, could I have still walked away from that flight? What would I have told them? What would have been my excuse? And what would I have been walking away from in California? What would I have been walking to in Rome?

Then the attendant behind the podium called across to the check-in desk, shrugging his shoulders and waving the short stack of papers in his right hand. The attendant at the desk released the intercom, fixed it back onto the wall behind her, and began sorting through paperwork of her own.

I took a long, calming breath and stared back into the waiting area. In the distance, in the first row of seating at the gate across from ours, I saw someone. He looked slightly younger than I was and was dressed in a navy blue UCLA sweatshirt and baggy Gap jeans. His headphones were glued to his ears as he skimmed an Italian-English dictionary.

I was seeing myself, age twenty, *Back to the Future* vision. I had just finished my short four-month semester in Siena which had culminated with a final week spent in Rome.

He put the dictionary down on the seat next to him and raised his boarding pass from his lap. He gazed steadily at it for the next sixty seconds. I knew he was reading only one word. *Rome.*

And I knew he was thinking only one thing. *One day...*

How could I have explained things to him? How could I have told him what I was doing at the very same airport these two years later? Yes, my Italian was slowly improving. Yes, I had made Italian friends. Yes, I had found a job. And yes, I was leaving it all.

I continued to watch him. He slid the boarding pass between the pages of his dictionary and began to drum on his thighs and nod his head as the faint sound of electric guitars escaped from his headphones. A smile broke across his face and he seemed to giggle ecstatically at the ceiling.

One day...

He would not have been able to understand—to grasp the reality of the situation. He was still in the middle of university; he was nowhere near the actual process of independently throwing himself over here. He had no idea what it would be like. He thought he did, but he did not.

He had not witnessed the invading carnival. He had not spent nights sitting mute among friends and understanding nothing of what they were saying. He had not found himself voiceless when yearning to give gratitude or support—to console or to impress. He knew nothing of the drugs and the darkness. He had not yet met *her*.

But as I watched him, I understood that even if I had explained things to him, even if I had sat him down and given him the truth and told him the why, he would not have cared. He would have been unyielding; he would have held firm. He would have told me that I could do whatever I felt like, and that I could leave if I wanted to, but that he would not. Because he knew whatever was going to happen to him—good or bad, kind or cruel, blissful or disastrous—it was going to be an adventure. An adventure so brilliant and so unforgettable it could only happen in one city. And for him, that city was Rome.

The speakers above my head crackled, and he was gone. I looked toward the check-in desk. The attendant breathed lightly into the intercom and placed her finger at the top of a sheet on the desk in front of her.

I looked down at my own boarding pass.

Departure: Rome FCO
Arrival: San Francisco SFO
Departure, Rome, FCO.
Rome, FCO.
Rome.
Alive.

"Good morning from British Airways. At this time we'd like to begin preboarding for British Airways Flight 117 to San Francisco, California. All passengers who require assistance boarding the aircraft and any passengers traveling with children under the age of seven are free to board at this time."

I felt the colossal weight of Excalibur resting between my hands, my fingers wrapped firmly around its handle, its blade finally stopped in equilibrium, my body at last untwisted from my first undisciplined swing. This time my strike would be more focused, more precise, more controlled. I inhaled deeply and held the oxygen in my lungs.

This would be choice. This would be my doing. Rome had spiraled out of control; I had placed far too much pressure on the people in my world here—unrealistic pressure, pressure which had extinguished their collective vibrancy. I should have been more proactive in maintaining control myself. I would not make these mistakes a second time.

"We would now like to begin boarding zone one. Passengers holding a boarding pass which reads zone one are now free to board the aircraft."

I exhaled, slowly, exclusively through my rounded lips.

I would choose to get on this plane. I would choose to reenter a world where I could fully express myself, one where I was articulate and linguistically powerful, a world free of legal constraints and budget nightmares. I would choose to return to California with everything I had learned, and it would be because my twenty-two-year-old self—sitting there ever so pensively in Rome's Fiumicino International Airport—*chose* to return, that I would ultimately build a life there, occupational and romantic interests included. I would be proactive regarding my life events. I would make my own relations.

I remained seated, staring at the grey carpet, my hands interlocked in my lap, my boarding pass pressed between my thumbs. My head cleared; my body relaxed.

In one swift motion I grabbed my backpack, swinging it to my shoulder as I stood and took off in the direction of the security screening. I liked trying to act spontaneous like that, as if it would somehow nullify my obvious overpreparation.

I made it about twenty feet and then spun back towards the gate, twirling on my toes, my head tilting skyward, my eyes pinched: a ballet of exasperation. I looked down at my boarding pass.

Seat 45H, Zone 1.

"Please have your passport and boarding pass available for the attendant. Zone one, welcome aboard."

I winced, spun again, and began resolute strides in the direction of the metal detectors. The security check was much busier than before, and I fought to dodge the oncoming travelers. The whole process looked so strange from this side: shoeless masses buckling their belts and shoving coins and gum into their pockets.

"Excuse me sir, you can't come this way." A security official appeared in front of me.

"I've already been through but—"

"Did you leave something here, sir?"

"No I need to go back through, like, *that* way." I made a waving motion toward the detectors. The officer appeared confused.

"Why don't you come with me this way, sir." I was escorted to a man at a makeshift workstation—a foldable desk topped with a laptop and a few stacks of manila folders—who appeared to be the head of the immediate security processes. The officer spoke to him.

"Mi scusi, Mr. Piccioni, il signore vorrebbe uscire all'-----." *Excuse me, Mr. Piccioni, the gentleman would like to exit to the …*

Mr. Piccioni turned to me. "Why is it that you must exit, sir?"

"I was on—well I am on a flight to San Francisco, but I need to cancel the ticket."

"Is there a reason you …" He trailed off while looking me up and down. I must have appeared harmless enough. "… vabbè. Sandra!" He leaned in his chair and yelled toward a young woman carrying plastic containers from behind a metal detector. "Potresti accompagnare il signore all'ufficio --------?"

He turned back to me.

"Sandra will accompany you to the service desk on the first level."

"Where the arrivals are?"

"Esatto. You will remain in this terminal, terminal C, and go always straight until the end where there are the duty-free shops. There is the desk to the right side. Sandra takes you."

"Okay, thank you. Grazie."

Sandra escorted me between two of the screening stations. A hundred faces in line watched me pass in the opposite direction. We rounded the corner at the end of the security area and then Sandra stopped. She pointed toward a set of escalators.

"Therah iz the … ah … eskilator to yorah lift," she said slowly.

I glanced at the escalator. Then back to her.

She pulled a packet of Marlboro Lights from her blue blazer and tapped loose a single cigarette. She placed it between her lips and looked up at me. "Lo vedi?" Her eyes widened, and she shook her head.

"Yes, yes I see it. Lo vedo."

With that, Sandra spun toward the pair of dual automatic doors leading to the passenger drop-off outside and lit her cigarette, leaving me standing by myself in the sparse concourse.

Oh, Italy.

I broke to the escalators, stepping onto the ridged metal which split into steps as I began my descent. I tried to calm my breathing. My heartbeat filled my ears. The metal united again and I stepped to the terminal floor. I looked up.

▲ Arrivi/Arrivals … ▶ Stazione/Station … ▲ Shoppe/Duty Free Shops

I flew through the terminal, stopping for no one, no automatic door, no luggage cart. My pace bordered on a run as I glided in and out of the pedestrian traffic. I reached the service desk.

"Hi. I need to cancel a ticket for a flight that is leaving."

"Do you have the ticket with you, sir?"

"Yes. I already have the boarding pass." I slid the pass across the desk toward Francesca: in her late twenties, Italian, wearing black-rimmed glasses and a dark blue blazer.

"You have already passed through the security check?"

"Well, yes. See, I was at the gate, but I can't go now."

My eyes caught a brown stuffed bear propped upright atop the metal filing cabinet behind Francesca. On its chest was pinned a red heart-shaped button with *British Airways* embossed into the glossy plastic. Its harmless face stared back at me.

You, Michael, are a moron. No one does this. You are such a screwball you have even Francesca here at the service desk confused.

"What is the reason for your cancellation, sir?"

My mind raced for a natural-sounding response. What had been that term I had always used in high school to tell the office I would be taking a sick day when I was not actually sick?

"Personal."

"Ehh. All right, just a moment to call my supervisor. I can't promise we will have your luggage off the aircraft and to you directly. Why don't you begin filling out this contact form for us."

Francesca slid me the form fixed to a clipboard. She took to her phone in Italian while I began filling in my first and last name.

Francesca occupied, I took a fleeting look past her toward the stuffed bear again. Its glossy black eyes watched me. I returned to the form.

Address.

You don't even have an address any more, Michael.

I'll use my old one, and just camp out there this afternoon.

You're being absurd. You can still make the flight. The plane is still at the gate; it's not too late. Apologize to Francesca; tell her you have made a mistake, and go get on that fucking plane like a normal fucking human being.

I placed the pen flat on the clipboard and glared the fuzzy children's toy directly in the face.

Hey. You're a fucking stuffed bear. Now shut it.

...

Good.

"Okay, Mr. Gyulai, we will go ahead with your cancellation. You are aware this will fully forfeit your ticket?"

"That's fine."

"There will also be a small fee for processing the return of your baggage this close to departure."

"And how much is that?"

I gripped the pen again, signed the bottom of the contact form, and slid the clipboard back to Francesca. She hit a few keys at her computer, turned her head to me while her eyes remained fixed on the screen, and spoke. "Fortyeight Euro."

I shook off my backpack, spun the combination on the lock of the side pouch, tore open the zipper, and grabbed the envelope from Giulia.

I extracted the eleven bills from inside and slid a single fifty across the counter. I then gathered the ten remaining bills between my hands, evened them with a few knocks on the desk, and shoved them into my right pant pocket.

"All right, Mr. Gyulai ..." Francesca held her hand over a piece of paper emerging line by jolting line from the printer at her side. She paused, the printer quieted, then she tore the page from the tray and placed it in front of me. "... we have your contact info and ..." she looked down to the clipboard I had left for her "... and your mobile number, so someone will call you within the hour regarding your belongings. All you need to do now is sign the bottom of this page to acknowledge the cancellation."

She took my fifty from the counter and slid me a two-Euro coin. I pushed it deep into my pocket and stared at the final form in front of me. It was a Neapolitan paper sandwich, thin white on top, followed by pink and yellow replicas. I signed.

Michael J. Gyulai

"That's it?"

"That's it. Have a nice day."

"Thank you."

I pulled my backpack from the floor and raised it to one shoulder as I made my way away from the desk. I was walking slowly now, folding my copy of the cancellation slip into fourths before sliding it into my pocket.

I fingered the ten fifty-Euro bills next to the receipt. With my other hand I pulled out my phone and looked at the time: 9:53 AM. I had a good jump on the day.

I was halted by a river of individuals flooding from the exit to my right. A flight must have just deboarded. They were streaming from the baggage claim across the hallway to the escalators leading to the train station. I watched the faces as they passed—two young couples, a married couple, three Japanese friends, one German tour group.

There was a break in the line and I dropped in behind two Australian backpackers, myself now heading with them toward the platform where I had arrived an hour earlier. The backpackers looked fatigued from traveling; they said nothing.

I stepped onto the escalator and we slowly began our descent toward the tracks. A banner stretched across the angled ceiling above us. The backdrop was a montage of tourist sites—the Coliseum, the Trevi Fountain, Piazza Navona, the Spanish Steps. A set of giant, bold-faced letters sprawled its length.

BENVENUTO

It was a word I knew.

WELCOME

978-0-595-47375-5
0-595-47375-X